VANISHING MONUMENTS

VANISHING MONUMENTS

a novel

John Elizabeth Stintzi

ARSENAL PULP PRESS
VANCOUVER

ARSENAL PULP PRESS
Suite 202 – 211 East Georgia St.
Vancouver, BC V6A 1Z6
Canada
arsenalpulp.com

The publisher gratefully acknowledges the support of the Canada Council for the Arts and the British Columbia Arts Council for its publishing program, and the Government of Canada, and the Government of British Columbia (through the Book Publishing Tax Credit Program), for its publishing activities.

Arsenal Pulp Press acknowledges the xʷməθkʷəy̓əm (Musqueam), Sḵwx̱wú7mesh (Squamish), and səl̓ilwətaʔɬ (Tsleil-Waututh) Nations, speakers of Hul'q'umi'num'/Halq'eméylem/hənq̓əmin̓əm̓ and custodians of the traditional, ancestral, and unceded territories where our office is located. We pay respect to their histories, traditions, and continuous living cultures and commit to accountability, respectful relations, and friendship.

This is a work of fiction. Any resemblance of characters to persons either living or deceased is purely coincidental.

Front cover design by Jazmin Welch and Oliver McPartlin
Front cover illustration by John Elizabeth Stintzi
Back cover and text design by Jazmin Welch
Edited by Shirarose Wilensky
Proofread by Alison Strobel

Printed and bound in Canada

Library and Archives Canada Cataloguing in Publication:
Title: Vanishing monuments : a novel / John Elizabeth Stintzi.
Names: Stintzi, John Elizabeth, author.
Identifiers: Canadiana (print) 20190228989 | Canadiana (ebook) 20190228997 |
ISBN 9781551528014 (softcover) | ISBN 9781551528021 (HTML)
Classification: LCC PS8637.T55 V36 2020 | DDC C813/.6—dc23

"No, there's no way not to suffer. But you try all kinds of ways to keep from drowning in it, to keep on top of it, and to make it seem—well, like *you*. Like you did something, all right, and now you're suffering for it. You know?" I said nothing. "Well you know," he said, impatiently, "why *do* people suffer? Maybe it's better to do something to give it a reason, *any* reason."

—*James Baldwin*, "Sonny's Blues"

CONTENTS

HERE

When the doctor calls I'm standing in the kitchen in my little house in Minneapolis, drinking the microwav'd ends of this morning's coffee, and as soon as the doctor says the words about Hedwig Baum—about *Mother*—the girl who runs away comes back into my bones. She takes over, like a surfer on a wave of fear. The first thing she does is put down the coffee and move me into the bedroom, to grab the old camera from its place atop the cabinet where I keep all my gear. As soon as she makes my hands lift that old, coated brass machine, and as soon as she's slung its strap around my neck—something that I do most days, without her—I know she's built up too much momentum to stop. To stay.

This camera, this old Leica III, was hers. Mother's. The mother whose dementia the doctor is telling me appears to have taken completely her already dwindling capacity for speech. The dementia she's been living with for about half as long as the seventeen years she had with me.

While the doctor talks into my ear, the running girl pulls out from under the bed the piece of luggage—luggage I don't think I've used since Genny and I went to Chicago, in 2007, for a talk I was giving on the body as an indirect object in figure-based art. The talk that came after I'd watched the I-35W bridge collapse into the Mississippi from the bridge beside it—the 10th Avenue Bridge—that I was driving across, watched the bridge and Genny's trust in engineering and infrastructure and our whole world fall out of sight. Luggage I hadn't used since I'd tried to take her away from here to pull her out of that.

"We've been keeping an eye on her," the doctor says, as the packing continues, "and she hasn't spoken, as far as we can tell, in roughly a week. Her responsiveness to being addressed has also decreased. She has had accidents. Well, more."

This is the first time the running girl has come to usurp my body since I ran away to Hamburg, Germany, in 1991, to escape Genny and the relationship I'd thought I was in, to try to get away from the me that I'd been living as, which had suddenly felt like a lie. The first time the running girl ever took over completely was when I ran away from Mother, from Winnipeg, with Genny, when I was seventeen. In the middle of the night, having removed my bedroom window with a pry bar. That was the last time I was there, in Winnipeg—almost thirty years ago.

That night was the first time the running girl grabbed the camera. The first time that girl got her way. Mother was not speaking then, either. But for a different reason.

I'm sure I've said things to the doctor. I'm sure I've been asking questions, for clarifications. I'm sure some part of me has, but I haven't been there to take note of them. The longer the conversation goes on, the more I've been following the hands, the more I've been using my legs to move my body through the house to let the running girl's hands grab what they want to. Bedroom to bathroom to bedroom to kitchen to bedroom to living room to bedroom. I cannot figure out what to focus on: the hands grabbing from my gear cabinet a lens for my Hasselblad and my old copy of Ovid's *Metamorphoses* that I stole from my high school library, or the doctor who is talking about a recent study about similar aphasia in patients with dementia. I focus on neither and fade into a relative peace, focusing instead on the breath in the body, until eventually the luggage is zipped up, ready, and I'm standing over it with my phone still pressed to the side of my face. I listen to the doctor, but there's nothing, just silence, because the phone call has already ended in one way or another without my realizing. I pull my phone from my ear and the side of my face is left with a rectangle of sweat.

I text Karen to tell her that I won't be able to make it to the collective's board meeting, that I have to go out of town. When she calls me a minute later, as I knew she would, I'm stuffing the luggage into the back of my little car. I stop to stare down at the vibrating phone in my hand until it stops, until Karen goes to voice mail. Then I close the trunk and climb in. I know that Karen won't call again, that she's going to rush to my house, to try and catch me, to try and get more information from me, but as I turn the car on I also know there's nothing anyone can do to stop me. The studio is a seventeen-minute drive away, in good traffic. I'll be heading in the opposite direction.

As I pull my car away from the curb, not knowing when I'll see this little house of mine, but not really caring about this house at all, I look across the street at Genny's house. I tried not to look, every molecule I own was instructed not to look, because I knew how much it would hurt, and I knew there was nothing I could do to stop that hurt from coming—for me, and for Genny. She will not understand, and she will also understand too much. I don't call her to let her know that I'm leaving, that I'm going back to Winnipeg for the first time since we ran away together. I know that if I called her to explain before I'd made it too far to turn back, I'd never make it.

And I have to. Some ancient signal has been sent up to rally me back. Some signal has told me that the road to Winnipeg, to Mother, will be too overgrown if I stay away any longer. The call from the doctor has proven that it has just turned from late to too late. The running girl has a history of doing things far too late, of running from one burning building into another's sparking start. But if I'm going to close any of the windows to my past, if I'm going to fight against the drafts, I have to go back right away. To make it to Mother, to that city. To pretend I've come back just in the nick of time.

As I head north, toward Winnipeg, I try not to think about Genny, sitting oblivious in her office, evaluating plans for this highway or that bridge, while I drive. I fail. I throw my phone into the back seat, out of reach, as I look at the clock and imagine her at this moment getting a call from Karen, as she drives toward the empty parking space in front of my house, letting her know that her partner has run away. Suddenly. Again.

While I drive, I keep telling myself not to look back at the phone, and by the time I fail I'm already too close to Winnipeg to turn the car around. This is happening.

Just north of Fargo, parked at a gas station, I finally pick up the phone from the back seat. The sky is dark, spitting softly on my car. There's a voice mail waiting for me from Genny, six missed calls, and a string of texts. It takes all that I have to text her back:

—*I'll call you tomorrow*

—It's Mother

Then I turn off the phone. I don't need it for directions. I've already memorized the route from all the times I stared at the map and traced my finger along the here-to-there. From all the times I put the addresses into Google Maps the last few years. From all the times I zoomed in and used the farthest tip of my body to trail all those highways north, all those directions. Transcribing that journey into me.

Home.

But before I pull out of the gas station I look down at myself, bound up and packed, in black jeans and a dark T. I go to the trunk and pull out a dress, a bra, and my makeup bag. I ball it all up and go into the station's bathroom and make myself that girl.

1

THE MEMORY PALACE

You close your eyes and turn around and there it stands, two storeys tall, board-and-batten siding, painted white too many years ago: your memory palace. The concrete walkway, with weeds growing through cracks from so many winter thaws, snakes up to the grey-blue door. A big portrait window stares out from the first floor, from the living room. Two small windows glare down at you from the floor above. Sometimes when you turn around to face the palace, you are outside the old picket fence, where the metal mailbox hangs, but most of the time the fence is not there, and you can walk right up to the front door without opening a gate that you never really knew closed. So you can go up the single step onto the landing, open the door, and go up the half step inside.

The rest of the street, the rest of the city—the world—is not here. You have to approach the palace excised from its contexts. Alone, as the house has never been. Without distractions, without other places to go to instead, this is the only place there is. There is only weather, if you choose to have it, but there is always wind. Sometimes blowing you toward the palace, sometimes blowing you away. The grass out front is long and wispy, moving with the wind like tendrils. Like a pit of snakes. When you approach the palace, you do not step off the concrete path, and on the path, you try to avoid every single crack. You fail.

Inside the palace—should you make it there—is everything in your life that you need to remember.

Twenty-seven years.

It has been twenty-seven years since I last drove across the border between Manitoba and Minnesota, to follow Genny as she started school in Minneapolis.

It has been twenty-seven years since I stepped on the sidewalks in Wolseley. In downtown Winnipeg. Since I stood on the bank of the Assiniboine River. Or the Red River. Or at the Forks, where the two rivers merge.

It has been twenty-seven years since I stood on the landing of the house, put my key in the door—since that key lifted the pins in the lock and turned.

It has been twenty-seven years since I saw Mother's chest rise and fall. Since I could not feel my fingers while I hung my coat in the hall.

I have carried the key for Mother's house with me every day since the night in August when I last walked away from that house—without locking the door behind me. I've carried it every day for twenty-seven years.

It has been twenty-eight years since I looked up at that Winnipeg sky, in the middle of the night, lying beside my best friend, Tom, on his lawn, trying to find stars.

It has been thirty-two years since I heard Mother laugh, thirty years since I heard her cry—horrible, deep, unhelpful sobs—and thirty years since I told her that I loved her and she mumbled incoherently into my ear.

Fifteen years ago, Genny and I had a connecting flight in Winnipeg when we were coming back from her father's wedding in Edmonton. But we didn't leave the airport. We waited there for six whole hours, watching tired but happy people—*happy* to be *home*—filing off flight after flight.

For twenty-seven years, the little key to Mother's house has sat next to the keys of apartments, offices, studios, and cars. Each of the other keys has changed, been replaced, each one but hers. It dangles beside the wheel. Clinking, probably, only too quietly to hear, as I drive.

It has been four days since I saw a photograph of Mother. Three weeks since I last called the home to get an update on her—when she'd still been speaking, somewhat. Eight years since she was first diagnosed with dementia. Three years since I coordinated with Dorothea, the day nurse I'd hired about eight years ago, to move Mother to the home. After she'd had what we'd agreed to call an accident and had to be placed in a controlled environment. One year since I started needing to take out loans.

It has been twenty-seven years—twenty-seven years—since I drove on this highway, the I-29. Only last time, I was going south. It's dark and I'm passing Grand Forks and I can almost see, behind the headlights I pass in the dark rain: them. Genny Ford and me: Alani Baum. Two kids escaping two untenable worlds. The staticky radio program playing, from a station back in Fargo, could well be the same exact one from that night. I know that if I don't listen closely, I can convince myself of that.

And behind Alani's eyes, in the car that passes by? The running girl. Inching away with the determination to stay away, but all the while starting the long, long odyssey that I'm now completing.

Before I got the call from the doctor, my life had gotten into a steady routine. I woke up, made Genny coffee, walked across the street from her little house to mine, made myself coffee, answered emails, went to teach, or to office hours, or to work on an exhibit at the collective's gallery, then came home and walked back across the street to Genny's.

After years of relative chaos, I finally felt like I'd turned my life into a machine. I took a step every day, at a set pace. I paid bills on time. I submitted grant applications weeks before they were due. I didn't miss the meetings with Ess to review hir thesis portfolio and the long essay ze was writing to accompany it. I didn't run to my office to find hir, frustrated yet doe-eyed, still sitting outside my door—under the name-plate that read MX. A. BAUM—forty minutes after I was supposed to be there, like I had throughout the first half of the fall semester. Instead, Ess began arriving to find my office door open, with me sitting inside it, ready to talk to hir about the folder of prints clamped under hir tattooed arm.

I wasn't myself is what I mean. I'd become a clearer-cut version of myself. I'd figured out how to appear ordered, found a way to make my body become a thing I could hide in again. I was stowed away. Exiled. My photography was suffering, by which I mean that—between teach-ing two courses and advising Ess and working at the collective—I wasn't doing it. My photography suffered because I didn't have any me to give, to pour into its form. Genny started distrusting it, I think—the new clockwork me. The spring's tension building up, clicking along to the time. She had never known me to be like that, not for so long.

That prolonged dissociation felt like a sort of vacation, as if my body was getting ready for something to happen. Something that you know is coming without actually knowing it, or without actually admitting to yourself that you know it. Like you've crouched down and put your hand on railroad tracks but can't feel the vibrations of the train coming around the bend.

But the whole time, some part of you knows that it is.

And then it hits you.

A few miles south of the border, static overtakes the voices on the Fargo radio station, and I switch through the channels, searching for another signal to the south of me. I listen just long enough to hear someone say where they're from, switching quickly away from any that strike me instantly as Canadian. When a station tells me it's in Thief River Falls, I stop. The signal has already started to lose itself to the buzz, but I can still make out the words. A woman talks about how the rain in northern Minnesota is probably going to continue for the next week.

The whole drive, I've been doing this: changing stations, mostly talk radio—to Sioux Falls to St. Cloud to Wahpeton to Fargo to, now, Thief River Falls—and sticking them out until they fade away. I want time to slow down, to convince me that I have more time to get ready to see Mother. I'm using the rain as an excuse to drive five miles under the speed limit.

At the border crossing in Pembina, I inch forward behind two SUVs and a pickup. When my turn comes, I roll down the window, letting in cool, wet air that chills me in the dress. A young man with pointy blond hair looks down at me sternly from his booth as I hand him my Canadian passport, my German passport safe in the glove compartment. The officer squints at the photo, looking back and forth from it to me.

"Where do you live, ma'am?"

"Minneapolis. I'm from Winnipeg."

"What brings you to Canada?"

"Visiting family."

He scans my passport into the computer and looks down at me, taps it against his desk under the window, glances in the back of the car. Softens a little.

"Cool camera you've got there. Some sort of special occasion?"

"Just haven't been back in a while," I say, suddenly feeling the weight of Mother's camera hanging against my belly.

"Busy, busy, busy," he says, tapping my passport. "Any drugs or alcohol?"

"No."

"Firearms?"

"No."

He stops tapping my passport, hands it down to me, eyes already on the car behind me.

"Have a good night."

"Thank you."

As I pull away, I realize the packer has shifted from under the jeans and binder I took off in Fargo and sits in plain view on the passenger seat. I pick it up with one hand and stuff it down a leg of the jeans.

Ess came to my office hours the second week of the first of my classes ze'd taken. The class was a studio course in portrait photography, and it was Ess's first year in the program. My office hours were from 2:00 to 4:00, and I showed up at 3:50. Ze was sitting on the floor in front of my door, fidgeting, working frantic on hir phone, and nearly fell over and hit hir head on the wall when ze noticed me come around the corner. As I apologized for being late, Ess talked over me, telling me how much ze liked the class. Ze cut right to the chase before I could even sit down at my cluttered desk: "Would you be willing to be my advisor for my thesis?"

I smiled at hir. I'd felt paternal toward Ess as soon as I'd read out the names for attendance and ze said: "Present, but I don't go by that name. My name is actually S.K.! People," ze said, turning side to side, to include the rest of the class, "just call me Ess." I'd felt paternal toward hir again at the second class, when ze had specified hir pronouns.

"I'm only visiting faculty, so I don't advise very often," I said. "And I don't really know your work yet."

As I said this, ze put hir hands on my desk, gripping it hard. It wasn't until then that I noticed all hir little tattoos, stick and poke, hardly visible on hir dark skin. I never asked if ze gave them to hirself.

"I know. I know. But I know your work. I've googled you so much. I stayed up all night looking at stuff. I tried to listen to lectures online. Your work is about bodies and mental health. Depression. Like in *Shavasana*—"

As soon as ze mentioned *Shavasana* I put my hands up, as if to slow Ess down a little, but actually hoping to stop hir in hir tracks. Ze'd not yet disclosed to me that ze was bipolar, but I could feel hir manic energy. But Ze continued hir sentence, saying things about my work I didn't want to hear, as I gestured, stopping only when ze hit the end of hir point.

"Okay. I'll talk to the department head and make sure they're fine with it. Send me your portfolio and a little write-up about what you have in mind for your project, okay?"

Ze jumped up from the chair, pulled off hir backpack, and took out a folder of photographs printed on cheap paper. Nearly slammed it onto my desk in hir fervour. I smiled at Ess, and picked it up. Ze stood staring at the folder.

"I'm not going to look at this now," I said. "My office hours are up. I'll email the head, okay? I'll let you know in class."

Ze stood there for a moment before realizing that I was asking hir to leave. Ze threw hir backpack over hir shoulder and beamed as ze backed out of my office. After a moment, I got up, went to the door, and called out: "My work—it isn't about mental health! It's about memory!"

From down the hall, at the stairs, I heard hir call back: "What's the diff?"

Sometimes when you come to your memory palace, the grass has grown over the concrete path to the door, writhing and hungry, and you can't bring yourself to take the first step. Sometimes the path is clear, and you walk down it—staring at your feet, trying to avoid stepping on the cracks—and then after a long time, you stop and look up and realize that the path has become a circle on the front lawn, with no exit and no entrance. So you have no choice but to open your eyes and leave the palace for the world.

But most of the time you do make it to the door, and lying out front like a welcome mat is a picture frame that holds a photograph. Inside is your earliest memory. Depending on the day, this memory changes. Before you open the door, you look down at it, and try your hardest to remember and relive whatever it is that you see there. To orient yourself to yourself.

Sometimes you get to the door and you don't look down. You forget, or refuse to, and you just open the door. Sometimes when you don't look, you step on the frame and break the glass with your bare feet, tracking bloody footprints into the palace.

Sometimes you look down and the frame is empty, or gone. But when the memory is there, after you look down at it and live through it for a moment, you open the door and take that long first stride up over the jamb. As you step over the memory and into the palace, try not to imagine the glass of the frame being cracked and stained from your previous failures to recall it.

Every time you enter the palace should feel like the first time.

I'm about an hour south of Winnipeg by the time I switch the radio to a Canadian station. Outside the car, between the little towns I pass through, the night slithers across the prairies unhindered. The water in the ditches keeps getting higher the farther north I go, my headlights bouncing off the surfaces in the dark. Flood waters are following me north because it's been raining in northern Minnesota and Manitoba pretty steadily for the last few days. I know this because my weather app has three saved locations: Minneapolis, Winnipeg, and Hamburg.

The rain is heavy and slow at once, and I can see no more than twenty feet in front of my headlights. Because of the darkness, I can't see behind me at all. All I have is forward.

A weatherman on the radio talks about the seasonal flooding that Manitoba is slipping into, talks about how this is not uncommon for May, and I grow tired of the talk, the monotony of the punctuation. I switch the radio to FM and stop at a Winnipeg station playing rock music. As I get closer to the city, the music gets crisper. The blurry road signs show fewer and fewer kilometres between me and the city, and the clock reads 1:24. In the end, the trip will have taken about nine hours instead of the estimated seven.

Eventually, the city arrives. I reach the perimeter highway and merge in an anticlimax that takes my breath. I turn onto the loop, counter-clockwise, and the city is little more than a short glow in the leftwards rain. I keep going, trying not to look left, until I hit a red light for my turn onto Saint Mary's Road, which will take me to the heart of the city. As I move into the turning lane, I can feel my momentum begin to wane. I am so tired. The turn signal is clicking. The rain is battering the roof. The whole highway is for no one but me.

As I wait for the light to change, as the sound of the turn signal bores through me, I scan radio stations and land on a new one, playing a song in French I can make no sense of.

I don't teach full time or tenure track because I don't have any kind of degree. When I was thirty I took a GED night class for a few months and passed the exam to close that conversation, but otherwise, I never went to school. The department head hired me as a visiting professor after I'd gotten a lot of attention locally, and more than I cared for nationally. A visiting professor who refused to stop visiting, who could run back to where they came from anytime.

I didn't want to teach full time. I had the collective, I had Genny, I had grants. I got by and lived lightly. My cupboards were bare but for whiskey and coffee beans. My fridge was empty but for beer, creamer, as well as 35 mm, 120 mm, and large format film. I took a lot of freelance jobs. I shot unconventional weddings unconventionally. For a while, I received a nominal salary as the executive director of the collective.

The only course I audited at the university was a seminar on Ovid, walking into the little lecture hall with my worn, stolen copy—the wrong translation—of the *Metamorphoses* under my arm. I had no interest in going to school for photography, or art history, or anything like that. My knowledge of the history of photography mostly came from stumbling upon it. I learned as I went: running into a colleague in the lounge who had a pile of photography books on the table and flipping through them. Picking up some famous names I hadn't known before—Weegee, Dorothea Lange, Diane Arbus, Robert Mapplethorpe —and striking up conversations with that same colleague, often as they were trying to take a break, scribbling down book titles to search the library for later. Delving deep into each photographer from there.

The only famous photographer I knew when I was hired to teach was Ansel Adams, because Mother hung a print of his in the hallway. It was the only picture hanging in the whole house: the moody land-scape *Tetons and Snake River*. Though I didn't know it was his until I ran away to Hamburg and met Erwin Egger, a photographer who held Adams—especially that print—in high esteem.

I didn't really have much interest in learning the many different ways photography was done before I first picked up a camera. I gleaned what was important from modern photographers like Wegman, Mann, my colleagues, or even the students in my classes. From Erwin Egger and Mother. I gathered the scraps of the history of the form, of tech-nique, like gossip. My contemporaries carried that history forth with them, corrupting it, bending it, and augmenting it in ways that worked better for their purposes. I learned everything I needed from that.

When I get to the door of the memory palace, the earliest thing I can remember—the beginning that I find in the frame—is often a sample from several kinds of memories.

Most often it's a memory of me making some definitive childlike action: like digging holes with a gardening trowel in the backyard of what would become our house. Other times it's a moment of fear: like sitting in Mother's arms, asking her where Ilsa was, the woman we lived with, and Mother was hired to care for, now that she had died. Sometimes it's the moment I came home from my first day of school crying to Mother because my teacher had informed me I was exactly a girl.

Sometimes the earliest memory has nothing to do with me, has nothing to do with a moment, but is simply the image of something I saw at some point, or something routine that my mind sampled or boiled down into a single, invented instance: Mother doing yoga in her studio, Mother taking photographs of happy couples in the living room. Sometimes it's a memory of being in a place, the feeling of sitting in that living room, of sitting in the hall outside the closed darkroom, of being beside a river, each without an event. Without any story to let the memory move.

Sometimes I get to the door of the palace and there's a memory from far later in my life, like the moment Genny found me stuck upside down in a child's swing in a playground in winter. Never the moment I got stuck in that swing, or the minutes after, but the moment she showed up, seemingly from nowhere, and pulled me free. Our first real moment together.

Sometimes the memory is even later: me removing my bedroom's second-floor window with a pry bar and climbing out of the house on a rope made of old clothes and bedsheets.

But sometimes when I sit down to remember it all, when I close my eyes and go to the door of the memory palace, I realize that my life never began at all. That the door into the palace is not there. Or that I am outside the picket fence, and the fence is fifty feet high and impermeable, with a huge *NO TRESPASSING* sign painted on it in letters taller than me. The lid of the metal mailbox opening and closing high above, laughing me out of my head.

When the light changes to green, I don't turn left but merge right and keep moving north on the perimeter to orbit the city. The weight of the day, of the distance, is crashing into me, and I tell myself that I want to try and find a weaker spot to break in, though I know that if I can make it all the way around the city, I'll drive all the way back to Minneapolis.

I drive around Transcona, cross the fat Red River I can't see in the dark and the rain, watch the blinking lights of the last planes of the night drooping onto the airport tarmac. I keep driving around the city until—two-thirds of the way through the circuit—in the dark ahead of me, I can imagine what I'm going to pass. Blurred orbs rise into my head, refracting through the rain: the huge stadium lights.

The Assiniboia Downs.

I slam on the brakes, thankful the highway here is dead. Ahead of me, I know there's an exit, that I can turn there without getting close enough to see the Downs, which of course would not be illuminated. But instead, I find a dirt access road over the median, where police cars probably station themselves. I break the law because it's closer.

I'm afraid that if I get any closer than I need to—if I get close to that huge mud circle where the horses race—I will be devoured by it. I'm not ready for that. I can barely make it as it is. So I drive across the lumpy access road and retrace my way along the perimeter, no longer fighting against the stream of time. As soon as I get to the exit that I know will take me toward Mother in the home in Kildonan—not to her house in Wolseley—I take it.

Slowly, after a few more turns, the home—a smaller than I'd imagined from the pictures online—shows up just beyond the intersection. The light at the intersection is red. The building is barely lit. There are bricks, windows, people inside I cannot see. Mother. Visiting hours are still at least five hours off, but I'll wait in the parking lot, in my car. I will see Mother first, before I go back to that house. Her house. Our house. The memory palace.

Ess took nearly all of my courses after I agreed to advise hir. Ze was starting hir thesis project earlier than most students—the first semester—and often made huge bursts of messy progress while manic. Sometimes, though, ze would miss a week or two of classes because ze wasn't able to get out of bed.

Ess's original project was about growing up queer and black on the outskirts of a small town called Peculiar, south of Kansas City, Missouri. Hir project—titled *Outside Peculiar*—was largely landscape photos from the surrounding area, with self-portraits crudely spliced into them. Many of the landscapes were themselves several photos stitched together roughly using Photoshop, because Ess used the camera on hir old, cracked Samsung cellphone. "A queer choice," Ess called it, by which ze meant one made out of necessity as well as against photography's normativity, against the fetishization of megapixel and sensor size and their conflation with "quality."

In the pitch for the project at the beginning of our work together, Ess wrote: "These open spaces and small towns in America are not often thought of as being black or queer. They are where the white and the cis and the straight are assumed to flourish. And they do. They are crabgrass in the spaces. They overtake. But if you stop and look at the soil, you see they are not the only weeds that grow."

I wake up in my car in the parking lot outside the home, Mother's Leica still around my neck, its old Summar lens folded into the body and capped, gut filled with the roll of film I'd been failing to fill for the last two months. Film that's empty because nothing of note came my way. No idea. No image. No body or variation in my psyche that needed to be pasted onto the reactive plastic. Nothing came to me but the old, thick fog of dissociation, the feeling that I was not myself, and if I were, I'd rather be dead.

My neck itches from the weight of the old leather strap. My packer and binder and clothes sit tangled beside me on the passenger seat. When I parked here last night, I didn't make a pillow out of anything; I just leaned my seat back and closed my eyes and eventually opened them to today rising into the grey sky.

Morning in this new place, clutched by the same old place.

It isn't raining right now, but it will. I open the door and stand beside the car, stretching, breathing out my popping muscles, shaking out my stiff legs, straightening the dress that feels wrong.

Exhausted. Terrified.

All I want to do is give up, get back into my car, and drive away. Turn on my phone and text Genny: *just kidding! be back soon.* But I know that I won't be able to make it. I'll just slow down and turn around again, get back here and turn around again, again and again. Slowly making it through the labyrinth of back and forth before my inertia surrenders to *here*. To her.

As I walk toward the home, the time between myself and Mother shrinks. Her camera hangs at my belly like a pit. The door opens and there's a nurse at a desk, in scrubs that are not supposed to look like scrubs, in the same way this home is not supposed to look like a hospital.

"I'm here to see my mother? Hedwig Baum?"

"Oh, of course," she says, standing up behind the desk and handing me a clipboard where visitors sign in. She's short, a good foot shorter than me, hardly taller now than she was sitting down. "She woke up a little early, but she's usually sharpest soon after waking," she says, while I finish writing a name that doesn't quite fit over me—*Allie Baum*—and put the clipboard down. I follow her down the hall. She walks so slowly.

"How long has it been since you visited again?" she asks.

"Sometime around Christmas," I say, because it's a shorter sentence than: *Never*.

"Well," she says, quiet, as we inch along a hallway of closed doors and cold tiles. "She's changed some since then, as you know. She has more difficulty hearing, especially lately, so you will want to talk a little louder than last time. But you will want to make sure to use a conversational tone. She responds better to tone. We also cut her hair, so don't be alarmed. She was having trouble with it being so long— getting it tangled up in things, tying it up in knots, trying to braid it. Things like that." She stops, looks up at me, smiles in a way that is supposed to feel warm. I don't tell her that Mother had never once braided her hair. "It's a lot more manageable now."

The door is open a crack, and beside it is an aging piece of card stock printed with Mother's name.

"Thank you," I say, trying to place a smile between us as I stare over her to the door. I start to move around her toward it.

"Would you like me to come in with you? Help you? I've worked with Hedwig a long time, and I know all the little tricks to get her to notice me."

I grab the door handle before that girl starts to panic, tries to tell my body to run away. "I'm fine," I say, forgiving her duty with a half wave of my free hand. "I still remember all the tricks."

I push the door in.

When I think about Mother, the first thing I remember is her body. Small chested, a dim scar on her belly from where I blew through her. Tall. Her long bright hair—brighter than mine. As much as I try not to, I can see her in my height in the mirror. Which is why I don't own a full-length mirror. Which is why I avoid them. Why I rarely try on clothes in a store.

When I think of her in motion, I imagine her body doing yoga. I imagine it through the bars of the vent between her studio and my bedroom.

After her body, I remember the feeling of her presence, the gravity she held in our creaky house. The gravity of the noise and the silence both, depending on the year, the month, the day. I remember being pulled back to that house after those long expeditions at night with Tom. Every time—every time but one—finding her there. Waiting up for me. And every time, not a single word between us.

What I don't remember is the sound of her voice. I've been trying not to. It's easier to believe she never said a word, that she was mute, than to think of her falling in and out of her muteness. First, because of the electric storm of depression. Now, because her brain has lost so much of its charge.

But as I've driven closer to her, I've heard her a little. Not the words themselves but her voice stacking upon itself in an unintelligible cacophony. Into static.

I walk into Mother's room, and there she is: a silhouette against the grey light of the window. She's sitting in a chair in a baby-blue blouse, and her hair is very short—*manageable*. Her back is to me. I don't know if she's actually looking out the window, and if she is, if anything is registering. I've never seen her stare out a window from behind before; I only ever saw her staring out a window toward me, at night, waiting for me to come home.

My eyes adjust from the dimness of the hall. I squint, try to make a distinction between her skin and the light. The door behind me closes with a click.

I approach, slowly, counting down the tiles between us. As I get closer, my memory of her body minimizes to meet reality. She's so small. Her shoulders are like wire clothes hangers, her wrists like thumbs wrapped in wrinkled pink leather. Her scarred hands are two collections of raw, bubbled webs. They're wriggling on her lap, the only part of her that's moving. When I stand over her, I can see that she's wearing a restraining belt that keeps her from getting out of the chair.

I stand over her for a while, taking her in, fascinated and hurt. Time has brittled her. Twenty-seven years gone, turning her long hair blank white, letting it be chopped off for convenience, to make her seem more put together. Letting it all be thrown away. No strand of hair on her head was there ten years ago. I imagine the nurse from the front desk, armed with scissors and grasping those long, drawn-out strings of Mother's dead cells. I imagine her clipping them all off.

I look down at Mother and I can smell her, that clean, hospital soap smell that lacks any breath of humanity. I could move my hand four inches and touch her shoulder. Just four inches and I could break through decades of gone.

I don't move. I stand in her soft shadow and forget completely what she used to smell like. I'm muddled as to how precisely her hair used to tumble down her back. Suddenly unsure what colour her hair used to be. Standing near her like this, silent, I hear my heart beating and realize the cacophony of her voice is gone.

Mother's old camera hangs off my neck. In the perfect dark of the camera's head the film stands dormant. The camera's eye jammed shut, capped, and collapsed into the body. The camera is a promise, weighing down at my belly, the thin leather straps digging into the sides of my breasts. As I breathe in, the camera gets closer to Mother. As I breathe out it gets closer to me.

Four inches.

I step back, quietly, even though I'm sure she can't hear me. I'll come back tomorrow. Someone in this body will. I turn and walk back toward the door, and as I go, I can sort of remember her again. As I near the door to her room, I remember my little hand buried in her tight palm, remember walking back from the liquor store with an empty wine box on my head. As I get back into the hall, I remember the smell, just a little, of chemicals and sweat and her when she came out of the darkroom, exhausted but sometimes smiling. The darkroom where faces, bodies, and angles all began to appear on wet, blank paper.

At the nurse's desk I somehow tell her, "Mother is asleep right now" and make for the door. Mother is asleep, her eyes open. She's enjoying letting the day into her head.

As I step out the door, into the cool air, I remember when the car stopped outside our house that morning and they carried Mother in— the man from Selkirk and Tom—to the bed where she would mumble. I remember the heat of the sun on my skin as I stood there on the lawn and watched. I wasn't wearing shoes. The dew was nearly gone, but the grass was still cool. I could smell it. Mother's hands were limp and one of her slippers sat empty on the sidewalk.

The light rising in the grey eastern sky is a false prophet. I get in the car. My bones fit back into the lumps of the seat better than they fit my body, as Mother's camera floats on the waves of my uneven breathing. As I put the keys in the ignition, I remember the man handing me Mother's keys and a bag of her personal effects—her purse, her Nikon with her fast 85 mm lens, her small coat—and telling me that she should not drive, but that someone should go and pick up her car from the Downs. Then, he handed me a bag filled with her medication.

I turn on the ignition, crank the heat, and drive, slowly, out of the lot and toward her house, away from the home where Mother is unaware that I just stood behind her, that I was only four inches away from her. I pull away from the home, south, toward the place where I grew up and ran from, the dark from which my light-thirsty stem grew wide, seeking the warmth of the sun. The horizon to the southeast of the city is dark and tall and endless. Widening. The waters of the Red and the Assiniboine are high enough, but more rain is still coming to drown us out.

History is, too.

2

THE HALLWAY

As you step across the landing and into your memory palace, the door always closes behind you with the same hollow sound. You can try to slam it, and you can try to slip it in slow and silent, but the sound of it closing never changes. You've even tried leaving the palace door open, but as soon as you turn away, it always falls back into place with that hollow gonging. A sound so unlike any other you remember Mother's house ever having made, so unlike any you've heard other doors make. You have met so many different closing doors in your life, but the door of the palace has a sound all its own.

To your right, once you've made it past that sound, are the stairs, and in front of you is the hallway. The hallway is bare because you think of it as a sort of memory thoroughfare, because you walk through it again and again as you navigate the palace. You must go through the hallway to get to any of the other rooms, so you think the only thing this hallway could really effectively remember is distance. Not the distance between the door of the palace and the door—which is only sometimes here—to Mother's old darkroom, not the distance between the door and the opening to the kitchen and the living room, not the distance between the kitchen and the stairs, or between the stairs and the front door.

Not these distances but the distance between people: the distance between you and Mother now, between you and Mother back when you still lived here. The distance between you and Genny now, or you and Genny when you disappeared to Hamburg, or you and Genny when all was well and good. When your days would string along, one after another, harmonized by care. Or the distance between you and Tom—then and now—or Karen, or students like Ess, or all the more often: between you and yourself.

The moment you hear the sound of the door closing behind you, you are already walking one of these distances. Some longer than others, some fluctuating depending on when and where you sit down to close your eyes to start your tour of the palace. Every time you come to the hallway, from any direction, the distance changes. These distances, unlike the rest of the house, lack event. Lack story.

But each of them is very important to yours.

I've known for a long time that I probably had no choice but to come back. I knew it the day I heard about Mother from Asha—her yoga teacher, someone who helped keep me in Mother's loop. Asha had taken Mother to the doctor because she'd been acting strangely agitated, forgetting to come to classes, answering the phone when Asha called with a voice that seemed unconvinced that they knew one another. That was when it started, almost ten years ago now. But I decided not to come back then, as the coil wound up, and hired Dorothea over the phone to take care of Mother and make sure she was taking care of herself, taking her medication. Doing that kept me away, kept me informed. And then, when Mother had the accident three years ago— when fear overtook the place where pity had been nesting—she could no longer stay in the house. I felt it so much then—this place tearing up the things I had left behind, trying to lure me back.

But then Dorothea told me about the home, a nice place that was not too expensive and not too religious. So I let the energy stay inside me, building up, and made a few calls and moved money around, and then Mother was transferred straight from the hospital to the home. She has never been back to the house, not since the paramedics carried her down the stairs and through the front door. They carried her out forever.

Since then, again and again, I almost came back here. I would be driving back from the university at night and stay on I-35 a few extra exits before looping back. I'd be downtown at a bar hanging out with Genny and some friends, and I'd step outside to get some air and walk onto a city bus that was heading toward the airport, only to get off after a few stops. I once sent my portfolio to a faculty member of the School of Art at the University of Manitoba—Cathryn Logan, an abstract painter—to see if they could find a place for me, even as a visiting professor. Three weeks later, after I'd contained myself, Cathryn called and told me that they'd love to have me visit the campus and teach a course for the department, and I told her sorry, something came up and my future looked a little less open-ended than it had. Two months later, after I'd learned that Mother was no longer able to move around on her own because she had fallen one too many times—trying to climb out of her bed at night but no longer knowing how to use her legs—I tried to call Cathryn back. But it was the weekend and she was not in her office. I left a long message on her voice mail, though I wasn't able to utter a word, except a whisper on the far edge: "Sorry."

It has been coming a long time, this return. I think I started slowly making my way back the day, the moment, I climbed out the window on a rope of old sheets and clothes and left in the middle of the night, at seventeen. Over the years, I've felt like Ariadne guiding Theseus through the labyrinth with a thread, only it was made of rubber instead of silk and was far too short, so after a while it just started stretching and stretching, to a point where it would either snap, marooning them, or finally amass enough energy to drag both her and Theseus out of the labyrinth completely. Back to the start.

As time has passed, I've felt like everyone in this scenario: Ariadne, Theseus, the Minotaur they are trying to slay, and the labyrinth itself. I have even been the thread.

So when this new silence of Mother's was placed before me, by the call from the doctor, the moment came. The running girl put Mother's camera around my neck, and as she did, the thread didn't snap. The force that had been building up was too much and I was pulled back here, to where I have known—in the back of my mind—for a very long time, that I would end up. No matter how well my life was going, with Genny. No matter that I knew how much impossibility was living in these river waters, in the walls, in the wet streets, and in each and every one of the strangers in this city, this city that misses no one yet makes sure to mark you permanently should you ever try to run away. This city that, as soon as you think about it after having abandoned it, you're doomed to—one day—find yourself dragged back to.

Because it's not done with you, oh no, not at all. Not yet.

Parked in the lot of a dollar store halfway down Main—a break on my way from the home in Kildonan to Mother's old house in Wolseley—I turn my phone back on to a half-dead battery and a roaming signal. Beside me, beside the bundle of the packer and binder and clothes, is a plastic bag filled with a few boxes of granola bars, two bottles of water, and a cheap book of sudoku puzzles I bought—an excuse for loitering, for letting myself be briefly marooned here. I look down at my phone and send a text, sit, and answer the phone when it rings.

"You're not sorry," Genny says. She lets that dangle. She's right.

"I am sorry, you know. I wouldn't do it if I didn't have to."

She breathes. I decide to breathe too, staring at the various signs advertising how cheap things are in the store.

"All you had to do was call. Karen fucking called, right away, right after you texted *her*. Only her. You can't just do that. You shouldn't just do that. Running off alone without letting anyone know where or why."

I watch a hunched old man make his way out the door, arms full. I worry I won't ever make it all the way to the house. It is so close; the air is so dense.

Genny keeps up the pause, and I know when one of Genny's pauses is building up to saying something she wants to say but also doesn't want to. That's what this is. "I could have gotten time off. It wouldn't have taken any time to pack."

"Stop."

"I would have. You should have let me."

I know that Genny is relieved as much as she's hurt. She doesn't want to come back here any more than I do. She does not have things to tie up here. Being back here would simply be existing among the sharp rubble of her past. There's nothing left for her to salvage. It's a city of pure emptiness to her, but the emptiness of my Winnipeg is what I've come back to try and save.

"You need me," she says, and it's true. There is nothing in the world that I need more than Genny. "I can drive up. I can fly."

"I don't need you," I say. "It's just a matter of figuring out every-thing here. With her, the house. It's just a matter of tidying up."

Genny breathes. So do I.

"And how is Hedy?"

"I haven't seen her," I say, thinking of the short-haired old woman sitting in the chair. If it weren't for her scarred hands, and her name on the door, it could have been any old woman.

"If I fly, will you come and pick me up from the airport?"

"No."

"If I drive, will you answer the door?"

"No."

Air. Dollar signs. Concrete. Time growing wide. I imagine that the phone against my cheek is actually Genny's face. Its warmth is hers. She is speaking directly into my ear. Whispering, whispering the same way she whispered in my ear the night I crawled up into her window after breaking out of mine, almost thirty years ago, when we drove all the way to Minneapolis together to start a brand-new life.

She hangs up the phone.

When Mother was diagnosed with dementia, I began researching things that are good for the brain. I started taking vitamin B_{12} and magnesium, running three times a week, eating more avocado and greens, as well as doing a sudoku puzzle every evening. I loathe sudoku.

I would wake up every other day at six, run three miles, and make us a breakfast of avocado on slices of roasted sweet potato. While Genny showered and dressed, I stood sweaty against the wall with a cup of coffee and had her quiz me: "When did we first meet?" "How many times have we broken up?" "What colour collar did my dog Hamm have?" I tried to answer as quick as I could. I tried not to guess. "Dark green," Genny would say, after too long a pause, peeking her head around the steamy curtain. Smiling softly at me before asking for a kiss.

Once, maybe a year after Mother's diagnosis, I was at a bar with Genny, Karen, and some other artists from the collective and went into the men's washroom and found an article pinned to a corkboard above the hand drier about how drinking whiskey can be good for your memory. So I dried my hands and became a whiskey drinker.

The next day I walked down to the liquor store at the corner and bought myself a bottle of rye, prescribing myself at least a bottle a week. The whiskey also helped me tolerate the nightly sudoku. A few days later, after work, I went to the mall and bought a stainless-steel eight-ounce flask and resolved to drink one flaskful per day, to portion my intake. I got it engraved: *A Prayer to Mnemosyne*, the Titaness who had—with Jupiter's help—mothered every single Muse, and whose name represents memory.

Isn't there something pretty about that? About the ways that memory itself can beget everything?

I can't afford to forget anything because I'm not finished begetting.

After sitting in the car after the call, not feeling ready to turn the ignition back on, not wanting to touch the steering wheel, not wanting to look in the rear-view mirror, not feeling ready for anything, I finally turn the key.

The rain has started up again. I back up the car. My head is fog, though I'm no stranger to this feeling. I have learned to trust that my body can make its way where it needs to go without my head's directions. So my car's nose turns, comes to the end of the parking lot, and when it's safe, pulls south onto Main Street. A hand turns the windshield wipers back on and the radio sings a song I don't hear.

Main turns to Portage, Portage turns to Canora. After skirting Vimy Ridge Park, the car keeps going, past the streets I know by heart, the names that may as well each be my name—Honeyman, Preston, Westminster—some marking the exact intersections where Tom and I stole the street signs when we were in high school. The last time I was here and Mother was not speaking.

Before I make it to my block, I stop in the middle of the lane. There aren't many cars at this time in the morning. A car comes up behind me and then slowly pulls around to pass, probably thinking I'm trying to park, or waiting for a friend to come running from one of the houses. Nobody runs out, to help me, to push my car the rest of the way. So I have to do it, let my foot move from the brake pedal to the gas.

Just before reaching Wolseley Avenue, I pull off to the curb and park. My umbrella comes up from the compartment in the door, and I'm outside with Mother's camera hanging from my neck like an anchor, the rain hitting my taut shield hard. I lock the car. The clouds are thick and the sun has risen behind them like an inverted horizon. The day has basically become just another night. I leave the luggage in the car, for now, and feel the walls of the house here, nearby, in this stormdark where all the wet dogs of the city are barking.

Taped to a tree is an image of a girl's face, laser printed onto green paper streaked and bowing from the rain, with the word *MISSING* in big letters over the top. I stand there, staring, wondering if it's a picture of me.

Two weeks or so ago, before classes ended, Ess was in my office brainstorming ideas for the outline of hir thesis essay and asked me: "What was it like growing up queer up there?"

I was very masc—bound up tight and my hair folded up on itself—gnawing on the cap of a ballpoint pen. *Al.* I leaned back in my chair and took a long time to start answering. Nobody'd asked me that before.

"I didn't realize I was. That's the short answer. I didn't grow up in a house that talked about things like that. Most of my time growing up, it was just me and my mother. She never talked about me as a boy or a girl or anything like that. She just, well, talked *to* me. Sometimes, when I was really little, strangers would point at me in the street and smile and say things to her, but I wasn't great at English yet. She understood, as much as she ever did. She'd say thank you but never translated their compliments to me. So I didn't realize that the ways I was feeling were queer. It's hard to realize that you feel different from how you're seen when the only pronoun you grow up hearing every day is *you*."

"I wish I'd never had brothers. Probably it wouldn't have fucked with me as much," Ess said, turning around and closing the office door to a sliver. "When did you learn?"

"I started school, and the first thing we had to do was take a tour, and the teachers had the class split up between boys and girls."

"And you picked?"

"Yeah. I lined up at the end of the boys," I said, feeling a flush across my chest as the pen cap snapped in my teeth. "None of the other kids said anything. My hair was short then, too, because I'd asked for that. But then one of the teachers came over to me and went down on one knee—I remember it like it was fucking five minutes ago—and she laughed and said to me, 'No, no, the girls are lined up *over there*!' and pointed to the other line. She smelled like peaches. She looked at me like I was stupid."

"Damn."

I spat out the pen cap and threw it in the trash can, leaning forward on my chair.

"When my mother came to pick me up I rushed at her, crying. She took me back home, where I could be myself. It's weird how much of me that house held. How much it does. It was often a hard place to be, but it was always an easy place to be *me*."

"You ever go back?"

"Never," I said, feeling an ache in my head where the memory palace stands tall, with its walls and floors and roof.

"Me neither. I haven't been to the house, at least. I was fourteen last time. I've steered clear of it, though I've been all over Peculiar since, for photos and whatever other things I feel I need records of," Ess said, cracking hir hands on the back of hir neck. "Do you plan to?"

"Never," I said, hearing the hollow sound of the front door of the memory palace closing.

So I walk up the concrete path of the house, through the rain, without my luggage, weary and very aware of the movement of my legs after spending all that time in the car, driving and sleeping. I watch my feet as I go, trying to avoid the cracks, trying to avoid making eye contact with the house. But I can see it anyway, standing in my head as it always has. At the door, I pull my keys from the pocket of my dress and check the number beside the door. I can barely tell in the dark of the rain if this is the house. I can't recognize it. But the number is right, and I put in the key and turn it, and when the door opens, I'm finally convinced. I step inside and close the umbrella. Mother's old Leica lifts up from my chest to my eye. I turn on the hallway light.

I think the reason the house was so hard to recognize is its complicity with the street's darkness. This house has never really been interested in participating in the dark, in seeming asleep, because whenever I saw the house from the outside at night, the living room light was on and the drapes were open. Mother would be sitting inside, every time, looking out, waiting. It was as if the house couldn't sleep without me inside it, and only when I was finally back—and up the stairs, and in my bedroom—did the light go off and the drapes get drawn.

The light was on in the house every time I came back, every time but two: the night I ran away and the first night Mother spent in Selkirk.

Inside the house, the dust rustles up from the wind of the door until I shut it. The dormant film wakes up, thirsty, and I close my left eye and look only through the viewfinder of the camera. I watch the dust move, as if it's being walked through, then settle. My hands go up to the shutter speed and the aperture and the focus and the shutter button and advance forward the film. The exposure is all guesses. My eye moves out from behind the camera to check the settings, to open or tighten the aperture, to see how many frames are left. I follow the dust as it rouses again and again throughout the house—the little gusts of breath, the house a slow lung—turning on lights and taking photos that I'm certain will turn out blurry and wrongly exposed. But that's not what matters. What matters is framing pieces of the house into boxes, is rolling those frames up into Mother's favourite little machine, is going into the rooms and seeing them bare and changed and the same. Is capturing this tour.

The hallway, long; the little closet door under the stairs, the same: frame one. The living room, sparser; the telephone table; the telephone: frames two and three and four. The kitchen, different appliances, same colour: frame five. I walk past the old darkroom like it isn't even there. I don't take a photo. The hallway again, from the other end: frame six. On my way back down the hallway, toward the door, toward the bottom of the stairs—in a moment when my eye is out from behind the camera—I see on the floor of the landing the memory of me digging in the yard, but as soon as I put the camera back up to my eye, it is gone: no frame.

The stairs are the same, the creakiest stairs still creakiest: frame seven looking up, and frame eight looking down. The top of the stairs: the huge armoire, still there; three doors, still there. Frames nine and ten and eleven and twelve. The bathroom is frame thirteen. Mother's bedroom, lonely, hungry, the bed still made: frames fourteen and fifteen and sixteen. The door to the studio is untouched. I cross it, with a wide berth, to my bedroom. I open the door to the dark: frame seventeen.

I turn on the light for frame eighteen. The creaky loft bed is still there—frame nineteen—with the vent near the ceiling that looks into Mother's studio—frame twenty. That vent that a child might look through so many times, but that someone should not look at now, because my old twin bed, coverless and yellowing with time, is frame twenty-one. And that window—the window that I removed when I was seventeen, that has been replaced—is frame twenty-two. The new-looking wood of the window frame seems like the house's newest scar, though I know that is not true. I walk over to it, and I let Mother's camera sit against my chest. I try not to see myself in the reflection in the glass and fail—fail to not look and fail to see myself looking back at me. It could be anyone. As I put my hand on the wood, I look down into the dark, cobwebbed corner and see it there. The pry bar, the little pry bar I used to remove the glass. Frame twenty-three. Frame twenty-four, also, just in case.

The wind I've always known moves through the house, moves along like a trail of words you can't hear, or like a trail of words you can't ever stop hearing but still can't make sense of.

I stand, looking straight into the uncoated eye of the camera. The man staring into the glass is rewinding the roll. When I hear the tail end of the film slip out of the spool, I realize how cold the house is. I let out a breath and see it squiggle into the emptiness like a soul.

Sometimes, when you go through the memory palace hallway, the length of it changes. Sometimes you can basically teleport from one end to the other, from the landing to the kitchen or the darkroom door or the living room, from that end of the hall to the bottom of the stairs. Other times, the hallway keeps stretching out ahead of you, and you walk and walk and walk, or you sprint and sprint and sprint, and you only ever make it halfway across. Times like these, you feel like Achilles chasing the tortoise, the tortoise with the head start that will never reach the finish line, the tortoise that he can never catch, because neither can advance more than half the distance between their destinations. You know that when the hallway is endless, it is taking up the irrationally infinite space between you and Mother, including the moments when you were both so close to the finish line but unable to cross it. You sometimes stop halfway through the never-ending hallway and try to run back, back to the front door, out of the hallway, and out of the palace, but once you're in the middle, both ends are taken away from you. When you find yourself in this hallway in your memory palace, you often end up collapsing onto the floor, and as soon as you hit the ground, you always hear, again, the door's foreign, hollow sound. When you pick yourself up, you find yourself standing outside the palace on the front lawn, among the grass that feels like hair and rises and falls like a breathing chest. And when you look at the palace, the door has completely disappeared. So you have no choice but to open your eyes, and come back to life, and give yourself up to the failure.

The concrete path, the door, the hallway. The house. I remember Mother stuffing me into down jackets and snow boots, hobbling me into the thick snow pants she'd bought for me at the thrift store.

"I bought it big like this because you will grow," Mother said when she first pulled them up my legs as I sat braced on the stairs.

It was late October, which back then meant there was already a foot of snow in Winnipeg, and the rivers were frozen. It was morning. I don't know where we were going. She'd bought me the pants with a too-big jacket because I'd outgrown the one-piece snowsuit I'd used for the last few years. I must have been around eight or nine. She rolled up the legs, took an open safety pin from between her lips, and started pinning up the rolls of extra length.

"If you buy big clothes, your body will know to grow into them. Do you want to be big one day, Alani? Like me."

I don't remember answering, but I must have, because that was back when Mother and I still responded to each other. My mind doesn't usually decide to remind me of us speaking. Instead, I remember thinking about my body getting larger, as she pinned the legs, and how hopeful that made me. I wanted there to be more room for all of me, I wanted my body to feel as bare and roomy as our house did, like

I could fit everything in. When I was in kindergarten, because it was too cold to have recess outside, our teacher brought out the projector to show us a documentary about hermit crabs. I couldn't understand what the voice-over was saying because of its speed and accent, so I just watched the crabs switching shells and started to think that's what life is like: you live as long as you can in one body, then once you can't fit into it anymore, you move to a new one. And someone smaller takes your place.

For a while, I didn't understand what growing up looked like, didn't know how it worked. For a few years after Ilsa died and gave Mother the house in her will, Mother helped other elderly people in the neighbourhood keep up their lives in their own homes. Over the years of looking after Ilsa and me, she had perfected her technique of caring for fragile bodies.

Before I was in school, or during the summer, I went along with her in the mornings and wandered around the old person's house while Mother was in another room, helping them get out of bed, bathe, eat, or take their medicine. I spent most of the time there either avoiding their mean old pets or walking around their living rooms, their hall-ways, looking at the family pictures on the walls. I remember looking through those photos for the old, frail things that Mother cared for and never once finding them.

I never thought that they could've been the result of one of the young bodies in those photos. After a certain age they stopped being documented, or else the newer photos were never hung. Mother hadn't ever taught me about aging, about time's effect on a body. I'd never seen a picture of myself as a baby; I don't know that I'd ever seen a picture of myself at all back then. I thought that everything was inside me, that as far back as I could remember was as far back as

I ever was. I assumed the people in the photos, in different stages of their lives, were each a different person. I thought I was going to be myself—a child—forever.

Nobody told me that I'd already been things that I didn't remember, that as far back as I could recall was not the start of me, and that my life would consist of slowly leaving myself behind. I hadn't yet realized that I didn't remember anything about the year or two we still lived in Germany. All I'd known was that whenever I looked at myself in the mirror, there I was. Back then, with that mindset, things seemed stable.

"What does it mean being big?" I asked, as Mother took my hands and pulled me to my feet at the bottom of the stairs. She tugged at the pants, put her eye close to the floor—her tied-back hair flopping onto the hardwood—to squint and yank at the pinned legs. By then, I knew people grew, that there was no escaping the body I was in. "Why do I want to do it?"

She sat up—the memory is tack sharp—finished adjusting one of the straps of the snow pants, pulled back a little, and looked me straight in the eyes. Her face was so close to mine. I can remember the smell of her shampoo, the weight of the snow pants hanging on my shoulders, her hands grazing down along them on their way to brace her against the floor with that swooshing sound of scraped polyester. I remember everything about that moment, everything but her mouth. I want to remember her smiling, but I can't see it. I can't see her mouth or the inflection that the words came out with.

"Because it is going to happen, Alani. Getting big. You should be welcoming and excited for things that are going to happen."

I wake up stiff and heavy and lift myself from Mother's bed, walk to the other side of the room, and turn on my phone, plugged in and splayed out on the dusty hardwood floor. Next to it are a few dead flies and ladybugs, belly-up. The dead insects are everywhere, riddling the windowsills and corners, as if they had each spent the last moments of their lives trying to escape the house.

It's morning, probably. The world outside the house is grey with rain. It's sometime between two nights, at least, and I'm here, dressed in half the clothes I brought, since the radiators took their time and there weren't enough blankets on the bed. My phone flashes its brands as it grumpily vibrates back to life. I don't like rain, don't like how it reminds me of the grey flatness life often takes—for people like me, like Mother.

Last night, after pulling the roll of film from Mother's camera and realizing how cold it was in the house, after grabbing my luggage from the car, I took another tour, cranking every radiator. I'm sweating now, in the blouses and the muscle shirts and the tight jeans and the boxer shorts and a long, pleated skirt. My phone blinks and sucks back the string of unread texts from Karen, none dated more recently than last night. I open them, so that she'll know I've seen them. I can hear the radiators knocking in the living room under me, in the bathroom.

—*Why aren't you coming to the meeting?*

—*Hey A whats up?*

—*Pick up your phone!*

—*Come on*

—*I'm going over to G's. Don't go dark, please?*

—*Promise.*

I don't text her back. I can't.

I check the missed calls and they are all the same ones I already missed. Genny hasn't tried to call again, since she hung up on me. I don't listen to the voice mail she left when I was driving up here. I let its notification hang over me, a very effective thorn.

I unpeel the many layers of me. The tall mirror that was once in Mother's room is no longer here, and I'm glad, as much as I feel like it's too big of a change. I undress to the amount of nothing I'm comfortable with. My skin starts to dry in the radiator air, and the clothes on the dusty floor around me look like the aftermath of an orgy. Boy clothes, skirts, and panties. My hair falls in front of my face as I look down, so I take a hair-tie from my wrist and pull it back. I pick up the clothes, brush off some of the dust—some of the fly corpses—and pile them up on the bed. Rain on the roof. Dust from years of abandon rustles up sneezes. I walk to the luggage and pull out the binder, the packer, but then put the packer away again. The electricity is moving in the walls. I can't hear that, but I feel it. I never bothered to cancel any of the utilities when Mother was put in the home, because I didn't think I'd be paying them much longer. I take off the bra and throw it onto the mess of the bed.

My old copy of Ovid's *Metamorphoses* sits at the bottom of the luggage, with a random assortments of things: floss but no toothbrush; a 150 mm lens for my Hasselblad but no camera body; half a ream of blank paper but no pencils; three empty film canisters, one with a roll already shot, another two with rolls of unshot Kodak Tri-X; a bottle of shaving cream with no razor; and a single eye's worth of fake lashes. Just in case.

The book is wrapped in my first real binder, whose elastics have been so stretched by time and use that it no longer keeps anything flat. It has long since lost its transformative powers but is tight with nostalgia. I got the binder after Genny and I ran off to Minneapolis, when I met Archer after a show and they told me where they'd gotten theirs. After noticing the bandages peeking out from under my arm, they said, "That's really dumb, but I'll help you," cementing our friendship.

I kept the book and that binder on a shelf in a cabinet at home, a small museum of artifacts from my life—the things that the running girl didn't end up ditching between the fires: A poem Karen wrote for me when I ran away to Hamburg, in purple permanent marker on her birth certificate—mirrored, so as to only be read through the bleed. The collar I bought for my cat, Darius, with his name and my name, but could never get over his neck for his claws and hissing. A bottle of cheap plum nail polish I stole from Genny's bathroom twenty years ago that has since become one dry piece of colour. A crumpled two-dollar bill someone gave me for a Polaroid print I shot—the first time I ever sold something I'd made.

Mother's camera, the old Leica III that I stole when I left this place at seventeen, was kept on top of the cabinet, not inside it, and not on that shelf.

I pick up the library-bound Ovid, unwrap it from the binder, toss it onto the bed, and then slowly pick through the clothes until I find something worth wearing. I leave Mother's camera sitting on the bedside table and carry the book downstairs. I sit on the couch—for the first time in decades, I realize—and flip through the pages, past underlines and marginalia riddles, from previous readers as well as me. The library loan card, still stuck in its slot in the front of the book, has yet to hold my name. My page-flipping eventually lands me at the poetry, and I skip past the first lines, the call to the Muse—*Of bodies changed to other forms I tell*—and rest on the lines about the creation, one of the many things that always seems to bring me back to this spine:

Ere land and sea and all-covering sky
Were made, in the whole world the countenance
Of nature was the same, all one, well named
Chaos, a raw and undivided mass,
Naught but a lifeless bulk, with warring seeds
Of ill-joined elements compressed together.

The words sink in like a mantra, and as I shut the book my mind feels the flurry underneath it all. I try and try to forget Mother—Mother in the home this morning and a thousand others before, each one a morning where I wasn't here. But I can't forget her, so she slides into the room and sits across from me. Her hair is short. She does not look at me, because she does not have a face, or any front at all. She is nothing but a silhouette with that short hair and her scarred hands, which dance on the armrests. She is quiet, bound in the chair by more than a belt, dark tendrils like ivy weaving her into it. I cannot look at her, or away. The radiators sound like a crowd trying to pound their way into the house.

I close Mother out with my eyelids. I take a breath, walk from the curb to the front door of the memory palace, and open it, stepping over the first memory without looking down. The sound of the door closing sneaks up behind me. It is always shocking; I'm never prepared for that sound.

In the hallway ahead of me a collection of distances rolls out. I begin to walk.

Somehow I make it all the way to the top of the stairs in the memory palace, remembering as much of the things I have designed the palace to remember. But as soon as I make it to the top—where the old armoire is—I can't take anymore. I sprint straight to my bedroom door, and opening the door opens my eyes.

Mother is no longer sitting in front of me. She and the chair are both gone, and I get up from the couch, leaving Ovid there face down, alone. Outside, the rain is getting heavier, darker. Inside, that gust of wind is back, rustling everything up.

I slip on my shoes and jacket, grab my umbrella, and run upstairs for my phone. After I check to make sure the voice mail Genny left me is still unlistened to, I look at Mother's camera on the nightstand. I don't remember putting the lens cap back on, don't remember collapsing the little 50 mm Summar lens into the camera's body, but I'm happy I did. It's hiding, too. I sling the camera around my neck and zip my jacket over it as I make it out the door. The umbrella *fwoops* open. The camera is an amorphous bump at my belly.

I walk south, streaming down sidewalks toward the river, and don't look back at the house. I do not need to look. I know that the house is following me.

The wind sprays a horizontal mist from the drooping trees along the Assiniboine River and my eyes squint to keep it out. Water will always find a way in. The umbrella doesn't help much here, next to the swelling river. I can only walk on the far edge of the muddy path, the only part that's still above water. My other hand holds my jacket closed at the throat, to try and keep the water from dripping inside the coat, down my chest, and onto the camera. I'm almost there, the place where the Assiniboine loses its name and power to the Red, where both rivers—thick and brown and quick—meet to traffic the province's water north through the rest of the city, to swell up the lakes, to tickle at Hudson Bay, and to end up as nothing but a frigid spit in the ocean.

The Forks.

There are a few people irrational enough to be on the river trail because no weather can slow a Winnipegger, especially not weather so dreary and moody. When someone is coming toward me, I walk off the trail first and let them pass. When I hear them walking behind me, when I can hear them over the sound of the rain, I walk faster. I don't look back.

I try not to imagine the river frozen and me walking down the middle of it. I do not imagine it.

I walk under bridge after bridge—cars splashing by overhead—and stick as close to the water as I can, going straight for the Forks. I ignore the market, the tourist trap, the things that are near the Forks but are not the real Forks, that are just the profitable capitalism of proximity. I steady my attention on the disappearing pathway, on the confluence where the Red takes off, emboldened after swallowing the Assiniboine, on the place where you can stand and stare at the water and be unsure which river you're actually looking at, where you can just look and be lost, knowing nothing certain except that the thing you're looking at is water, is river, is moving. That's all that can be said about them. The names, any words of distinction, for places like these stop making any sense.

A raw and undivided mass.

I stop on a piece of high, dry land out of the way of the few people trying to walk the river path. I stand there and stretch my spine, pulling at the cap of my head until the word "mountain" jumps to mind, until I'm barefoot in the yoga classes where I tried and tried to learn to move and hold my body like Mother always did. The rivers are both mud brown, and the rain has decided to slow down a little. I can see the far end of the bank. I try to remember which neighbourhood of the city that would be, but nothing comes. The words for specific things fall off into the flux. I take my hand from my collar, pull my phone from my pocket, and call Genny—speed dial.

I know that she's at work, that her phone will be silent, and even if she was not and her phone was not, she still would not answer. I know all that. But I switch to speakerphone and hear her recording say, "This is Genny Ford, leave a message," and when I hear the beep I hold the phone out toward the rivers, the Forks. Little whirlpools swirl not thirty feet from me as the water spins along the rocks set at the edge of the path—rocks that are now under water—to try and keep the rivers from eroding the path away. To try and keep the space.

I stand there, with the phone recording at the far edge of the umbrella's protection, recording whatever little sounds the mic might be able to transcribe into the message. Then I force myself to yell: "The Forks!" before I can turn the phone around and hang up without saying anything, because I don't want to fall off the edge of her world, our world, as much as everything feels like it's beginning to pull me under. Or rather, rise above me. That the chaos, the too-much, the teeming that is the foundation of everything is bubbling back up. The dark place that makes people grow quiet.

When I turn around to leave, I'm glad that Mother's house is nowhere to be seen, that it has not followed me all this way. But its creaking has sunk into my head again, hasn't it?

I think it is my bones themselves, that sound.

The sun has almost set and I'm so tired of the rain by the time I make it back to Mother's house. On the way, I stopped at the grocery store to get some food and some things to clean and dust the house with. I stopped by a restaurant on Sherbrook that was not there thirty years ago and ate a sandwich alone at a corner table where the waitress called me ma'am. I wanted that moment to drag out, to skin me with a dull blade, rather than come back to the house. But once I carried my grocery bags past Walnut, I couldn't stop walking. These creaky floorboards have a terrible magnetism.

As I walk up to the door, I put my bags down on the ground so I can put my hand on the knob. When it turns, the door opens. I didn't lock it. From the open door comes a huge whooshing sound of air escaping, rushing past me, as if the house had been holding its breath. I turn around, to see where the wind is heading, and the world blinks out into pitch-dark night.

I'm there on the sidewalk, scrunched into a stiff denim coat, and it's raining and my feet are worn out. I'm fifteen or sixteen. Tom is holding his umbrella over me. His other arm holds his jacket to his chest, conspicuously hiding the street sign we just finished removing from its post atop the stop sign. I can remember the intersection—Palmerston Avenue and Lenore Street—but not which name we ended up taking for Tom's collection. That specific part of the night is gone.

From here, nearer to Wolseley Avenue, we can't see inside the house, into the lit window, to see Mother sitting and waiting. I don't think to look at the darkness at the door to see if someone is standing there, watching me.

"You're sure? It's still early," I say to Tom, trying to convince him as a means of making him stay longer, though we're both running on the last dregs of our fumes. He looms over me. I'm not short, but he is a lanky giant. It's around two o'clock and we've spent the last three hours—at least—walking, hopping over deep, endless puddles.

"Yeah, I just don't think so. Del has been trying to, you know, do things with me again. She quit Thursday. For good this time, she says. I should get a little sleep."

I feel the weight of Mother's camera around my neck, and when I put a hand to my belly to touch it—under the cover of Tom's umbrella —I'm briefly at the door, feeling the lens cap through my coat. Then I lift my hand from my belly and I'm back with him.

My hair is buzzed down clear to the scalp. I am shivering. Tom has not lost his hope, and that is why I love him. He and I are impossibly different. I squeeze my way within his umbrella arm and his tall body. I don't remember my hair getting buzzed, but it happened that night— this night—before we went out walking. I am no longer the person who wanted that done. The want is trapped in fog.

I can feel the pressure of his umbrella arm on my back, the hidden street sign pushing against my shoulder. And then I feel myself pull away; I watch myself do it. I feel the wind on my head, feel the rain knock into it as I move from under his umbrella toward the brightest house on the dark lane, toward the door. I try not to look at the lit window, where I know Mother is sitting, waiting for me. Tom and the whole world behind me disappear and everything is quiet, silent, as I can't help but look in the window and see her looking up at me. *Allie.* Me. I stop moving.

I shake my head, feel my hair long and tied back, so I go inside and untie it, sitting dry on the couch with the grocery bags at my feet. The living room light is off, and outside is nobody. I lie down on the couch and attempt level breathing. Dust, dust, dust. I can imagine them going to the door, taking out their keys, unlocking the door, hanging the jacket they stole from Tom's house, and climbing up the stairs. I can picture the light switching off in the living room and hear the sound of the stairs measuring her ascent to her own room, to her own bed. Mother.

When my breath evens out I get up, flip on the living room light to combat the encroaching grey, go to the closet under the stairs, and pull out Mother's vacuum. It's a different vacuum than I remember, but it has been kept in the exact same place.

I plug it in and push it room to room, sucking up the dirt, the dust, and all the dead bugs.

3

THE LIVING ROOM

The walls of your living room are covered in memories. Layers of them, framed like photos, or windows. Memories from everything: your exile in Hamburg, your school days and late nights near Tom, the long summer weeks, the days at home, and the countless hidden journeys into your various darks. In the living room hang the scenes of your life—the living scenes. The people in the framed memories move and speak. When you walk into the memory palace, as you come down the hallway—for as long or as little as that takes you—you hear the memories looping in the living room. If you listen closely, you can pick up which memories are going to be the loudest.

Framed above the phone table is the memory where you are sitting on the docks of the Elbe near Cuxhaven while Erwin Egger takes a landscape photo. He is shooting on his Hassy, and the wind is blowing your hair. You are not looking through your own camera—Mother's old camera—that you set up on your tripod, because you just can't find the beauty in bare, unpeopled worlds like Erwin can, not at all anymore. Erwin finishes his shot, comes over to you at your tripod, and tells you to stand at the end of the dock. You do. You stand there and you take your clothes off, because that's how you prefer yourself, in photos and in life—imprescriptible. At the edge of the memory you hear young dock workers walking along the shore, commenting on the lucky old man. Erwin finishes the shot and the memory rolls forward again, mostly the same, though the angle is a bit different.

Beside that one, blossoming across the walls and sitting on the floors, are memories of you climbing in and out of windows. Genny's, mostly. In Minneapolis, when she lived apart from you in a place that did not welcome guests. There's the memory of you climbing into Genny's window in Winnipeg, too, the night you two left. In a few it is Tom's window, for fun, and in one—sitting face down on the floor in front of you, which you lift up to check—it is your own. As you kneel to that memory, you don't see yourself in it. You just see the makeshift rope. You just see the room, beginning a second life without you in it.

Whenever you lift this memory, the rope snakes out from the frame and begins to weave itself into and back out of every single memory in the room. Binding memory to memory like a web. The rope winds itself around your body, like the ivy that Ovid uses as one of the sensible flourishes of Bacchus's powers. Only it doesn't transform your body into some wild aberration. It just takes over the space around you until it finds your throat and tightens up until you're dead in every single one, while the rest of the memory keeps replaying.

Eventually, the rope will web across the doorways, trapping you, so you want to make sure that you leave the living room while you still can. If you're trapped inside, you know the web will tighten around you until you are unable to get away. Pulling memories from their frames on the wall into a gibbering mass with you at the centre. If you don't get out while you can, the memories that you built the palace to acknowledge—to remember and then pass by—will become even more your only world.

Mother never told me anything about Germany, about leaving, about our life before, about us coming here and what the plan was if she hadn't found the job caring for Ilsa, the old Belgian woman whose children had transplanted her from Antwerp into a relatively cheap house in Wolseley when her husband died. I don't know anything about our life before we lived with Ilsa. My earliest memories are of living in this house with Mother and a woman who spoke only German and who was dying very slowly.

The job working with Ilsa was probably hard to fill, since she required a live-in nurse who could speak German, and because her children were dreadful and did not pay as well as they could have afforded. It was all obligation and appearance to them. But Mother still took the job, and somehow, she didn't hate the work, I don't think, despite the fact that since I was a baby, her whole life revolved around keeping two fragile things at either ends of their lives from dying.

I remember Ilsa having the air of a sage: her eyes set in deep sockets, her hair thick and dark and long and rootlike. I remember Ilsa and Mother always talking, frantic and tired. I remember sitting outside the door and listening, though all the words are gone. Mother may never have talked more in her life than when she lived with Ilsa, but despite that, when I remember that time, I can only see their mouths moving. That past is almost completely silent.

We lived in Ilsa's house with her for nearly half a decade. She hung on as every mechanism in her body started to fail. If it wasn't for Ilsa, I suppose Mother might have turned to photography sooner. But I'm not sure working in photography was ever what she wanted to do, even though a year or so after Ilsa died she ended up shooting portraits in a little studio she set up in our living room.

I don't remember Ilsa's children except that when they were in the house, they rarely talked when I was in the room, and they demanded that Mother speak English to them. They hardly climbed the stairs to see Ilsa but instead stood on the landing and were briefed by Mother about how Ilsa was. Occasionally, they would come and, with Mother's help, carry Ilsa down the stairs to a wheelchair and whisk her off to some function of theirs. But I don't really remember their presence but for the feeling of sprinting upstairs, or ducking into doorways downstairs. I remember running down the hallway toward the living room or through the kitchen to the backyard when I heard their feet approaching and their keys jangle in the door. I remember them most vividly in my fear of them.

Despite the fact that I vacuumed and dusted everywhere in the house last night—everywhere except Mother's yoga studio and her old darkroom—by the time I woke up this morning, the dead flies and ladybugs had already begun to repopulate the house. Legs and bellies to the roof—to the grey, wet sky above—back in the same corners and atop the same sills.

I go back downstairs and pull out the vacuum, plugging it in and unplugging it as I drag it through the house, sucking them back up. I wonder if, at night, they dragged themselves out of the vacuum's tube. I wonder if I should take the bag to a stranger on the street and ask them if they can see them in there: the dead.

But I don't do that. I go to the kitchen, put the bag in the trash, tie it up, and put it outside. Then I come back in and put the vacuum away.

After Ess and I started working together on hir thesis project, I rationed hir to two visits to my office hours a month. Ze kept it up, kept meeting goals for having new pieces to show, rarely skipping any, even if ze hadn't been able to make it to class that week. By the time ze stopped coming to class altogether last November, ze was pretty much finished *Outside Peculiar*, aside from hir essay.

One day, at the far end of the two weeks ze'd missed, Ess didn't show up to our meeting, which had always been set for the two hours before class. I closed my office door and called hir. The call went to voice mail. The voice mail message said: "Can't answer the phone right now. Prolly dead."

The only thing that delayed my sprint to my car was looking up Ess's address on my laptop and running over to the administrative assistant to tell her that I had to cancel class, last minute. I handed her a sticky note with the room number so she knew where to go and in big bold letters wrote the word: *EMERGENCY*

From life in the house with Ilsa I also remember the backyard, where I would dig with a little gardening trowel Mother got me for my fifth or sixth birthday—which are some of my earliest, stable memories. I would dig all sorts of little holes, cutting through the weak turf. I remember the smell of the grass clippings and unearthed soil. I remember the tall wood fence that separated the yard from the alley, except for the opening where the car could pull through to park, where Mother's old car is now. These days the fence is drooping in, but back then it was stalwart. I remember Mother sitting on the back stoop and watching over me, with the back door to the kitchen open, listening for Ilsa's call—*Hed! Hed!* Our life was so much simpler, both of us seemed so much lighter.

I didn't remember why I wanted the trowel until my ears got reacquainted with German while I was in Hamburg. It was a warm but overcast afternoon and I was biking over the little bridges crossing the city's capillary canals, down thin residential streets, when suddenly— halfway there, in a quiet neighbourhood—a woman who was watering a hanging planter on the absolute tips of her toes called out to her friend on the opposite sidewalk in German, "I wish I were taller!" And that word *"wünschte"*—wish—brought me back to my little face pressed against that tall wood fence, pressed to the place where a knot had fallen from a board, where I could see a man digging a hole to plant a bush in the yard across the alley.

As that word came back, the doors in my head opened up and the past slipped in. I kept pedalling, remembering how I called Mother over from her station on the stoop and pointed to the little hole, say- ing, in German, that I wished to be a digger. Though looking back now, I think in that young moment I just wanted to be *him*.

I was surprised, when that memory came back to me, that the feeling of looking through a barrier at something I wanted to be was significant enough to return. But that's the feeling I could be chasing when I put my eye to a camera's viewfinder. It's a feeling that has lived inside me all this time, invisibly, pulling me along.

On the way to the kitchen to heat up a can of soup, I stop in the doorway of the living room, where the soft grey light is lounging across the floor and the furniture, and there I am: sitting on a little stool against the wall, and the light is gone but for the sudden blast of the flash. Mother lowers the flash and sets it on the floor, as my eyes fill with blank spots. I'm in the doorway, too, so old. I'm six or seven. I'm naked.

Mother looks down and scritches a pencil on the yellow pad at her knee. I cannot hear the real sound but an assumed one fills the space. She looks up at me, then adjusts the exposure on the camera on the tripod. But there's no camera there, so she just readjusts the air, hair tumbling down her other side. An older woman is dark in the doorway, the camera that Mother is using looped around her neck. She doesn't look over at me. She's looking toward the blacked-out window.

I know the words I've got are hers. The head on my shoulders, that Mother is photographing, isn't any more mine than my body. Isn't anyone's.

Mother looks up at me, finger to the camera's invisible trigger, flash held out to the right of her. My right.

Click: brilliance.

I rub my eyes, Mother scribbles on the pad, I jump off the stool.

"Ey," Mother says, looking up at me. My feet don't feel the wood underneath, but it still hits them. "One more. Get on the seat, Alani. Please."

"No," I try to say. "*Nein.*"

Mother puts the flash on the floor again and opens her mouth. Words fall out and align themselves in the space between us, obscuring one another. I do not understand them, but the little head on the little body does, climbs back up onto the stool. Mother puts her eye to the empty tripod and refocuses, then recomposes. She lifts the flash back up, and I ask, "What is it a camera does?"

The flash arm slackens. Mother, the look of her, is mostly falling hair and assumed movements, assumed flesh, but now I see her face: less burdened, less ravaged—but than when? I'm filled with the doorway's life, the doorway's forgetting, but when Mother smiles I can see it, there, on her face. A turn of the lips. And just like that, I realize how much pain smiles can cause.

"They, hmm ..." she says. The woman in the door has disappeared and Mother's Leica is on the tripod. It has always been there. "They sort of take time, and they hold it still. So it is easier to look at."

I squirm at the words I know and do not know, because Mother switched to English after Ilsa died and I am still trying to catch up.

"What is the word 'time' mean?"

"*Zeit*," Mother says. Her voice is not her voice. She has been recast, borrowing the inflections of some voice in my head. The smile floats above her head, like the blank spots in the eye after the flash has pierced them. Her smile is looming everywhere I look.

"*Zeit*, time, is a sort of river of moments you float down. And I do. Everyone does."

My heart races. I know it's not happening, it's only remembering, but I feel that moment in me, the terror of it, of realizing that I'm living on sprinting water, past blurring riverbanks. I remember the tempo of that little human's heart. Mine.

"But I can't float," I say, and the flash breaks the moment open and spills me out to now: a middle-aged woman—person—in a doorway, her camera sinking in at my belly and the day dragging its way over hardwood and upholstery. The stool is gone. The tripod. But the camera is still around my neck, gazing. The wind in the house feels like it's grabbing the back of my head, as if it's about to push it down into a trough of water, as if I'm some drunk cowboy in a Western that it wants to sober up.

The little girl's little naked heart is bolting. It wants out. But someone called it a rib cage for a reason.

The only thing that is superimposed onto all of the memories in the living room of your memory palace is Mother. She is standing in each of your memories, staring at them, at things she knows nothing of because you didn't tell her about any of them. She stands, in each of the compositions, waiting, as if she were a still photograph sutured into the motion of life. But you think she is simply standing still, you think if you look at her hard you could see her blink or breathe, but you can't bear to. She is just there, everywhere, waiting with a patience that only those with a sickness of the mind can muster, waiting for the occurrence through which all murky things will clearly mark themselves knowable. Waiting for an answer to life in the living movement of another.

Mother stands perfectly exposed in your memories; everywhere you look she is perfectly clear and stark, even in the memories that are faded—old or boring things that were on the brink of being lost when you first built this palace. Things you don't grab quite so desperately.

Despite being everywhere, Mother never looks at you as you move through the memory palace. She stands in the memories, not always in focus, waiting. You can't tell if she's judging your memories. You can't tell if she can see them at all, despite standing within them and staring. But you know she's there. You can hear the familiar silence of her.

After cancelling class, I drove hard toward Ess's place with both hands. I'd been once before, when I picked hir up for the opening of the collective's show on flatness that ze had a piece in.

It didn't take long to get there. I put the car in park, left the key in the ignition, and ran up the wood stairs that went up to hir tiny studio above the garage.

I tried the door. It was locked. I started knocking, and thankfully, Ess opened the door before I had to start pleading for hir to let me in.

"Hey," I said, standing there catching my breath, staring at Ess in hir underwear looking too tired to be alive. "Let's go for a drive, yeah? Let's get you help," I said. "But first, let's get some clothes on you."

Cicero, a famous Roman orator, practised the mnemonic technique called the method of loci—also known as the memory palace—to help him remember his long, complex speeches. Cicero did this by imagining his rhetorical points pinned onto memorable things in a perfect re-creation of his own palace in his mind, which allowed him to picture himself walking through the rooms he knew so well, visualizing things in his home that represented different movements in rhetoric. When walking through his imaginary mansion, while standing in front of a huge crowd, Cicero could recall long, meticulously constructed speeches with grace and eloquence—as if speaking with a natural and spontaneous brilliance. Through this technique of pinning memories into intimately known places, the mind becomes capable of incredible feats of memory.

A few years after Mother was diagnosed with dementia, I began attempting to compose a memory palace that could contain all the remembrances that I felt made up my life, made up myself, out of the terror of eventually losing them. For a long time, I tried different houses—from Tom's to mine in Minneapolis—but ended up using Mother's, despite it being a bit small for all the things I needed to remember. I didn't want to use it, but after a while I knew that it was a place whose walls I could trust would always be standing in my head. That no matter how far, or how close, I ran I would always have it with me. Because it already had so many of the memories I wanted to hold onto storming through its walls.

When Ilsa died, she wanted the house to go to Mother instead of her children. For almost half a decade, Ilsa and Mother talked and smiled and wept and gossiped and lived together. Though I can't hear their voices, I'll never forget their faces together.

Mother cried as they carried the body from the bedroom. I stood in the corner of the room, staring at the bed, the bed that I don't remember really seeing empty before that moment. I must have, but that emptiness felt different. I don't really remember Mother crying much since then—aside from after her return from Selkirk. Ilsa's children were a string of shadows cast along the wall outside the door as I watched Mother cry, kneeling in the middle of Ilsa's bedroom floor, as faceless men carried the body out of the room.

But then, perhaps I was the one crying, and Mother was simply kneeling in respect for her dead friend. Mother began packing our stuff that night, but two days later, Ilsa's daughter came by, more annoyed than sad, and handed us the deed to the house. I can't imagine how much that must have hurt Mother, thinking that Ilsa—a phantom she cared for and consoled for so many years—had, at the end, thought to try and buy her love. Mother must have thought of that deed as a letter saying, *Please remember me.* But maybe that's just something I would think.

In the following days, while Mother and I were grieving in the emptiness, a crew came by and carried all of Ilsa's things from the house. The place grew bare. They carried out pretty much everything but the beds and the armoire on the second floor, at the top of the stairs. The armoire was well crafted, by Mennonites, but it wasn't an antique. It wasn't worth the effort.

The house was transformed from a home into walls surrounding space, space that we would hardly make a dent in ever filling up. It always seemed like we'd only recently moved in, because we were not a family who had things to fill houses with. We had what we had, which was mostly just each other.

Before Ess was admitted to the mental health centre, I put a hand on hir shoulder and told hir, "The wave of bullshit will come, but it won't get you. I know people who have come through here and were treated just fine. And don't worry, I'll come visit you."

After the nurses took Ess in, I went back to the waiting room and called Genny. My heart was racing, remembering the sound of footsteps on those tile floors, the sharp sound the backpack made as it was placed on the floor at the front desk. And the sound of a zipper opening to show what had been packed. What had nearly happened.

I told Genny where I was, quickly adding that it was for Ess. "I was really scared ze might have already done something," I said.

"I'm sorry, again, Genny."

"Allie," Genny said. I stared out the window toward the grey November day. I felt a breeze circling my shoulders, tugging at me a little. "Do you think, after all this is over, you will let hir apologize to you?"

"No," I said, thinking about Mother in bed after Selkirk, thinking about how she never apologized either, how I never wanted her to. "You're right."

"Good. Are you stuck there? Or are you coming by for dinner?"

"They just took Ess back. I'll come back to see hir tomorrow. I'll be there soon."

Sometimes while you're walking around the living room, remembering all the memories framed on the walls, on the floor, the landline on the phone table rings, reminding you that it exists. Its ring adds to the mutterings of the people in the memories on the walls.

Sometimes you pick up the phone, and sometimes you do not. Sometimes when you get to the phone, the receiver is stuck to the base and you cannot answer it, and you cannot pull its plug from the wall, because it's not plugged in at all. Sometimes you answer it and you can hear yourself, muttering things you do not want to hear. Things that you said to the boy in the mirror, or the girl in the mirror, or to yourself outside of it. Horrible things.

Sometimes it is Genny, and she is trying to talk to you, but she cannot hear you respond. She gets frantic at your quiet, you get frustrated with your unheard noise, and she hangs up on you.

Sometimes you pick it up and it's quiet and you begin to talk and you get frantic. You ask why they called if they don't want to talk. You go from scared to angry, but before you hang up—an action that always throws you out of the palace—you mutterspit into the phone: *Mother, Mother, Mother*. The last thing you hear before you slam the phone down is her, on the other end, stop breathing.

I check my phone, but Genny hasn't called. I try to call her again and fail. My fingers want to, want to follow their path and bring her voice back, but can't. I consider listening to the voice mail she left as I drove north, imagine the worry—the nostalgic weariness—in her voice and don't listen to it. My nerves rack. I put my phone down. I can feel the house start to close in around me, the pressure making my ears want to pop.

It comes back to me, the wind. It puts a hand on my back and pushes. I surrender myself to it. I do not look at it. I let it take me.

A coat, car keys, an umbrella—the remains of the afternoon. But as I open the door, I feel the running girl swirling through my head, and I go back into the house and grab Mother's camera and the *Metamorphoses* from the couch.

I stand outside the house. The wind pushes at me, but I don't move. I let it gather its momentum. I know the direction it wants me to go.

I walk to the car to go see Mother.

Every time I went to visit Ess in the centre, I made sure to ask hir how ze was, specifically drawing out what annoying things were happening to hir so ze could vent about it to someone who'd been there: casual but excessive misgendering, prying and semi-judgmental and semi-racist questions about hir tattoos.

"But I feel like I'm coming out the other side," ze said, a week in. "I'm sleeping some!"

A few visits in, I told hir that I'd talk to the department and see what Ess could do to make up for the lost weeks. Ess disclosed to me an interaction ze'd had with one of my colleagues, who'd asked hir to stay back after class to talk about a project ze had done for a course on experimental film. She told Ess that the project ze'd submitted felt a bit unfinished, a bit unrefined, and that she was giving hir the opportunity to work on it for another week to tighten it up.

"It was fucking impossible for me to get it that done," Ess said, rubbing hir hands on hir forehead and looking down at the table. "Doing more—the idea near *killed* me. Feel stupid just admitting it."

"I know. I get it," I told hir. "I'll talk to her."

"Al," ze said, placing hir hands on the overly clean table between us, tilting hir head up to me a little but not quite meeting my eyes, "I don't want special treatment."

I smiled and put my hands on hirs.

"It's not special treatment. I'd do it for anybody. It's just treatment."

After ten days, Ess was out. When ze was back on hir medication and rested up—with a bundle of class deadline extensions—ze told me that ze was doing a new project, even though *Outside Peculiar* wasn't finished yet.

"Peculiar isn't going no place," ze said, sitting in my office for the first time in months, a few days before the fall semester ended. "But I want to do something about being bipolar and queer. And, yeah, I know we've done all this work, I just—"

"I'm totally here for it," I said, interrupting hir. "One thing I've learned about art is that whenever you see smoke, you should chase it to the fire before the fuel is gone."

The nurse at the desk pulls at the neck of her scrubs, centring them.

"Your mother just woke up from a nap, so you may want to wait for half an hour before going in. She tends to be a bit clearer once she's had a chance to wake up."

"That's fine," I say. I sign in. Beneath my signature are the pages and pages of visitors who have come to the home since I did last.

Al Baum.

I hand it over and the nurse smiles, reads the name. "Was that your sister who came in the other day?"

"Yes," I say, turning around to the waiting room chairs, and then half turn back to say: "Allie's my twin."

All the chairs in the room have a sag from all the waiting done here. There are new magazines and old magazines, folded up and worn. I imagine all the people coming and going, all those names between my names, coming in and waiting, waiting upon each other's impressions of waiting. I sat on them, too.

I think about going to the car and grabbing the book from the passenger seat, from beside Mother's camera, but I don't want to risk leaving. I need to practise staying.

The television is on, set to a Winnipeg news channel. I catch the tail end of a story about how a sinkhole—the size of one lane—that opened up on St. Mary's Road a few days ago was finally filled in today. A slide show of still photos of a huge hole where the road had been hollowed out is running over the headline, the subtitles.

But then, just as they're cutting to an interview with someone who witnessed the sinkhole breaking the road, the screen switches, and a red *Breaking News* banner comes up, overlaying a grainy film clip of a boat going out onto the Red River toward a railway bridge, the railway bridge just north of the Forks, just north of where I'd been only yesterday, holding my phone to the thick spring swirling. I could have turned my body and seen that bridge.

The banner says a body has been found there, in the water. The camerawork from shore is shaky, zooming in on the boat past the point of clarity. For a moment, we are intimate with the pixelated engine, with the rolling turbidity of the muddy, swollen river that is licking at the boat's fibreglass hull. For a moment, the scene is abstracted, as the camera loses its bearings. Then the image cuts back to what appears to be the beginning of the shot, the distant pan of the river, a boat just leaving the banks, a slow and shaky zooming in.

The waiting room is quiet, the television muted. The only sound is the nurse at the desk occasionally rapping at her computer's old mechanical keyboard. I can hear every stroke of her fingers, dancing, slowing, stopping, resuming. I can almost feel the weight of her eyes in her head as she glances up at me, looking over at her from the television, and pulls her closed lips into a hospital smile.

Not a hospital. A place where the bad attempt to gracefully get worse.

I wish I were her.

So as I wait, I watch the same news break, again and again, in a steady repetition of itself, with hardly a detail added. I can imagine a few journalists scrambling to make copy to keep people watching. The subtitles run again and again, talking about the rains, the flooding, the incidence of bodies being found in that river. "... likely got disturbed by the fast waters." "The Red River is known for its ..." "... last June, some may remember ..."

"Mr Baum," the nurse says, pulling me up. "You should be fine to go in and see your mother."

For a second I don't move, just look at her, and then I stand.

"Remember to talk loud but conversationally. She responds best to tone, so you don't want to seem like you're yelling at her," the nurse says, standing and moving toward the hallway. Mother's hallway. "Though I'm sure your sister told you all about that."

I give her a hospital smile.

"We don't talk much," I say, waving as I go down the hall to let her know I don't want her to follow me, thinking how a body has suddenly appeared on my horizon, dead.

I stand by the door, its kickstand propping it open. I go in.

It's a horror how many people slip into our lives simply as bodies. Simply as broken vessels, sunk. How many people in life are not important until they are gone, until they are at the point when we're unable to retrieve them. It can happen in an instant, people invisible or unreachable only showing up through the violence of their leaving, becoming a kind of palimpsest.

Mother is sitting up in the bed, and I go and sit down in a chair beside her.

She is so tiny, in the bed, with her face staring out from her head cocked slightly away from me, to the window. I can hardly stand to look at her, but I do. I can recognize all the parts of her—the arms, the eyebrows, the lips—but not all of her together.

The first day I came here, I could hardly recognize her. Then, I could only recognize her hands, hidden and moving under their bubbly scars.

I take up the loose collection of bones that make up her hand and rub my thumbs along the atonal wrinkles of the scars. I try to open my mouth but can't. She looks away from the window and down at my hands holding hers, as if confused, either by my holding it or by her hand itself. The other chair is still staring out the window, and Mother is not in it. She is in the bed, and I am holding her.

Twenty-seven years break. I feel her blood pulse in her palm and her muscles tense. I loosen my grip but keep holding.

My teeth start to hurt from holding everything in. My hands do their best to draw back and not shatter her. Something in me, some dissociated fury, grows an awareness of her fragility before it is allowed to reach the end of my arms, before it can get to the headquarters of my hands, my fingers, and before it can reach the tip of my tongue or let go the muscles of my jaw. I'm paralyzed by a swell of intensity, a break in the numbness, invisible, just at the brink of expression. I can feel it moving through me like a fire.

I don't say anything to Mother, small Mother, in the bed. She looks like a pen hung over the edge of a jeans pocket by its clip alone. If she lifted her arms over her head, she would be sucked under the covers, deep into a pocket beyond my reach. She looks at our hands. I look up from them to her.

Time. The doctor is in the room now, introducing himself, talking about how he's doing his rounds at the home today. He is sitting on a chair on the other side of Mother, asking her questions she can't answer.

"How are you doing, Hedwig? How are you feeling today?" She doesn't say anything. She looks away from my hands. He talks loud, with bad tone. "Have you and Al been having a good chat?"

I want to kill him, the way his sentences fall out of his so-doctorific face, jagged and clause-less. I imagine it's the same way he talks to his dog. After he's done trying to talk to Mother, he turns to me and tells me about her, talks about her bluntly and honestly, as if she were not there, as if she cannot hear him. I try not to listen. He talks about the progress she has made into her dementia; the word he uses is "progress." I am not here. He tells me that Mother's slow progression into severe neural degradation is gaining momentum, and that from here—the recent loss of speech, added to her loss of mobility—the speed of her disintegration will only increase.

"I can't really see her going more than a year at this rate, Mr Baum."

I can feel her hand in mine. I can feel her moving. Beneath my skin, another version of myself is on fire. I am not who anyone sees.

I don't look at him while he talks; I just search Mother's mute grey-blue eyes for her. I have imagined these eyes a lot over these years. I have thought most of her eyes and her body in a static motion, in her yoga studio, as I watched her through the vent in my bedroom.

The doctor is gone, and I'm not sure how long I've been here. I don't know that I said anything to him at all. My chest is tight, my skin a facade.

I let go of her hand, and I start to shake. I get up and steady myself on the wall and back away. Mother looks my way for a moment, and I bolt, before she can try again to recognize me.

I go through the doors without looking at the nurse, stumble outside into the rain. I put my head in my hands and my hands through my hair, pull all the pins out of it and let my origami'd head fold down to my shoulders.

Shook free of myself, I bolt again. To the car. I get inside and try to remember how to breathe.

I can still feel her hand in mine, loosening under my hard grasp before I dropped it. I breathe out and try to breathe in but just breathe out again. My car starts to fog in the cool world of rain. I see the pixelated boat, abstracted on the water, going for the body at the bridge, trying to collect information that might lead to knowing something more, and to feeling less.

I look over at the passenger seat: Mother's old Leica stares up at me from atop the Ovid—and in seeing the camera and screaming, I do not scream at all.

4

THE KITCHEN

The knife drawer in the kitchen is stuffed with old negatives. The drying rack is overflowing with fresh darkroom paper, and the taps flow with fixer, stopper, and developer. The sink itself is filled with a calm and palpable darkness, a darkness you can put your hands inside and lose them in until you pull them back out. In the cupboard, instead of plates, you have panes of glass that fit the stacks of empty frames. Instead of cups, you have bundles of recycled wire, handfuls of nails, for hanging. Instead of pots—instead of ingredients—you have the enlarger, developing trays, slide viewers, tongs, replacement bulbs. You have stretched string from one edge of the kitchen to the other, so that you can hang your wet remembrances to dry. In the fridge you have canisters of undeveloped film. In the fridge, you keep things you've been meaning to process.

Most of the time, when you step into the kitchen, the room ends there: cupboards, a sink, a fridge, then a dark gap you spin past.

The kitchen is the factory, the place where you come when you have recalled something you need to add to the palace, or when you need to fix something that you already hung up in the palace, either because you've reason to believe that it is inaccurate, or because it is fading and you need to meditate on it and pull it back to sharpness. Sometimes, you just enter the palace from the back door that leads straight into the kitchen and do nothing else but work.

The kitchen is your palace's darkroom, though it is bathed in light—because to be in complete darkness when processing the memories would be the same as painting the walls of the palace black, and the floors black, and the ceilings black, and the stairs and everything, such that no room would reflect the light to allow shadows or depth. There would be no getting through it alive.

I am in my car in the rain, south on Pembina, in the parking lot of a Midas auto repair. The last half hour comes back to me, in reverse.

There is honking, I am turning off Pembina into this lot without using my blinker, without really slowing down. I'm coming south, I'm turning south onto Memorial from Portage, instead of going back to Mother's house. I am almost merging into a reckless red Volkswagen bug, I'm turning onto Portage from Main, I'm driving south on Main and hitting the brakes for a yellow light gone red and hydroplaning into the intersection at the same time a couple crosses the street underneath the insufficient cover of an umbrella, my car slowing just enough to spare them. When the car stops, my body keeps moving, ahead of me.

I'm turning onto Main, turning out of the parking lot of the home, starting the car, screaming, climbing into the car, running away from Mother.

I am here because I was heading south. It was raining. I was trying to make it out of the city.

I call Genny, but she doesn't pick up, and when I reach her voice mail I don't leave one. I go into my voice mail and delete hers, and the new one I have from Karen, without listening to either of them. I turn off the phone. I beat the edge of it against the steering wheel and scream some more: for stopping, for not allowing the energy to break me out of this life. I toss the phone onto the passenger seat with the *Metamorphoses*.

The radio is on: "*All the information the police have given is that the body belonged to an Indigenous boy, a teenager. It's likely that the high river waters brought him up. At this point, police are not ruling out suicide.*" More words spout before they go back to the weather.

One day, the weatherman says, this rain will end.

The city becomes a funnel, a sinkhole, and I know that I've lost my chance to escape. I put the car into reverse, into drive, and pull out of the parking lot and head north, toward the hole, toward the drain, toward the house.

The spring after I turned fifteen, the year after Mother came back from Selkirk, I thought I could run across the Assiniboine River on the flow of broken ice. At a bend, the pieces were coagulating, and I thought—being bird-like—I could make it across.

I don't know how much I actually believed it was possible. One thing I wouldn't have admitted at the time was that I wasn't worried about what would happen if I couldn't make it, if I failed halfway through. When Tom and I, walking along the river trails, saw that clog in the turn of the flow, my mind instantly jumbled into a pure, selfless curiosity, and the discovery of the possibility—or impossibility—was enough payoff to justify the act.

Tom didn't humour my idea at first, but he came around because he knew that if he didn't, I'd come back and do it alone. Maybe he also knew I'd make it nowhere, and that as long as he stayed, there wasn't much danger. All I know for sure is that he knew I was stubborn, so after not too long, we went down from the trails to the riverbank. I took off my coat and stretched. It was midday and we were supposed to be at school. The wind blew a chill across the shattered river, and Tom stood there, holding my coat, trying to look supportive while feeling angry and afraid.

What happened was that I basically just jumped into the near-freezing river. I didn't catch a firm footing for even a second. The first moment my foot reached the ice, the second moment I was under water, the third I was above again, and by the fifth I was in Tom's arms, being lifted up the bank. Once I was out, Tom wrapped my coat around me and carried me to his place. I was laughing through my chattering teeth while he shivered curse after curse under his breath, occasionally looking down at me and shaking his head into a smile.

He drew a very warm bath for us, and after we had warmed up some, naked under blankets, we lowered ourselves into it. The bath overflowed immediately because Tom had forgotten to account for two bodies' worth of displacement. I laughed and pulled him back down into the tub with me just as he was about to get out and try to stop the stream of water that was snaking out under the door.

"The damage has been done," I said, feeling his muscles lose their intensity, surrendering into me.

We sat in that tub until we got warm, then chilly again, then got out and dried off. For the next hour I watched Tom try to clean up the water before Del came back from work. He followed it out the bathroom and down the wood stairs; the water had to turn to go down them. Tom complained to me about the skewed foundations, how he always felt that the house was trying to tip him out into the world.

I watched while he mopped, his long body slowly descending stair after stair, and thought it a magically unimaginable result of a reckless moment. I sat at the top of the stairs in a blanket, knocking my feet against the wood, atonally, and whenever Tom looked up at me, weary of the drying, I stuck my tongue out at him, and he smiled.

There's no parking in front of Mother's house, so I'm sitting in my car, idling in a spot a few streets over—on Ethelbert—listening to the radio. The night is coming on again, promising to be wet and long. People pull in on the street; people pull out. Someone in an SUV lurks behind me, thinking I am going to move because my car is on. We sit here, in a sort of stalemate. Eventually, they honk. Eventually, they honk again. Eventually, they speed past.

Who do they think I am? Do they not see how surrounded I am?

The radio says there's going to be a vigil at the Forks tomorrow evening, for the dead boy. In protest of all those who continue to be lost. The host makes light of the rain, of how the Forks might be under water by then. It is not a surprise. This is the world.

I want to turn off the car, but I can't bring myself to. Mother's camera sits beside me, turned over, still lens-capped, to keep it from watching. All the mirrors are turned far away from me.

After Ess came back from the centre, and kept up hir medication and therapy, ze started hard at the new project. Ess titled it *NON-POLAR-BI-BINARY*. Ze wanted to give a sense of what it was like to live through two identities people don't understand. Ze wanted to talk about living between the poles of gender and mood. Ze wanted to have photographs that were manic and queer next to art that was depressive and near trite. It was whiplashing the viewer that ze was after. It was trying to make them feel like ze did—thrown around from one end of hir head to the other, every single day.

Over the holiday break and the last semester, Ess filled hir portfolio and worked harder than I'd ever seen hir, which was saying something. After every meeting, I told hir that ze should go home and get some sleep. Ze looked exhausted, but despite the bags under hir eyes, I could tell ze was feeling a contentment I'd not seen in hir in a while.

"How is the fire?" I would ask Ess when I ran into hir in the halls.

"Still burning beautiful," ze'd always say.

That's the thing my life has been missing, the reason why I haven't been making photos. Why the first roll I've shot all year is the one I took when I walked into Mother's house. I haven't even put film back into the camera, but I can smell a little bit the smoke, here. I know there's something here that will cause me to ignite.

I want it to happen, and I am terrified that it will.

It's nearly two in the morning by the time my car runs out of gas here on Ethelbert. Over the last six hours or so I turned the car off only a few times, because I saw police driving down the streets. I didn't want someone to come to the window and ask me questions I couldn't answer.

I have been sitting here, with the overhead light on, reading Ovid. Leafing through to passages underlined or marked with questions, by me or whatever kid checked it out before I stole it, whose name is probably still on the library card. Medea, Bacchus, Midas, Philemon and Baucis, the creation, the epilogue. I've been picking up the book, opening it, reading a little, then putting it back down, overwhelmed. As the engine died, as the gas light beeped for the last time, I opened it to Daedalus and Icarus. Exile, hubris, and open sky. Daedalus was telling Icarus to follow him, to fly the middle way—not too high that his wings would melt, or too low that the sea's spray would weigh them down—as the engine stopped and it got so quiet. So I put the book down, letting Icarus live on a little longer, and turned off the ignition to keep the battery alive.

The rain has let up, and the neighbourhood is dead. I get out of the car. I don't lock it. I put Mother's camera under my jacket and hide under the umbrella. I head west, away from Mother's house. Every step I take I feel like I slip five steps back, but my body moves forward, and I try to pretend it is carrying me even farther away.

These streets at these hours are years of me, quieter and lonelier than I remember them. My feet hitting the curbs, feeling the rise and fall of the sidewalks—it is a tempo I once had, that I used to slip into with Tom every chance I could.

Tom. The body knows, and walks me north onto Home Street: blocks starting and ending, most of the windows asleep.

I stop and tilt the umbrella back so I can see the dark rectangular building with the tiny porch light at the tip of a short awning: windows, darkness, angles.

This is where Tom's house used to be. I didn't know, of course, that his house was gone, torn down—with the houses of his neighbours on both sides—to put in this little apartment building. The address misappropriated and split into unit numbers. I haven't talked to Tom since before I jumped continents for Hamburg, back when he was someone I had keeping a loose eye on Mother. I didn't call to tell him that I'd left the States, that the phone number and address he had wouldn't be any good, even if I ever came back. And when I did, it was only to find that his phone number—Del's number—was gone, too.

When I started to construct my memory palace, I went through a few houses before I ended up at Mother's. I tried mine, Genny's, and even Erwin Egger's in Hamburg, but none of those really felt right. I used Tom's house for a long time, though. It was a house I always knew as a mess, a house so old and poorly built that almost every single floor was drooping in at the middle, or tilting to one end. The door to Tom's bedroom couldn't even close all the way because of the way the house leaned. So it wasn't possible for him to lock it, and most of the time he had no reason to. It wasn't so different from Mother's house, except for the very important fact that it was *not* Mother's house. Which, for a long time, was a very important distance for me to preserve.

Tom's house worked well as the palace, particularly because it was well suited to holding early memories of Genny. But eventually, when I went into the palace I started thinking more and more about Mother's house, about Mother, and as soon as I heard how much further she was slipping away, I started adding more memories about her. And as I did, Tom's house began to get blurry. I stopped being able to picture the walls that held the things I had put there. Instead, the memories themselves stretched over the gaps and became the walls, but that became too much. You need the empty space between memories to make a memory palace work. After Tom's house failed, I decided to try using Mother's, and it was then I realized the ways memory can have a life of its own. Memory itself has the power to tell you what you will remember. The remembering place makes such a difference when it's the place where the memories were made.

But Tom's house is gone. Where those beautiful old wood walls once stood, there are now four storeys of cinder blocks and concrete.

The building obscures the light milked sky, which on cool nights in the summer we would sometimes look up at, our backs on the dewy, unkempt lawn, while Del was inside, drunk and angry, or soberly not-alone. We would watch, Tom and I, as a small collection of the brightest stars slowly burned their way through to us.

"Only the best," I say, looking up at the ceiling of clouds I cannot see.

I stare at the blackness, a blackness I must make sure not to fly too close to. I walk away from the place where Tom's house was and try to imagine that nothing has changed, that no time has passed, and that by the time I get to the corner of the street, I could turn around and see his lumbering silhouette waving to me, walking toward me, as we readied for a night in the dark together, stumbling these streets.

I don't turn around to see him waving. I drag myself down toward Mother's house, but when I'm about to cross Ethelbert, I put all the force in my bones into turning, into making my way back into the gas-less car. But I can't. The turn happens a street too late, onto Mother's street, so I try hard to pull back and end up walking up the back alley, to the rear end of Mother's car—a brighter shadow in the opening of the dark fence. I pass the car, rusting in its little back lot, my hand grazing the wet white paint as I walk toward the back door of the house that leads directly into the kitchen. I freeze. Distinct parts of the memory of this door reconnect: hand, stove, tines, a sharp and furious pain in my left thigh.

By the time I'm going again, I'm walking around the house to go in through the front door instead. I'm taking off my raincoat, hanging it up, and holding the camera like a bowl of warm soup as I climb back up the stairs to Mother's room. I recall pain burning into my thigh. I stand in the doorway, looking at the rough sea of the covers on the flat world of her bed. I feel wings on my back, a melted worthlessness, heavy, like a backpack filled with an ending.

I have not made it very far, have I?

I could say this out loud, but it wouldn't make a difference. The house can hear me even when I don't say it. Silence is the language this place knows best.

When you come into the kitchen with memories, you pull them out of your head like canisters of film. You slip them into the dark-filled sink and work them with touch, only. You work them until you can feel that they have taken the shape you want. You work them until you can hear the memory's noise resonating up from the sink. Until you can smell it, taste it. Until it is as good as happening in that exact moment. Then, you yank it up from the dark, hold it up to the scrutiny of light.

When you underwork them, you pull the memories from the sink and it takes a while for you to see the full picture. The memory doesn't make enough noise, doesn't move quite fast enough, to seem like real life. Framed and placed on the walls of the living room, these underworked memories would simply fade out. You would skip over them with your eyes. You would not hear them participating in the cacophony of the room.

Sometimes, though, you overwork the memory, and it is too perfectly re-created, which means that the second you pull it out from the sink you find yourself engulfed by it and it alone. It becomes too immersive to be able to be housed within the palace, so when you pry yourself out of it, you are back in your life rather than the palace.

To make a memory right and ripe for the task of being remembered, you must bring it to the brink of being fully realized, just under a perfect re-creation of life. That way, you can climb into the memory, relive it, and still be able to climb out into the palace.

I lie in Mother's bed, thinking about the dead boy in the river and feel the gap where that distinct, innocent piece of me has been missing for so long. The piece of me that went grey and fell off when I ran away to Hamburg.

My phone is in the car with Ovid, and I am naked here, thinking about water. Sinking. Exhausted by life.

I stop breathing, try to forget my body exists. But Mother's camera is around my neck, strangling me to remind me that it does.

The first night I went over to Tom's, the first night we took to these streets and stayed out late, I was still a few months from thirteen and Tom was going on fourteen. We had met about a year before, when he was sitting in Mr Whipple's art class, still at work on a pretty bad painting, and I walked in at the tail end of the group of classmates for mine. His painting was bad partly because he was working with his left hand. His right was in a cast because he'd broken it that week on the side of a kid's head, a kid who was probably at least two years older than him. But Tom was already a giant. He overheard the kid saying some things that he didn't like, things that Tom refused to repeat to me, so he just snapped and went nuts on him.

It was mid-January that first night, deep into winter. Neither of us really wanted to go home after school. Del was drinking again, and Mother had slipped back into quiet for the last two weeks. That was about as long as she'd ever stopped talking, the usual maximum that her eyes slipped behind the grey veil and she turned ghost. But I couldn't stand it, and each time I could stand it less. She'd stop scheduling portraits, stop leaving the house, stop doing much of anything besides wandering room to room, doing yoga, and sleeping. I hated it, hated how it drew me out and toward her, such that I would talk to her about all the pointless, stupid little things in my head in hopes of hearing her voice, in hopes of being addressed and acknowledged. I wanted her to listen to me. I wanted her to tell me to shut up. It made me feel stupid, how much I tried to bait her out of it, how much I tried to bait her toward talking to me. I couldn't stand being in the house with her silence, and after those last two weeks, I decided I wouldn't stand it anymore.

Tom and I stayed after school, in the art room, for as long as Mr Whipple was willing to stick around with us. I crammed myself into the school's tiny leaky darkroom, trying to remember the timings of the agitations, and Tom sat at an easel nearby. We talked to one another loudly through the door, while I tried to string the rolls of undeveloped film onto the spool, and he tried to paint a self-portrait. By then, I'd been shooting for a while, with cameras I borrowed from the school and film I either bought or lifted from drugstores. I'd mostly take pictures of myself through mirrors, or set up the camera on a desk and make dramatic faces at it. I was obsessed with looking at and archiving myself. I made no sense to myself; my limbs felt unlike my limbs, my neck not my neck, my lacks not my lacks. I've always been enamoured with the stranger of myself. Sometimes I'd also take photos of Tom, painting or sitting around. Every shot had people in it.

When Mr Whipple had to kick us out, Tom and I scrunched deep into the heat of our coats and wandered around. We went downtown —down Portage—and walked to the Red. As it got dark, we wandered down to the Forks and out onto the thick ice. People were skating up and down, and we walked on the trail beside, going up the Assiniboine.

We didn't talk about what we were doing, why we were doing it— we just did it. I distinctly remember the night progressing, and slowly losing feeling in every piece of my body but my heart and my head—though my face was good as gone. We ended up following the Assiniboine's windiness to the edge of Omand Park, climbing off the ice, and turning back into Wolseley.

Eventually, we did make it to Tom's; we were too cold. But by the time we got there, Del—tall, looking so much like Tom but sallower— had passed out on the couch. Tom went to the kitchen and ran his hands under lukewarm water to get the feeling back, and then picked up the bottles surrounding his mother. He got a chair and put any bottles that still had alcohol high up on the top of the kitchen cupboard.

"I want to give her a chance to realize what she's doing," he said, holding back the emotions from his face.

Once the feeling came back to my hands, I went draped a blanket over Del. Tom fixed the blanket so that it was double layered over her feet. "She's got bad circulation," he said, to the sound of us ascending the uneven stairs to his bedroom.

When Tom and I got into his bed to warm up, I thought that maybe I'd never go back home. That maybe I would just no longer live with Mother, that it was clear she did not care about me, did not love me. That she was a dangerous thing to be near, that the middle distance I needed to keep was too far from her. How could I help her if she couldn't even say a word to me, couldn't tell me what she was feeling? I warmed up next to Tom, feeling at war, and then got out from the covers to raid his closet for his loose, faded Iron Maiden shirt. I climbed back into bed, resolving to stay with them, with Tom and Del. Resolving to become Tom's real brother.

"Tom, I don't want to go back. I don't want to go back, not ever."

"Then stay."

His bare arm was next to mine, our arm hairs tangling, our bodies yet unmarked. I wanted my skin to open up and tie itself to his. I wanted to no longer be myself, I wanted to be Tom, I wanted to feel straightforward and clearly cut. But I couldn't. My lot was trapped a few streets down.

"Tom, will you walk me home?"

"Of course I will."

I had this sense, walking back that night, around two in the morning, that our house knew everything about Mother, knew her, and I believe that it still does. Just like the story in Ovid about the reeds that whisper the secret of King Midas's ass-ears on the wind, like spores. Only instead of reeds, it was the walls of our house, it was the walls that were already built but were rebuilt by our living inside of them, by our having stormed and infected them with our breathing, with our quiet proximity. They knew everything, those walls, knew us each better than we knew the other.

I knew, walking with Tom, a very short walk, holding his hand through our gloves, that by choosing to go back home that night, by returning to a house that did not feel filled with love so much as sorrow, that did not feel like life happened in it at all, I was losing myself. I knew that I had made my choice: to come back forever.

When Tom and I walked down that street, the living room light was on and the curtains open, and Mother was sitting on the couch, staring out toward the night. I went to the door, unlocked it with my key, went inside, and hung up my coat.

The second choice I made that night, knowing that I would be forced to repeat it again and again, was that I didn't go into the living room to see her, to confront her, about how my love for her was destroying my ability to stand being around her. Instead, I went straight up the stairs to my bedroom, where I sat with my back against the door and listened to her flick off the light, lock the front door, come up the stairs, and go into her room.

I didn't realize then that Mother's silence would continue, past those two weeks to another six months, to when she went to shoot photos of horses at the Assiniboia Downs and ended up in Selkirk.

The air outside the house is silent this morning, but the wind inside is howling at my back again, pressing me close to the gas range, turning it on to boil the kettle for tea. I slip in and out, remembering, pressure breathing as if a window is missing in the palace and the front door is ajar. I'm double exposed here: standing near the stove with the kettle and—at fifteen—heating the tines of a fork on the burner. The exact same burner. No matter the water, the tea, I can't stop the kid from heating their fork the same way they saw their mother do it, heating it until the warmth wanders up to undermine their grip on the handle.

The kettle is starting to rumble, preparing to whistle; the kid lowers their jeans to the knees with their free hand. Then, Mother is there, possessing them, overflowing them, hiking up her skirt. The inner thigh that the kid presses the steaming metal of the tines to is both their thigh and their mother's thigh at once. I feel the sizzling flesh, too, the teeth biting hard the bottom lip, the wailing inheld, the kettle uneasy and beginning its scream. They are both here with me, burning and squirming, attempting to feel, attempting to feel alive after coming back from the dead into a numb life. I'm leaving my belt on; my hand grips the buckle, to either guard it or be ready to yank it off. I see the wounds on the kid, on fifteen-year-old me. I stare at them, at Mother's flesh superimposed there, which we only saw happen through the window one night, at fourteen, in summer, when I was coming into the house from the back door—a few gargantuan months before the kid does it, too. Even though I'm standing here beside Mother, I can only see her filtered through the grime on glass.

I don't take off the belt and peel off my jeans. I don't want to see the scar again, from one of the first times I tried to wear Mother's pain, to follow after her. The kettle, the kettle—*Yes, I hear you*. I remember when I was fourteen and Mother came back from Selkirk, remember helping her into the bath day after day, and counting the collection running along the inside of her left thigh. I knew the number then but cannot recall it now, can only recall the depth and the leather of hers, a testament to her commitment to containing pain, the tine of each scar like a bar in a prison cell. I remember her going over to the sink and washing that fork as I walked in the door, remember again her wailing soon after she came back from Selkirk, her dam burst, having returned from the dead by taking pills that seemed mostly to make her more erratically and visibly despairing. I'd sometimes find her wailing in her sleep, hot steam bursting from the roiling hell in her chest. Sweat draws rivers down the side of my face: her long skirt dropping back down to a knee, a pair of jeans hoisted back up to a wincing belly, tears running down my face. Water running from a tap, boiling hot. No soap.

Three hands kill the burner at once, but only mine lets a belt buckle free to reach for a kettle's handle as the whimpers cease, and only one mouth yelps at the grasp of the too-hot handle, only one brain reminded of the lesions caused by reaching out when it is already far too late.

When you walk into the kitchen, you like to imagine that you have full control over all of your remembering, that you have the capacity to keep things bright. You like to think that while you go to the cupboard to fix the broken glass of the photo from the landing you stepped on, while you attempt to reprint a photo from the living room so it won't have Mother in it, watching. But you know that as good as the print looks in the bright kitchen, as soon as you retrace your steps to bring it into the living room, Mother will slowly burn her way into the composition. Just like you know the stove is there, in the corner that you don't want to look at, spewing its deep, red shadows. Just like you know there are holes in the walls, around the windows, under the door, where the wind sneaks in. When you stop to look around, you can feel it encircling you.

It was May then, too, that night when I was fourteen and came back to the house and the living room lights were off. I remember Tom walking me to the door, equally surprised that Mother didn't seem to be up and waiting for me. I figured Mother was in bed. It was after four in the morning, a bit later than I was usually out. Tom and I had spent the night listening to records while he painted the fifth painting of a banana in a week, the same banana in the same spot, only getting riper and riper. The music we played while he painted was loud, but we could still hear the bed creaking in his mother's room.

When I got inside I went upstairs and went to sleep. All the lights in the house were off.

In the morning, I went downstairs to the phone and saw the tape in the answering machine was full. I rewound it and played it back. A crackly voice came on and said, "I'm calling about Mrs Hedwig Baum. Don't worry, she is okay." That was how the message started.

The voice was a doctor who said that Mother had been admitted to Selkirk Mental Health Centre that afternoon—the previous afternoon, Friday—after she'd tried to climb over the fence at the Assiniboia Downs. She'd been hysterical. The voice said she was stopped before she could make it over, had been weeping and yelling in German. I could hear the hooves stomping the dirt in my head. He said that she had been placed under full-time watch, as she seemed to have broken into a severe depressive state. He said she was going to begin receiving therapy that evening. He left a number and said to call as soon as I got the message.

But I didn't call back, not right away. I rewound the tape so that the answering machine could record over it again. I sat down on the couch. I stopped sitting and stood up on the couch. I went up to Mother's room and checked her cameras. The Rolleiflex and her old Leica were still there, which meant she'd taken the Nikon, which meant she'd been at the Downs to shoot for the newspaper, since that camera was the most dependable for action. I slung the old Leica around my neck, went back downstairs, and called the doctor; I thought if I didn't, they'd send cops. I was surprised they hadn't already.

But they must not have known that I was alone.

The man I talked to, who wasn't the doctor—the doctor was busy —told me that Mother was resting. They'd given her a round of therapy the night before and would give her another that afternoon.

I told him I would be staying with my friend Thomas Roux. I gave him Tom's address on Home Street and phone number, told him the good times to call if they needed to get in touch with me. Then I hung up and went to the darkroom, took Mother's film out of the Leica, and loaded it up fresh. I didn't call Tom; I just went over.

I stayed with him for three days, watching him paint that banana again and again, the last time almost fully black, before deciding I had to leave.

"I called the hospital and she's coming back this morning," I told Tom on the Tuesday. "I won't make it to school, but I'll call you later."

I went home and listened to the answering machine. There were some clients calling about scheduling portraits, mostly for students graduating from high school that spring. They'd seen Mother's ad and liked her price.

When I showed up to photograph these kids, kids who were older than me, the parents were a bit confused, but I handled the camera well. I had watched Mother do it. It wasn't so hard, and they were clearly too uncomfortable to ask if I was really her. I'd introduced myself: "Hey, I'm Hedy Baum—sorry for being late!" They paid me the upfront amount, and I went home and developed and printed the good shots in the sizes they wanted. The next day I called them and said they could pick them up: "Already?" Of course. I was a professional.

I did that for a few days. Then, I don't remember what.

Next thing I knew, I had a buzz cut and Tom was yelling at me in my living room, for lying to him. The hospital had called and told him that Mother was going to be released on Monday. It was Saturday then. He ran to my house as soon as he got off the phone. He was still panting as he yelled.

Tom stayed with me until Monday. We didn't go to school; we just waited. I took lots of pictures. I liked using Mother's darkroom, her camera.

When she came home, driven by one of the nurses, she looked tired and blank. The nurse gave me the keys to her car and said that an outpatient nurse would be visiting her daily to make sure she was doing fine and taking her medication. Tom stood in the doorway and helped Mother into the house, guided her upstairs to her bed. After the nurse left, I sat beside her while Tom went downstairs and made her some tea. Her camera was around my neck. Her keys were in my pocket. I don't know if she noticed. We didn't talk, but she did. A little bit. What she said was very quiet and I couldn't make out most of it.

Later, Tom and I took a bus to the Downs and he drove her car home. That night, he slept on a pile of clothes on my floor.

According to Ovid, after Icarus did not heed his father's warnings to fly the middle way—melting his wings and falling into the sea—Daedalus just kept flying. Had he followed Icarus down, Daedalus would have also broken from the middle way, and the spray of the sea water would have weighed his wings down, drowning him alongside Icarus. He saw his son falling from too high, calling out to him—but what could he do? He had a course to keep. How could he join Icarus when there was a pathway, a jet stream, a method of breathing possibility stretched out ahead of him?

Ovid writes that once Icarus was dead, Daedalus was no longer a father. Icarus was, then, no longer a son. Who was punished by this identity stripping? Who lost their identity first, and then entangled the other in that loss? The blame is murky; they were victims of each other's hubris. One drowned because of the other's invention; one robbed the other by means of rebellion.

As his son plummeted, Daedalus kept flying, kept course. But every day following Icarus's screaming and gurgling in the sea, Daedalus probably imagined himself as a huge bird, swooping in and saving him, grabbing his body with his feet like an eagle. At night in bed, unson'd, he would put his wings back on and, in his dreams, go circling, diving, invincibly putting his toes around his son's spine, lifting him up, carrying him face forward through the wind, so that he might look at the life ahead of them, as Daedalus pumped his way to the mainland, stretching out to the unreachable horizon. With his toes inset, Daedalus would feel his son's heartbeat, the heartbeat keeping Daedalus a father. Daedalus's protection keeping Icarus a son.

And every time, before he could reach the mainland, Daedalus would wake up, his arms broke-tired and grounded, tipped with feath-erless fingers, his face sea-swept and weary.

I let my burnt hand run under the water at the sink and look out the kitchen window to Mother's car sitting patient in its spot. My palm in the cool water has that shrinking feeling of slapped skin. I feel it, feel very here in this body, drown it, look up toward the cupboards above the sink and remember this is where Dorothea hid the keys: behind a coffee tin on the near-empty top shelf. I turn off the water, grab a chair from the kitchen table, climb up onto the counter, and look behind the empty can. And just like that, here they are.

It's exactly the same place I hid them, when Mother came back from Selkirk and couldn't be trusted driving yet.

I walk out through the back door to her car. Of course, of course, it doesn't start. Nothing happens with the key in the ignition: no lights, nothing. I sit in the driver's seat and sink back to the day Tom drove me and the car back from the Downs. That was one of the last times I was even in this car. It has hardly changed, though it smells of mildew and there are little explosions in the back seats from rodents chewing through the cushions. There's also that dirty fog that windows get from static time. This car probably hasn't been driven in nearly a decade.

I pop the hood, stand in front of its open chest, and stare down at the battery, the stopped heart. I put my hands on it, where the lead clamps onto the nodes. Positive. Negative. Ventricles.

An older man walks by in the back lane. I catch his eye for a second and know he's one of those old men who wander around life looking for someone with an open hood. He stops walking and smiles at me. His blue eyes are tight mouths of wrinkled deltas, his smile wide and kind and fake-toothed. His shirt is longer than it needs to be, his raincoat too short, and he's in black rubber boots that go all the way up to his knees. I look down at his hands: in one he has a repurposed grocery bag with the wooden hat of a large nutcracker coming out the top, eyes wide and staring and blue, too, and in the other hand is nothing but a grip that could hold the ghost of a leash. A clear and palpable absence. It's Saturday, just past noon. This man has probably been to a yard sale. I smile back at him and lift my hands from the battery.

"You her son?" he says, shuffling over, nodding to Mother's house and looking at the hood.

"I am. Al," I say, waving, not wanting to offer my hand to shatter the memory in his grip. I also don't want him to put down the bag.

"I'm Blaine," he says, pulling his face from years ago back to here.

Blaine comes over to the hood and looks in, tells me he used to see Mother walking west on Wolseley every few mornings—toward Asha's, I know, for yoga, but do not say. He lives just down the street, he says, across Wolseley, where Mother's street changes its name, curling off into an avenue—like the Forks, where the Assiniboine River loses its identity to the Red.

He asks me how Mother is and I tell him she moved a few years ago, to Ste. Agathe—the name of a town south of the city that I passed on my drive in—because we have family who can take care of her. The truth is we don't have family anywhere.

I tell him I think the car's battery is shot, and he says of course it is, that's what happens. "If you'd like, I can go get my car and we can try and jump it up."

I nod. Blaine goes off, and I just wait here. Staring for a long time at the back of Mother's house, at the second-floor window that seems so much lower now than when I scaled down from it a lifetime ago. Studying the folded mat of the back lawn's grass before Blaine makes it back with his truck, chugging along slow, squelching through puddles in the rough back lane. He pulls up as close to Mother's car as he can, doing something like an eleven-point turn, and gets out so that we can string his cables to both car's hearts. We stretch them out between the two and they aren't long enough, but I rifle around in the back of Mother's car and find hers. Both cords lock teeth in the middle, then Blaine gets into his old truck—as old as Mother's car, the bed filled with plastic totes, the passenger seat peaked with bags—and revs it up. I get in Mother's car and turn the ignition over and over. It coughs. It screams. It knocks and shudders. But eventually, it comes to life. I let the key stop starting it and it stays, snorting. I get out of the car and give Blaine a thumbs-up.

I smell smoke, a little, and can't quite tell if it's coming from the car or from inside my head. I want to ask Blaine to come over and sit in here and smell, but I don't. I unhook the cables from the battery, go over to his truck, and thank him.

"My pleasure," he says, winding his cables into a loop. After, his free hand returns to its leash grip.

"I'm going to drive the car around to make the alternator recharging the battery more entertaining," I say, and he smiles at me through the window as he puts the truck into gear.

"I'll see you around, Al," he says, then pulls out down the alley and away.

I get back in Mother's car and go, hit Portage, turn west. The car curdles along the street, and I can tell from the way it drives that the tires are probably low. The gas is old, the oil too settled in its old head, but it's moving. I keep going west toward the edge of the city, and when I cross the perimeter, for a moment, I feel technically out—but only out enough to make it to the Assiniboia Downs.

My whole life feels like I'm retracing steps.

I pull into the empty parking lot, into an estimation of a place where Mother parked the car before Tom and I came to take it home. It's around two in the afternoon, and there are no races today because of the weather. Running the track would be sprinting through deep muck. The place is vacant.

I picture Mother watching the seamless ease of the motion of the horses. I try to place myself in the destructive quality of it.

I turn off Mother's car, get out, and look at it sitting there. I don't lock the doors, and I leave the keys on the seat. Around the Downs, huge posts hold spotlights high like a ship holds cannons. Chain link frames the parking lot, keeping people from getting out to the track without going through the building, past the line of betting tellers.

Here, contained but open-aired, is the place where firm beasts ran tight circles. Where firm beasts still do. Where short men stand up on glazed backs and beat forward, forward, forward, faster. The place where, years before she went to Selkirk, Mother brought me with her while she took photos for the paper and then led me up to the sides of the winning horses, asking if it would be okay if I reached out to touch their hips, their shivering, hot flesh.

Here, contained in the loop behind this fence, is the place Mother, alone, sadfrantic, tried to throw herself under the hooves of beauty and power and God.

I turn away, from the car and the Downs. I want the things that the Downs remembers to stay here.

I start to walk back toward Winnipeg—the city of puddles—along the wet highway. I cross again into the perimeter and walk east until I make it to a gas station where a taxi is filling up. I wave to the driver and he nods to me. I approach and ask him if he's working.

"Yes, ma'am," he says, so I keep walking until I find another, ten minutes later, spitting, as the bound pressure on my chest no longer feels like a natural phenomenon at my ribs, as the packer becomes nothing but a blank weight.

When I finally make it back to Mother's house, I open the door to my memory palace.

I was around ten years old when Mother started doing yoga, and I started to spy on her. She turned the empty room beside my bedroom, the room that had been Ilsa's, into her studio, and if I climbed up onto the rickety loft bed—which I was not supposed to do; Mother didn't trust it—I could see her through the grates of the air vent that came up through the wall between us, breathing fresh, tinny air into both rooms. I'd sit up there, wary and still, not wanting to make the bed creak or crash, and watch her bend, fold, and pause in the naked dawn light. For a lot of my life I connected the smell of circulating air with that image of Mother. When I hear a heat vent blow or an AC unit turn on, I can see her, through the vent's bars in my head, turning and stopping and writhing in the light.

Around the same time, I began to be bashful about going out into the hall to dress in clothes from the armoire. I stopped on a morning when I woke up late, just after Mother had finished her yoga and shower. I opened my door and found her in front of the armoire. She was naked. She didn't notice me standing in my room, staring out. When she'd started to practise yoga, she seemed to lose her ability to sense my presence in her world. So I just stood there, stalled in the dark opening as she dabbed herself with a yellow towel and pulled out clothes. She was a tight, unabashed form, and I was completely blown apart at the sight. Her muscles were ready yet reticent, her breasts enviously small, and she had gotten a control over her body that I only later—many years later—realized was a clue to how her mind was chaos. I recognized it in her when I first saw it in myself. She started doing yoga around the first time I remember her going silent, when her depression began to overtake her. But even so, and perhaps because of this—this dark shadow that had been chasing her, that had finally gotten its dimness on her, and that was trying its damnedest to destroy her, to minimize her into nothing—she was completely beautiful.

I remember that moment vividly, her standing in front of the armoire, the way her long hair spun and curled behind her, how she rested her weight on her left leg. How the scar on her stomach, curving, insinuated that I'd been difficult her entire life. I felt ashamed. I felt like a poor copy of her. That image of her seemed to stand there forever, until it didn't, until it turned back to her bedroom without noticing me.

That felt like the story of our lives: one of us turned away while the other, unbeknownst, stared from the corner, sharing our nerves in the quiet hurt.

THERE

A heavy thunderstorm has drowned out the light, turning dusk to near-midnight as I climb out of the 10 bus and open my umbrella. Earlier this afternoon, to the west of the city, the last hours of the light were stabbing at the belly of the far edge of the thunderheads as they rolled in, allowing only pinholes to break through. The storm horizon was buzzing and flashing artificial, was the same as the sky is now only farther away, was someone else's weather. But not anymore. Now this wet, thundery climax has become mine.

I'm dressed in black, umbrella to toe. When I got back from leaving Mother's car at the Downs, I walked into the gusty, creaky house and made my way to the closet in her bedroom, where I ransacked the few clothes that remained and found a black silk scarf and a long-sleeved black blouse to wear over my black jeans, matching my tar-black boots and black cotton gloves. No raincoat, no protection from the slanting wet but the umbrella. I can't protect myself from it all.

I walk south toward the rivers, reach an intersection, and wait for the light, crossing a few seconds after it tells me I can, because I can't not imagine my car careening through the intersection the other day, with me inside it. I make it across the street, the unfinished Canadian Museum for Human Rights lurking in the raindark to the left, flash-bulbing into view, and continue toward the Forks.

I did not bring Mother's camera. As soon as I got home from the Downs—before I raided her closet, finding also an enlarger under a towel, and her old radio—I walked down to the end of the hallway to the darkroom's door and opened it only enough to slide the camera in, along the floor, and closed it tightly after.

The flashes come and the thunder follows instantly. I know how to measure the distance of lightning by its separation from the sound, and this lightning might as well be striking us. Those who are gathering at the Forks, despite the weather, for the vigil.

I walk past the market to the rivers, to the pitch-dark Assiniboine and the pitch-dark Red, knocking heads and spilling over, turbulent, at the feet of the small crowd. A sea of umbrellas, grey in the dark, some lit into colour by flashlights, or cellphones, and some bravely guarding flickering candles, but many just monochrome roofs bouncing back the darkness.

Most of the umbrellas have at least two people underneath them. Some have more. I may be the only person here who is completely alone. I pause, looking out over the crowd, small but determined. I stand there for a while, just watching, just feeling all that pain. All that weather.

I wrap the scarf around my head and lower the umbrella so that nobody can see me, so that I become little other than a legged torso in the dark, then walk toward the little people in their little dry islands.

I walk through the crowd, stopping sporadically to place my gloved black hand softly and quietly on someone's shoulder. I don't speak. I don't squeeze. I just set it there, one person at a time—so briefly—and then move on. Some jump, some point their flashlights my way, others are quick and place their warm, soaked hand on mine. Some speak toward my silence. *Sorry, stop, thank you, why.* Many don't. Many just stand, faces toward the dark in the quiet and the pummelling rain. I weave through, slowly, toward the rivers and back out, to the fringes, to the stragglers and passersby. Short shoulders. High shoulders. I find people by their feet and the sound of the rain on their umbrellas and think about the rivers I grew up near and all the stories of their hunger, of the people who joined their flow, by their own choice or by another's hand, stories that happened again and again, with different names and dates and bodies. Stories that could almost be clichés if they weren't about real breathing people dying, stories that slowly prod a deep-tissue bruise you develop even if you never knew any of the people who died. Most of them vulnerable people, most of them Indigenous people, like this boy, many of them murdered.

I walk, reaching out. I let my old city's grief, a segment of my old city's grief, flow over me.

The first time I did this was back in 2007, when the westbound lane of the I-35W bridge collapsed into the Mississippi River at rush hour, killing 13 and wounding over 100 more. When people gathered there for a similar vigil, drenched in bug spray instead of cold rainwater, I reached out to the hurt in my adopted city. I wanted to feel present in the reality of the moment with them, with each of them, and hurt along-side them, to try and understand, while knowing it is always impossible to fully embody someone else's hurt. But I tried to imagine it.

I move through the crowd like a sort of monument, but one that does not declare itself as a monument, and does not declare its intention. A monument that stands for no real motive but what it invokes in context, a monument that's here as much for itself as for anyone else. I walk through the crowd, remembering hugely the void that I carried around so heavily when I ran away to Hamburg. The void that I still have, of course, but have grown better at carrying.

I wander through the crowd, remembering and forgetting and getting distracted as much as anyone here. But every time I stop and rest my cold, gloved hand on someone, I feel here with them. At every touch, the grief swells back into me, and I still try at every point to do the impossible: to understand. But the thing that makes me a good monument is that I don't understand—that I don't pretend to know, or to know any better. I am nothing but here. I am nothing but here, with them—with *us*—trying.

An hour passes, maybe less or maybe more, and I'm fully soaked. I pull the scarf down from my face and put down my umbrella, because there's no reason to fight the wet, and I walk away, alone, back toward the bus stop. The thunderheads have moved on, and I can measure the distance of the lightning in miles—ten, fifteen, thirty—as I wait for the 10 bus. By the time the bus shows up, there are a few people with umbrellas I let get on before me. The bus is warm enough to make me realize how cold I am. How empty I have been, and for how long.

I dig my hand into my pocket and find the small packet of transit tickets I bought when I got groceries the other day. They are soaked, flimsy, dimly bleeding. I look up to the driver and hold them up. He shakes his head and smiles.

"You can dry those in your microwave at home," he says, closing the door behind me and pulling away from the curb. He looks tired, and I grab the bar nearby, trying to drip away from the aisle.

"Just don't do it too long. I did it once with a page of a letter the mailman left on the step in the rain and it worked just fine but was still a little damp after. So I tried it with the second page and set it for just five seconds longer and left the room, and when I came back the page in the microwave was on fire."

I think of Mother's hands, the letters she used to get from Germany. And then I think of the letter Genny left for me in the mailbox just before we ran away to Minneapolis together, the letter I did not open and read until it had staled to poison.

"Did you put the fire out?"

"Yes," he says, making the turn onto Portage.

The light ahead, at the intersection of Portage and Main, goes from yellow to red. The warmer I get, the more I start to shiver; the more I shiver, the more water drips down.

"But I never did get to know what that second page said."

5

THE DARKROOM

There's one room in your memory palace, at the end of the hall, where you never go—one door you wander past without being able to turn to it. You like to think this is because going in the room would ruin the continuity of the stream of remembering, but you stumble back and forth over your own paths anyway, so that's hard to believe. You think you know what's in there, but the truth of that thought is impossible. The door cannot open. The door is warm. You like to think that the room holds the memories from before your first solid one, a swollen room of fluxing sensations and fragments you've lost access to. You like to think that's where the memories are all in German and too foreign for you to live now. But you don't often believe this, because as you sit in the real house and take the memory tour, you place your hand on the wood and sense that maybe you're on the other side, mirroring yourself. But this sort of contemplation of the room only happens when you are a certain version of yourself. Only sometimes, when you're most boy or most girl, do you feel that negative presence, only then do you see the knob, do you try the knob, do you push the door. You know that the door never locks, that the lock was broken before you came to this house, and that the force that is holding you out of the darkroom is a kind of Newtonian resistance. Equal and opposite. While you stand at the door—when the door is there—you can picture it, on the other side, paper thin, twisting you at bay.

I first learned about the Monument against Fascism in March of 1991 from a boyfriend of Karen's, a couple hours before she dumped him. His name was Eros, and he and Karen had been dating for a few weeks. Karen's interest in him stemmed partly from the novelty of his name— *Eros*—and partly from the fact that the Minneapolis winter made it hard to meet new people.

We met Eros for the first and last time when Karen brought him to an opening for an exhibition in a chilly warehouse where some members of the collective had pieces. I was showing a few prints, and Raya—an installation artist, and the third brain of the collective's founding triumvirate—had built short, bulging, phallic sculptures on the floor, which everyone tripped over less the drunker we got. When Eros and Karen showed up, Raya refused to shake his hand. Raya saw men as significantly lesser beings, and nearly all of her work external-ized that. The unavoidable phallus was almost always a central image in her work, which I always respected, even though she was the kind of feminist who thought genitals were key to defining a person. As I grew bolder in presenting myself—on occasion—as a man, that belief became one of several major tensions between us.

By the time Karen arrived, we already knew that she planned to break up with Eros after he drove her home. She had kept dating him an extra week because she didn't have a car, and she wanted to make sure she had a ride to the show, not wanting to try and trust the bus like Genny and I did. Eros was short and quiet with dark hair, long eyelashes, and a square jaw. A few weeks before, Karen told us that he worked for the city as an assistant to the public art manager. Karen gagged when she said the words "public art."

When Karen introduced Eros to us, he smiled. "I've heard a lot about you all," he said, unzipping his coat in the cold warehouse, then zipping it back up.

As soon as we were introduced—*Raya, Al, Genny*—Karen grabbed Genny by the arm and followed after Raya, leaving me with Eros. At first, he took a quick step to follow them, then stopped abruptly and looked over at me, as if he were about to ask me what he should do next. I felt a kinship with him, with the way he moved and was unable to move, with how I knew his fate.

"Women," I said to him, pointing a thumb and shaking my head.

Karen spent most of the night hanging out with Genny, and I ended up talking to Eros. We wandered through the exhibit and I asked him questions I knew the answers to, and he told me how he aspired to climb the ladder until he had the power to commission public art. While we wandered past explicit, queer art of all mediums in a non-venue far from the centre of things—navigating a smattering of phallic sculptures on the floor, sipping wine—Eros talked about being involved in making art as accessible and approachable as possible to a general public. He felt it was important to connect people, and mend the wounds of society, through art.

Then, Eros started to talk about monuments—about the Monument against Fascism that he'd studied in a class on public memory in university. The Monument against Fascism was a twelve-metre-tall, one-metre-wide aluminum column clad in a thin layer of lead that was installed in Hamburg-Harburg, Germany, in 1986. The point of the monument was to let people inscribe their names with metal styluses tethered nearby, and pledge themselves against fascism. Once the section of the monument within reach was filled up, the column would be lowered farther into the ground, so as to offer a fresh canvas.

Eros said the monument was already halfway gone. "The point is that the monument won't be there forever. Once it's gone—vanished —the people will be responsible for keeping up its memory. I'm not sure a monument that disappears works, but it's interesting."

I couldn't help but feel sad at the irony of a vanishing boyfriend telling a guy he'd probably never see again about a vanishing monument. I couldn't help but feel sad about how part of me didn't really want him to vanish, not because he was particularly interesting, but because of how much he reminded me of Tom. I felt that Eros carried himself with a similar resignation to being a man. As if he knew he was a man, that it was fine, but it wasn't really all that important to him. I always had a sense that Tom was uninterested in trying to defend or police being a man, in himself or in others. It was what he was, not what he was invested in.

I think Eros already knew something was up with Karen but had resigned himself to that fate, too. We met back up with our girlfriends after maybe an hour. Raya continued to ignore and avoid us. I got tipsy enough to trip over the sculptures on the ground less. Everyone got tipsy enough to be comfortable in the world we were in. To forget, maybe, that time was so limited. That, like monuments, people could also vanish into nothing but a fading stain in the brain. Like the fog of our breaths in that cold, warehouse air.

At the end of the night, Eros offered to give Genny and me a ride home, and we crammed into the cab of his three-seater pickup. Karen sat in the middle and Genny sat across our laps, yelping quietly whenever the truck hit a bump. I couldn't see Eros as he weaved over dark ice and snow, slipping occasionally but not crashing. We all talked, but we didn't talk about anything.

I never saw Eros again. When he dropped Genny and me off, I got out of the truck first, and as I started making my way to Genny's door in the sub-zero night, she grabbed my arm and held me to wait on the sidewalk with her. The door to the truck was slightly ajar, and the windows were too foggy from breath to see through. It had started to snow, transforming the moment into one that felt too much like Winnipeg. After a minute, Karen climbed out of the truck and closed the door behind her, Eros pulled away. She looped her arm in Genny's and dug her chin into her scarf. Before we walked into the oasis of Genny's apartment, I looked over to see the tail lights disappearing into the falling snow a few blocks down.

Karen never mentioned Eros again. She got into a new relationship a month later with a man she'd sold drugs to, who ended up stealing from her before breaking her heart. I didn't think of Eros much after that night, but I'd find myself thinking of a monument being lowered into the ground, of the challenge to remember things removed from view.

I would think of Eros again the day the past rushed up to meet me, to undermine me—when the running girl came back and decided that we should go somewhere far, far away. When she decided that monument was something she wanted to see.

According to Genny, the first time she remembers ever seeing me she was very drunk and fucking Tom. I walked in on the two of them, having come over to Tom's to see if I could borrow a pair of his boots, to try and while away the night. Tom—furious and wasted, too— proceeded to yell at me, telling me to give him back his clothes, which I was wearing, and leave.

I was sixteen, then. That was one of the times when my hair was buzzed. Mother had bounced back from her time in Selkirk, and I'd slipped back out to the end of the line, to the far edge of my unstable orbit.

That moment seems like something I'd remember, but I don't. From that day, I only remember fragments, when I stood in the hallway of Tom's house, wearing an overly long white dress several sizes too big that I'd taken from the mess of Del's room. I also remember the walk back home with nothing on but that dress and my winter coat in January. I remember, the short spectre of Genny, swaying, with every article of her clothes half-on, tugging them as if she had to fight her clothes to get them on. Then I remember she vomited in her hands.

And I remember the aftershocks of that night, when I went over to Tom's the next morning to apologize and return his mother's dress. I brought a garbage bag with the rest of his clothes that I'd taken over the years, just in case we were actually through. I let myself in his house again, as I always had, and went up to his room to find him: bloodshot eyes bagged, and painting. He didn't say much as I came in; he just stood up, patted the sides of my arms as if verifying I was real, and led me over to sit in the diffuse light that beamed into the room. He replaced the canvas that he'd been dabbing at since waking up hungover.

As soon as he sat down behind the blank canvas on his easel I opened my mouth, but he said, "No" and picked up his brush. He said he didn't want to paint me with my mouth open. I sat there with the apology welling up inside, the violent shame that arose from what is now a dark gap in my head reconstructed by hearsay, the hearsay of two people who were trashed at the time. I had to have remembered it, then.

As Tom painted, he told me about Genny, about the mistake he'd made bringing her back after the party he'd gone to. He'd been a virgin.

"She was so passive," he said, putting the wood tip of the brush in the middle of his forehead and pointing the bristles toward the canvas, tracing in the air. "She was like a corpse."

I gave him a look.

"I mean, I'd assume."

We laughed.

"Fuck," he said, slashing the painting with the brush, his red eyes squinting. "Now you've got some laughing in your portrait."

By the time Tom was finished painting, the words of the apology were gone and we were balanced again. He turned the easel and I stared back at me from the canvas in a dimly grieving way. The anatomy was as skewed as it always was for Tom, the colours more impressionistic than flattering, but it contained me in a way that I loved, contained my image like oil held in a fist of water. Me, removed from fleshy congruency. And somehow, at the last moment, my laughter had snuck in.

Everything is looping as I wake up shivering and sweating in bed. I sit up and feel dizzy, look around to the rainy mid-morning light slanting in at the window and realize that I am not Hedy Baum. I'm not, no. I am Alani. I'm in Hedy's bed, but I am not her.

My sinuses are full, my brain too heavy. I am boiling alive in my own body.

I lie back against the pillow and open my mouth: "Too much rain. I can feel every bone." The ceiling is a blank white swirling. My scratchy throat drips. "I got here a few days ago. Hedy is my mother, not me. I am in Winnipeg," I talk myself out of her and back into my skin.

"Genny is not in Winnipeg, and she is not talking to me. I am not an engineer, like Genny. I'm a photographer, but not a photographer like Mother. I'm a photographer like me. Annie. Annie? I'm sweating. There was a dead boy in the water, and I don't think I'm him, either. I'm a monument."

I close my eyes and try to fall back asleep, but I find myself thinking of the memory palace, dragged by a dark hand through room after room, and every room is on fire. There is so much smoke, so many hands, so many versions of myself that I've tried to keep straight over the years, that are laughing and screaming and turning to ash. I am being pulled by my scalp, through the first floor, then up the swelter-ing stairs until I'm thrown into my bedroom. The pry bar is still there, in the corner, so I wrench off the boards holding the windowpane among the flames, pull it out, and try to climb free, but as I do my foot catches and I can't get out of the grip.

I don't want to turn around, so I do, and open my eyes to me drown-ing. There is water in the room with me, over my nose, in Hedy's bed, in the house.

Or else I'm stuffed up and crying and just forgetting to breathe.

After Mother tried to kill herself, after she came back from Selkirk, I woke up in the house every day to less of myself, but no fewer versions of me. The bed felt crowded, yet nobody spoke, nobody looked at one another. Every morning after that—when I would have to drag Mother out of her bed and draw her down the stairs and pull the blinds closed and sit there, watching her take her medicine—I felt a generalized sensation of lessening. I got smaller. Loose ends shrank and broke off, and then there were only more of me. I was a collection of frayed ends, ends that had no communication with their roots.

I fed Mother. I pulled her up the stairs. I put her in the tub. I told her about school, about my classes, about what I was reading and all the lessons that I hated. Her face was there when I talked to her. I put her to bed and sat there with her for a little while, breathing. And every time I sat there with her I thought about smothering her with her pillow. I loved her too much, and not enough. As a concession, I kissed her on the forehead, and as I did I pressed her head into the pillow. When I pulled away, a blank print appeared, and by the time I turned out the lamp, I could see the place where my lips had been rouge up with Mother's blood.

The same blood that had sprinted from me.

That heavy, mute time was when Tom and I started to drink. Not because we were cool, and not because we were interesting, but because we had to do something. We mostly siphoned from Del's various stashes, particularly the stuff that Tom stole to try and force her to be dry for a few days. I drank less than he did, mostly, and he talked more than I did, but we both took turns wearing each other's wounds. Some nights I'd drink too much, and when we went to parties I'd dance too close with too many girls. And sometimes he would be sober but completely silent. Other nights we were on a level, both half sharing, both half-drunk.

We were trying to understand our mothers by shadowing them. We rebelled by following suit. They were the lit room and we were the dark world behind glass, staring, unstared.

Eventually, Mother got back into herself. Slowly, she regained her capacity for locomotion, played at agency, started working again. Wore a personality and had enough energy to fend for herself and, finally, to fend me off. Then she started trying to talk to me again, but it was too late. Someone had walked away with my throat.

I could barely say a word. When we were out alone, Tom would tell me about things that were going through his head. When we were out on the streets, when we often couldn't see each other besides as the negative space of bodies blocking lights behind them, he would talk about Del, who was in a vicious cycle of falling into new men and then falling out of them into drinking. She was either too hopeful to give Tom the time of day, or she was too drunk to see him. We both loved our mothers so much, if only because we could not reach them or do anything to help them. We cared about them and watched them break themselves down. I didn't talk about Mother. Not much. I mostly just muttered irrelevant things, or communicated by touching Tom's arm, or simply followed him around as he lorded over the streets as the thin, stooping giant that he was. I'd started reading Ovid's *Metamorphoses* around that time, basking in the gods, their petty lives, their vengeful transmutations—relishing in Actaeon, in Pan, in Bacchus—and one night, when we were throwing sticks into the Assiniboine, I told Tom that I thought he might be some kind of willow tree given human form. He might have smiled; it was dark. I felt heat. We stood there in the quiet of after, throwing dead limbs of him into the river's midnight tumult.

I started to drink more. I stayed out later and later and stopped avoiding strangers at night. Not that they were much of a true danger, anyway. I did less and less at school. I stopped taking pictures. I skipped school more and was alone more often, wandering the streets of Winnipeg's midday. Downtown, the Exchange, Broadway. Tom was never as willing to cut school as much, never wanted to stop learning. He cared about everything: about his future, about himself, about me. I felt like a string of film with no lens to gain focus, no cage to keep light from burning me blank.

At the parties we stumbled into, I was the one people were wary of. I was a bad influence. I was unstable. Nobody knew if I was going to come in a skimpy dress or an old, ratty suit I'd nicked from a thrift store. Nobody knew how to address me, to reach out to me, without making me angry. So people parted a path, nodding, whenever I came through a door.

I don't remember many of those parties. Not now. When I stepped into a party, I stepped into a largely unrecorded state. I was too lost, too abstracted from my centre—or else I was already too drunk. Once, I ended up breaking a rib dancing because I'd bound myself up too tight and flat with hospital bandages I'd stolen from Mother's old nursing supplies, which transitioned into a month of hiding all the clues from Mother, which transitioned into a month of Tom holding me down, dragging me to his house or to the edge of the river, trying anything to make me settle down enough so I could heal. There's a calcified bump there now, from the breaking and half healing and half breaking again, just below my left breast.

I couldn't look at myself half of those days. I wanted the many-ness of me gone. I was everything, but I wanted to be one simple fucking thing. I was sick of manoeuvring between. I never felt welcome in my body, except for the moments when I did, and by then I didn't even want to be. I wasn't welcome at some of those parties because people were afraid of me. Of who I was and who I could be. Of how uncomfortable I made people, people who wanted to feel chaotic without having to be in the presence of a purer essence of it.

I was always out late, but no matter what—no matter how drunk I got, no matter how bad I wanted to disappear—I'd always show up back home, and Mother would be waiting for me in the living room. Sometimes, before going to the door, I'd just stand on the sidewalk and stare into our house, at Mother staring out the window toward me but not seeing me. I knew she could only see herself reflecting off the night. The look on her face was tired. She would be wearing anything from a dress to next to nothing. Sometimes I'd stand there for a few minutes, until I caught wind of something walking down the sidewalk toward me—some dark other at the swelling edge of night—and then I'd run to the door.

The door was always locked, and I'd always have to dig my key out of an inconvenient pocket of my jacket. It took a lot of fumbling, but I never once knocked. No matter what, though, no matter what evil ridiculousness my mind could conjure bearing down on me, I turned the key just as reluctantly. Opened the door with the usual hesitance. Hung up my ratty leather coat with just as steady a hand, and then walked upstairs, into the dark skull of the house, with my feet knocking deliberate and hard. Echoing.

I have the duvet, I have the old radio from Mother's closet—cord wound around my neck—and I am sliding down the stairs on my butt, one at a time. Every time I stand up, I feel like I should fall over. I want to be downstairs without having to go downstairs. I want water, want to be on ground level, want to keep my eyes open so as to keep the fire in the palace out of this real house. I slide down, stair after stair, saying, "Excuse me, excuse me" as I pass by the other versions of myself that have come back here. Then a little breeze comes down the stairs, grazes my hair matted to my sweathead, and I turn around—nearly at the bottom now—and all the legs I just scooted past are gone but hers. Mother.

She is walking up and down the stairs, one hand on the banister and the other holding the papers, envelope-freed, forgiving their two folds flat. She comes all the way down and steps through me, turns back up. Words, Mother's mouth moving, noises coming out without her being able to stop them, words that I can't hear. Words I could have heard, words I did hear but couldn't have known. A language I'd then lost sense of.

I'm at the end of the hall, coming out of the kitchen, standing by the darkroom door. I'm maybe nine. Or eleven. I'm either on the brink of blood splitting my body open or surviving in the wake of it, surviving and deaf to her, deaf to all but the creak of the stairs while she reads aloud. Like she always did, sucked up and immersed in language in a way I could never be, because I'd already lost that language.

I watch her come down to the bottom of the stairs, watch her turn around. Mother is so young, my age. I can hear her get to the top of the stairs, and then I see her at the bottom, her old radio's cord wrapped around her neck, sweaty.

I hear the papers waving as she goes up and down, hear the house move with her, hear her feet on the stairs, her butt as she scoots down—or, as I do—but the rest is her secret, her life, a ritual she will keep up for years yet. Until before Selkirk, until we started going to the liquor store for cardboard boxes, to hold the river of letters that have stopped coming.

The house's wind is trying to get my hair out from the sweat. I'm stuck inside me at the bottom of the stairs, wrapped up in cordage and duvet. I'm growing, stretching to the sky like a thistle stalk, wearing boy clothes at the other end of the hall—hand-me-downs from Asha's son.

Everything is too short on me and life is too long. Mother is at a different level of existence, out of sight, and I am down here, scooting along the floor toward me, growing into the way the world wants me. And then, just like that, I slip back into the kitchen and the house goes quiet. When I scoot my way into the kitchen, I'm nowhere to be found.

I pull myself up to the sink and put water in a tea-stained mug. I drink it down hard, gripping the counter like a cliff edge. I drink two mugs' worth and then grab a third and let myself down and scoot to the living room. As I go, I can feel the photos, whispering. I plug in the radio and stretch it up near the couch, where I lie, with the duvet. I turn on the radio and then look out the window to the grey morning.

Looks like we'll be getting a small amount of rain tomorrow and Monday, but we may see the sun again starting Tuesday! And boy howdy, do we need it. Back to you, Joan.

I want the sun, not the fever. I try to remind myself that the sun is still shining out there; it's just unable to break its way to the ground. It is tripping along the tops of the clouds. But the idea is ruined by clouds framed in plane windows, light coming in as beams so hot until the plane turns to fly into them. Away.

"Boy howdy," I say, closing my eyes, breathing hard through my mouth and reaching down to the mug I set on the floor.

"Howdy-boy-howdy, back to me."

What I count as my first real memory of Genny makes no sense without the story of me walking in on her and Tom. On the way home from Tom's place late one night, in a state of sad lightness, I decided to stop at a small playground. Nobody was around and it was snowing fat flakes. I climbed the slide, hands hovering over the sides as I slipped the slow descent through the tiny snowdrifts that were stacking up on the sheer metal. I reached the bottom and scooted off.

But I still didn't want to go home, so I went over to the children's swings and thought, *Yes, I can fit in the tiny harness if I try*. I climbed up on the seat, braced myself between the chains, and slid my legs down to above the knee before I finally got jammed in, lost my balance, and fell over. The snow continued to fall in a quiet, blanketing laughter as I wriggled on the ground, trying to escape.

Moments before I was going to begin calling for help, small gloved hands appeared and pulled the swing from my legs. Attached to those small hands was Genny. Once I was free and upright, we looked each other in the eye, both of us completely conscious and sober for the first time, and embarrassed, not because of the absurdity of that moment but because of our recognition of having met before—the anchor I now can't grab hold of, the demolition I know only by the presence of the rubble and the rumours of the blast.

On the short walk over to her idling car, to the little heat that we would sit in together for an hour before she dropped me off at home, we offered each other our names. The air was so cold that we watched them as they migrated across the distance, like little boats drifting into the path of a storm.

It's morning, I suppose a new one, and Mother's landline just rang with her doctor. When it rang I was lost to the noise, still feverish, half sleeping but back to myself. I was able to stand up from the couch and step over all of the memories stuck to the floor to get here, to the little table in the corner, where this same phone has always been sitting.

The doctor is saying that he meant to ask me, when he met me at the home the other day—"Nice to finally meet you, by the way"— if I could sign off on him putting Mother back on antidepressants, since she's certainly no longer capable of communicating the consent herself. He thought that, considering her case, and especially with her history of severe depression, they might be able to help her. "Some studies show that antidepressants can help with some of the more aggressive and agitative aspects of the disease," he says. "It's impossible to tell, actually, which parts of her suffering may be dementia and which are symptoms of depression. Perhaps the aphasia is purely a side effect of the depression. Perhaps we could get her to communicate again, at least."

I sit here in Mother's old house, listening to him, watching the memories pop in and out on the empty walls, still feverish and growing dizzier the more I sit upright, and realize he's paused to hear what I have to say.

"Oh. I don't know. She really hated them before."

"Things have changed," he said. "She's not the same as she was, and the drugs are better."

"I don't know. I don't know."

"You can think about it if you want. You have my number, you can ca—"

"No." I remember the months after I started them, before I quit. I remember the incontinence, the lack of appetite, the weight gain, the excessive dissociation. "No, let's not do that." The numbness, the anger. "I don't think it's worthwhile. Not at this point."

"Oh. All right. Well, do let me know. I have colleagues who say it's worked wonders for similar patients, and I can recommend an excellent medication."

The rain outside won't stop. I remember boy howdy. I remember the weatherman's crackling promise.

"Let me know," he says again, after a moment.

"I have. I have." I knock on the door of the palace. "Oh, an old friend of mine is knocking at the door. I completely blanked about him coming over. I've got to go, sorry. I have to go now."

I hang up the phone, stay sitting there at the little table and look out the window, to the front yard, to the empty walkway. I am hungry and nauseous.

At the end of the call, the mailman stuffed soaked flyers into the mailbox attached to the little fence in front of the house, and then kept walking down the street. Waddling.

I get up and stumble to the couch, flop back to horizontal bliss. I wrap the duvet around my neck and close my eyes and the door opens and I take a step into the burning house, lower my head at the landing, and get dragged through the fire and the flames again.

Most times, when you go into your memory palace, the door to the darkroom simply isn't there, and you don't think about it at all. As a rule, you don't like darkness in the palace. You don't trust it. You think of film, and how when you open a camera's shutter, the darkness is mapped into a complete transparency, a lack of opacity created by the light of the scene not choosing to burn those portions of the film black. How when you develop the negative, darkness becomes the empty space between the images, between the opaque transcriptions of light.

In the negative, darkness is a lack of information, which is why you tend to overexpose your photos by at least half of a stop, to try and encroach some form onto the darkness, to get more information. Because you know that most darknesses are not total, that most darknesses have some slow wiggles of light eking around in them, that you would just have to stare long enough into to find.

But you're afraid that the darkroom is the place where the things you don't know, can't know, or don't want to know, stay. It is a room housing a very rich lack, an abyss you know would only repay your patience in pain.

My stomach wakes me up and drags me away from the couch, away from the talking radio, to the kitchen, to the cans of soup I bought the other day. My body is weak. There's a dirty pan from the last can of soup, from before the vigil, before this sick, still on the stove, and I open the easy tab of the new can and pour it in, turn on the burner, and move along the counters with my hands, in case my body decides to fall over. I get to the sink and turn on the tap to fill the mug I brought from the living room and drink the water up. Then I pour a mugful into the soup. I breathe through my mouth.

I look out the back window, through the rain of the afternoon leaving, and notice the space where Mother's car was. Where my car could be. For a second I wonder where she is, where she could be driving to, whether she'll be coming back. I remember doing the same thing after listening to the answering machine the morning Mother never came home.

There's nothing in the backyard but the bad grass and the old charcoal barbecue. I don't think that was even ours, and doubt it was Ilsa's, but it has always been there.

I hear, in the lull of the soft rain, the sound of a cat, far off, meowing. Hungry, lonely, elsewhere. But perhaps it is my stomach, because the soup is burning—I can't smell it, but I taste it in the air. I stir it with a spoon and turn the burner off.

It is with great skill and no grace and all the energy I have left that I make it to the kitchen table with the full pan, that I sit and wait for it to slowly cool and then start to eat.

I was twenty-seven when I started taking antidepressants. I'd been working hard, as a cover. I carried my cameras around with me all the time and spent so many hours in the darkroom, chemical fumes settling into my skin. Genny thought that I was working, that I had stumbled into a brutally encompassing idea that was threatening to slip past me, but I was just trying to make it through. I was terrified. I slept badly and woke up and went to the darkroom and talked to myself all day. I thought about jumping off Hennepin Avenue Bridge with a small boat anchor in my backpack. I bought the anchor and the backpack and the rope, but I couldn't do it, and the only reason was that I couldn't do that to Genny. She would have thought it was about her. She was too much in love with bridges, and with me.

I thought about lighting a fire in the darkroom with the door locked. I had a wide array of ideations, and when they got too strong, that was when I stopped taking photos, moved almost exclusively into the darkroom, and started printing photos without film. I did it with grave focus. I enlarged light onto blank paper and pulled prints of various grey tones from the baths. I took my camera out empty and set it up on a tripod. In the studio I set up massively elaborate shots: insinuations of violence, insinuations of release, insinuations of blankness. I spent hours fussing over an empty camera. Every time I wound the camera I felt the complete lack of tension, as huge strings of the efforts of my days slipped on undocumented. I didn't want anyone else to know. I spent about a week going in and out of the darkroom, hardly eating, printing and printing, and then I tied a noose in the rope, tied the rope to the anchor, packed my backpack with the anchor and the rope, drove to the centre—the same centre I would drive Ess to so many years later—and told them to please help me.

The fourth day I was there I called Genny and she came. I could tell that the first thing she wanted to do when she saw me was slap me. She brought Hamm with her and we sat on a bench outside and I watched her cry. I watched myself watch her. I watched Allie watch her. Then Al. Everyone was there, and nobody could empathize with her. So we pet her dog. So we kissed her skull.

When I eventually surfaced, blowing back and forth with the dissociative numbness and incontinence of the medication, seeing my therapist two times a week, being watched by Genny, I called the show of near-blank photos simply *1997*. It was my first solo exhibit since *Shavasana*; the others were all with the collective. The photographs set in borderless frames in three rows lined the entire gallery. Some were grey, some were pitch black, but many were completely blank. I'd numbered them, counting down to the first, which was the only one I'd done with anything other than the light. For one brief moment while exposing the paper, I had put my hand between it and the light of the enlarger, then pulled it back, horrified by the gesture. Looking at the print, all you can see is a slight lack of uniformity that's not in the others, which were done in such profusion to try and wash the taste of that first reaching from my mouth.

6

THE STAIRS

As you go up the stairs in the memory palace you are a ghost passing yourself—yourselves: at different ages, in different clothes, with different expressions. They bump into each other and push at one another as you ascend. Alani, at five, is digging through the floor at the bottom of the stairs. A girl at fifteen, with fists, is yelling at a nineteen-year-old boy, who bites his lip at her. Someone, who you somehow know is twenty-seven, is punching the wall very quietly, blood coming down her knuckles. Most of the youngest ones are yelling, laughing, loud. The teenagers are either screaming or completely silent. One of you cries at all the commotion, near the bottom step. They are the first one you step through, and as you go up, you keep turning to look back at them. They are so sensitive that you wonder how they ever survived so long, so softly, among all these stiff phantoms. On the walls, lining the way up to the second floor, more and more of you jump out of picture frames. A long-hair boy, a hoodied elsewhere, a short-hair girl, older and younger. Every permutation is you.

Many pick fights with one another, and you want to stop them, but you're translucent. You have no agency here. All you can do is look and walk forward, one step at a time, through them, feeling what it is to be each of them.

The opportunity to have any effect on your life has passed. At this point in the tour—should you make it this far—you often think of the quotation about how life must be lived forward yet can only be understood looking back. Something like that. You watch conflicts boil between your parts as you take your steps up and up. When the conflicts peak, the players explode into ash and are reborn, mumbling their way back up into their climaxes. You want to break them up, but they are stuck, stuck on repeat. You take another step. Sooner or later, you will make it to the top, though sometimes, like the hallway, the summit never gets any closer and you collapse. But if you remember not to look at the empty frames on the wall where they each climbed out, you have a better chance of making it. If you look, the staircase will spiral out into empty bone. The wind will pick up and a door, somewhere, will slam—with a sound you never get used to. And you'll end up trapped, by one side of the door or another.

It's my seventh day here, a Monday, and I wake up in Mother's old bed, with all the covers chucked across the room, naked. It's barely day. My fever broke sometime last night, but the cranked radiators gave my fever to the house. I woke up into a hot world and thought the fire that had been moving through the memory palace had made its way into this house. Had sparked from my body, which was moving through both. Then I heard the radiator knock from its place up against the wall and remembered veins of iron, of brass, remembered hot water and that first cold night here. So I got up from the bed and walked through rooms opening windows so that the house could breathe.

As the weatherman promised, it's still raining. The window in the room is open, and the rain is dripping down the sides of the roof like sweat, and somewhere nearby a cat is yowling. Their throat sounds dry and hoarse in the rain.

I sit up and stretch. I breathe into the bends and snap myself out of the ache of waking and into the sore of being awake. Into the sore of being awake here, in Mother's bed, having survived the worst of the fever. I hadn't slept in this bed since the nights I spent here alone, at fifteen, when Mother was in Selkirk and I didn't know when or if she was ever coming home. And before that, it must have been at nine, when there was a storm so bad several small tornadoes were gouging at the outskirts of the city. Mother and I watched the clouds from my bedroom—those tight dog-nipple clouds—as they began to explode the horizon. I was brave until night came and I could only see the world in flashbulb bursts. I've always wanted to do a portrait that way, with a camera open in a dark room, waiting for the sky to pop. Several times I've set it all up and sat in a room in the dark, waiting, as a cloudy evening went off into a dry night. Every time, I remember that night when the hail threatened to break our walls in. How Mother held me so tight while we slept in her bed.

The cat is yowling as I blow my nose and dress myself loose. I look at myself in the bathroom mirror across the hall and hate it, go back into the bedroom and put my hair up and bind myself up prairie flat. I kiss the light lipstick I'd thought was right onto the corner of my fist, bend down to my luggage for the packer. Even now I can feel wrong a few times before I even start a day.

I go downstairs and start closing windows so it doesn't get too damp or cold. The air in the house has gotten a little fresher since I got here, diffusing the old stink of stale dust. A smell of abandonment, of piled time.

When I'm closing the kitchen window I hear the cat again. The rain is there, but it isn't compelling. I look out to the backyard, and beyond the overgrown, blown-over grass and under that rusted old barbecue in the corner, near the hole in the fence—which has become one of many holes—the cat stares at me, mouth half-open. It yowls. I yowl back—at pitch—close the window, and open the back door. The cat and I stare at one another around the falling droplets of rain. I leave the door open, go to the front hall for my shoes, and grab one of Mother's umbrellas.

Before I got Darius, my first and last cat, I hated all of them. There always seemed to be something insidious about them. I met Darius because of Karen, the first Minneapolis person I'd clung to. She'd worked at this shitty café that barely sold coffee and I'd loiter there while Genny was at university. Karen did performance art and I kept trying to get her to pose nude for me. She also sold drugs in the art scene, and is about the least gay girl I've ever gotten close with. One day, when we finally became friendly enough, she brought me over to her place and there was this fat, white Persian cat there. Darius had been her roommate's cat until her roommate moved out and left him there. I hated him. He was such an asshole, hissing at everyone, running off, then coming up and rubbing against your leg when you finally stopped cursing at him. Then as soon as you'd give in and pet him, he'd just run off again.

I unfurl the umbrella at the back door and go halfway to the barbecue. The cat is a deep ratty grey, thin. I kneel and put my hand out, half the backyard away, and the cat disappears through a gap in the corner of the fence where the boards have rotted out. I stand up and go back inside.

Whenever I went over to Karen's place, Darius was there, battling it out with me in a game for attention I never quite learned the rules to. Eventually, when Karen finished running a draft of a performance by me where she was trying to read verses of the Bible with a mouth full of thumbtacks, she told me I was very much like that cat. I told her that was bullshit and she spat blood into her kitchen sink and put down her Bible, moving her long ponytail from one shoulder to the other. She just stared at me, quiet, with a little red trickle down the side of her lip.

I pick up two chairs from the little table in the kitchen and take them outside, trailing along the back lawn to the barbecue in the corner. Little oases. I go inside and find masking tape in a drawer and a box of garbage bags under the sink and use them to construct a long canopy leading up to the open back door between the chairs, end tables, floor lamps, whatever legged thing I can find in the house and bring outside. The sun is rising over the houses now, a thin fog wisping through the wavering rain. The cat is quiet.

I knew Karen was trying to get rid of that cat, but I still decided to take him when she asked me to. She was moving and didn't want to have to take it to a shelter.

She told me, "It'll teach you something about yourself. About loving yourself. About what it feels like to love someone like you."

I open a can of tuna, one of the relics from the mostly barren pantry, and put it on the kitchen floor. The cupboards were usually bare even when Mother and I lived here. It never quite felt like we'd settled into the house in a forever sort of way. I go and sit on the couch in the living room and wait. Then I notice Mother's old standing mirror in the corner of the room, reflecting the darkness of the corner to itself. I set it up so that I can sit on the couch and watch the door for the cat. I look down at the floor at my feet, at a small collection of dead flies tangled in a dust bunny nebula, which must have been under the coffee table before I carried it outside. The cat has not yowled in a while and I wonder if it left. I should have put out some water, even though the little animal is probably soaked to the skin. The rain picks up again, and then slows. I hear it spatter the garbage bags outside. Soon, shadows start in at the doorway.

When I took Darius from Karen, I was barely scraping by, and so was Genny. She was busy with her studies and I saw less and less of her. We lived apart, like we always had, and I was feeling like my life wasn't quite right, like I wanted to disappear, back to Winnipeg, or farther, into some different flat, strange world. Iowa or Saskatchewan or Texas. I wanted to look out my window and see nothing but sky. But then, just like that, I had this asshole cat to deal with. He scratched up my legs until they looked like the hash marks of a prisoner growing weary of noting down his days. He peed in my shoes. He gnawed open my feather pillow one day, so when I came back the whole room was fluttering. I yelled at him. I cursed him.

I named him Darius because he didn't have a name that we knew, and because I wanted to prove to myself that I wasn't stupid. That I knew things about history, since history and art were the classes I skipped the least. He was a Persian cat and I wanted to feel Spartan against his aggressions. I hissed at him a lot whenever I was home during the day, and when I went to bed, he snuggled up beside my skull. I woke up with my face in his hot belly and scratched him awake, and we would sit there on the floor as he ate and I counted up my dollars and wondered which store nearby I could go to and snag some film. Then, most of the time, he'd scurry under the bed and swipe at my ankles as I got ready. All my socks had bloodstains.

Every day I came home to him, and years later, when I tried to move in with Genny, Hamm—her Blue Heeler–Doberman mix—got in a fight with Darius and snapped his ankle. I realized how deeply I loved him when I broke up with Genny over that, for a few weeks, despite the fact that Darius had asked for it by swiping at Hamm's nose. By the time Genny and I got back together, Darius and I had already moved into another shitty bedroom on our own.

The cat is standing in the hall, in the corner of my eye, like a scarecrow. They're looking through the house, wary. I don't move. The cat goes past me like a wet ghost, and I get up quick and move for the open door in the kitchen. They bolt the other way, up the stairs. I go outside and bring the furniture, dripping, into the kitchen. I close the door after each piece so that the cat can't leave. When I'm done, I see no sign of the cat and wipe it all down with a stiff, dusty towel.

The house is dead still. Hot toward feverish and surrounded by the cool spring day. The rain is tapping the shingles of its crown. The only thing different is that now, somewhere, there's another heartbeat hiding.

The first time I saw the sinking Monument against Fascism, at the tail end of the summer of 1991, I thought I'd never leave Germany. Whoever had just arrived that day in Hamburg as me, whoever was standing there in the mid-afternoon summer heat believed that what surrounded them was the strange landscape of their new life. That all the people they'd been fractured into, all the people they'd loved, all the people they'd destroyed and left behind on another smoky continent, were precisely that: left behind. I'd removed myself from my life so forcefully to find myself there, a stranger in a pedestrian mall in a country so foreign to me yet somehow intrinsic to me, looking up and down that dark lead monolith.

The skin of the monument was scrawled with names, sentences, scratched images carved in with the metal styluses tethered nearby. There was graffiti. The markings stretched from where the monument met the ground to the highest reach of the tethers. There were many empty spaces between the names, still bare and waiting. More room stretched toward the sky, out of reach. There was still time.

I stood near the monument for a few minutes but didn't add myself to it—unsure what name might come from the twitching of my hand. Fortunately, the cab driver, who had understood enough English to get me to the monument, was still there, idling. I got back in, beside the kennel that held Darius, and he drove me to a hotel that charged by the week. We crossed tiny bridge after tiny bridge to get there: short spans over the trickles veining the huge city. Every time we drove over a little bridge, I felt like I was transcending my previous life, transcending Genny. I remembered her and felt beyond her reach. The cabbie sang along softly to the radio. When we got to the hotel, I tipped him, unsure how many deutschmarks would be too generous. He got out and dragged my single piece of luggage to the door of the tall building. The same piece of luggage I have with me here.

The rooms of the hotel were closet-sized and ancient. Each floor had a mixed bathroom on either end, each with a thick-curtained tub to insinuate the possibility of private bathing. But the rooms were very cheap. The woman who rented them out had a necklace of keys and a languorous German tongue in contrast to her sharp, hopping English one. She muttered everyone's name as she passed the doors—names rooted in many different languages—flicking through the numbered keys on her necklace.

"Alani Baum," I told her, when we reached the door whose key was the first on her necklace that had two copies. The name had slipped out before I could catch it and hold it in. The passport's name, the name I signed bureaucratic documents with, the name that was used to demarcate the official body but that was rarely ever used to identify the flesh. But I didn't know who else I could have been.

She opened the door to the tiny room and I put Darius down on the counter. He whined. I muscled my luggage up onto the tiny bed beside the tiny window looking out north, toward the sea. When I turned around she was gone. I heard her muttering the names down the hall, their order reversed.

I closed the door, opened Darius's kennel—though I knew he wouldn't come out until he'd acclimated—and looked out at the over-whelming strangeness that my world had so thrustingly become. A day before, I was not here. A week before, I had not even entertained the chance.

It felt like there was much less of me, after leaving Genny. I sat there, in the tiny room, trying to acclimatize to that, too.

For a long time while I was in Hamburg I felt as if nothing from before could reach me. As if the distance from both Mother and Genny allowed for a brutal slash-and-burn kind of reprocessing. As if I'd become pastless. That first day, I stood there and looked out toward the city that was nothing to me, nothing but a vessel holding little known but the monument, nothing but a single thing I learned about from a man who skirted briefly along the edge of my life. Hamburg was a landscape I felt I could fill with a new life, unencumbered by my many concentric pasts.

But though an ocean is wide and can keep most flesh away, it's hard to hide for long from the ghosts of the things you've pushed to the edges of your mind. An ocean may be inconceivably vast, but a brain is composed of nothing much but inches.

There's nowhere to run.

Once I've towelled off everything in the kitchen, I look at the mirror in the living room—see half of myself reflected by the closed door—and realize that so many things in the house are out of place. The mirror, the kitchen table, the few remaining magnets on the fridge. Things that are no longer where they were—or where they are, at least, in the memory palace.

The first thing I do is go to the sink and turn the tap on just a pinch so it drips water a few times a minute like it used to, before Mother must have had it fixed. Then, I go to the fridge and start moving magnets around, back to where my gut tells me they should be. The magnets I don't recognize I set aside to throw out. One of the new ones—a photo of Niagara Falls, someone else's souvenir—holds a piece of paper with phone numbers for emergencies: ambulance, police, poison control, Dorothea, and Asha. I listen to the sink drip, throw the magnet out, and put the page in my pocket. Then I remember the pad of paper that used to sit beside the phone in the living room, where I would sometimes doodle when I was talking to Genny or Tom, so I go and I put it there. Beside the phone is the answering machine, which no longer has a tape in it. The phone is no longer plugged into it—a skull that nobody tells stories to anymore.

I hear the sink drip but cannot hear the cat roaming the house. The house's creaking has not given them away yet. They must be hulking, hidden somewhere. I blow my nose into a wad of tissue.

I pick up the mirror, take it back to the stairs, and start to carry it up to Mother's room. Dorothea probably moved it down. Perhaps Mother no longer wanted to be confronted by herself first thing in the morning.

As I climb the stairs, I watch myself in the mirror and have to slow down so I don't trip over my feet. All I can see is me and everything behind me.

Even if my muscles still know exactly how to steer through this house, even if my legs remember the height of each stair with precise accuracy, even if my body remembers the exact number of steps, navigating the house with the mirror—and myself—in front of me is harder than it would be if my eyes were closed.

So partway up the stairs, I close them, and make my way to Mother's bedroom. Before I reach the corner of the room where the mirror used to live, I trip on my luggage, the contents spilled out on the floor. I nearly drop the mirror as I fall sideways onto the bed. My eyes open into a surprised look I don't want to see. I'm staring down at myself, two bodies sandwiched between mattresses. I get up and put the mirror back where it goes.

With the mirror restored, the room is hostile, different, so I make the bed, then stuff my luggage with all my things and carry it out of the room. I stand in front of the armoire and look over to my bedroom and then over to the stairs. I sneeze. I feel the cool, wet air enter the house from the windows, rehydrating the dry, radiator-heated air.

I could leave, couldn't I?

But I can't. My car is on Ethelbert. It's out of gas. By the time I fill it up, it will already be too late.

I carry my luggage to my old bedroom, imagining the surroundings of the house only as they pass me: life as a delayed reaction to having lived.

If my life were this house, I'd know exactly where I was going without having to look at where I'd been. But instead, all I do now is scratch out a semblance of who I am, with no foreknowledge of the way forward through the fog.

I don't remember my first kiss with Genny, and I'm not sure I believe her story. According to her, we kissed at the New Year's party of a mutual acquaintance. I don't trust that I would have done that, kissed a girl out in front of people. I also don't trust that she would have done that. All I remember from that night was that Tom was supposed to show up, but he didn't, because Del was angry at him for coming home late a few nights before—because we were out trying to steal street signs with pry bars we had smuggled from the hardware store—and said he had to stay in. So when I went to the party alone, a lone girl, among people I didn't know at all, or had hardly spoken a word to in my life, I went straight for the alcohol.

It's strange to feel as if you do not share the same beginnings with someone, when their first memory is inaccessible to you. All I know for sure is that the first time I kissed Genny, inarguably, was weeks later, in her car, three days after she saved me from that swing set.

Sometimes the stairs in the memory palace are empty, and sometimes they're too full. There are times when you disbelieve in the many forms you've taken, when you believe you are one thing and always have been and always will be. And there are other times when you don't believe you're anyone at all. When it's the former, your path is unhindered and the walls are lined with mirrors capped in photo frames. You just go up the stairs, like in the real house, and stop at the top. When it's the latter, the stairway is like a crashing sea, a river nameless and sourceless; nothing but turbidity and power. The walls are torn blank, the frames shattered, your memories drowned out of their angles. You forget how to float, your transparency is no safety, and you are simply accommodated in the moment, feeling your skin turn wet and other. You become a tincture, dissolving into the unlabelled mass. Teeth clenched, furious at believing that there is any such thing as an identity at all, you don't believe in you or in anyone else. It's just a tsunami of images. You break from the palace and mock the many names you've used, the many costumes, the many gestures you still drape over yourself in attempts to signify a shift inside. A shift from one vast nothing into the same. From one scream into its synonym.

I go to the armoire and open it: dust and muted detergent, polished-wood touch, hinge-creaking. Mother's unrecognizable clothes hang in its familiar gut, where my clothes used to be. So many places she could place herself, so many places she was placed in, so much so far from her. I let my hand snake toward them, grazing. I let it shop. Long, quiet-coloured shirts; dry, stiff leather jackets; blouses that have forgotten Mother and moulded to the hanger's shape.

As I hear the wind coming up the stairs, I find myself sixteen or seventeen, and Tom and I are heading into a thrift store in Saint Boniface. I cannot read the name of it, sprawled above the door in redacted blackness. I probably forgot the name by the end of that year, when I was waking up every day in Minneapolis.

"I like buying clothes that have stories I don't know," Tom says, or said once and the sounds are just replaying in my head, as we walk from Del's car to the store's door.

We're either swaddled in fat coats for heat or dressed as scant as we can get for summer. I'm a boy, bound up but not packing, not yet. If it's summer, I'm sweltering; if it's winter, I'm shivering.

We're inside the store now. Tom is wearing dark sunglasses we snagged from another thrift store, west on Portage, not far from the camera shop I've been working at part time since Mother came back. Tom has his arm looped in mine, pretending to be blind. A French-speaking mouth has greeted us, and their eyes drag along after us. I smile. Or I did. We are at the men's racks. My hands are losing themselves in the fabric.

Tom is bigger than me, as thin as me but so tall. He stands behind me, muttering, "Hey, that button-up, the blue one. What size? Grab it for me," and I take it and model it against him. He feels the fabric, presses it to his chest. Perhaps his other arm is full, his winter coat slung over. Perhaps mine is, too. His head looks straight out, pretending his world is blank, but his eyes look straight down at me. "What do you think?" I can see the dim pupil'd blueness peeking.

I pull shirts and jeans. I avoid shorts and anything that shows any flesh but my arms. Crewnecks, turtlenecks, slacks, button-ups, everything in blacks and greys. I feel the eyes floating around the store, surveilling, mistrusting, trying to unfold me. My heart has revved up by the time we have armfuls of clothes, hangers clanging, and head into the biggest of the two change rooms together. We're undoing our boots, and I am as close to the far corner as possible, half-naked. Tom is shirtless in his own jeans, still wearing his sunglasses. He is holding an arm span of blue.

I dress and undress and re-dress. I do not turn to the mirror until most of my skin is hidden, not wanting to see my wrapped-up chest. Tom occasionally asks, as I'm trying on men's clothes, "So, how does it look?" projecting his voice as if on a stage. And I say, "Those black jeans look good on you," or "This blue button-up looks very dashing."

I'm sixteen, or seventeen, stuck in other people's stories in a tiny room with my best friend, playing blind. I am the man in the mirror, costumed in pre-worn histories, feeling an ache to get out of here and go see Genny. Either we have been seeing each other for a little over a month, or we are getting ready to run away together. Either I am keeping my only secret from Tom, or creating the environment in which to do that.

The store is quiet and it might be mid-afternoon. It's either summer, or we've cut from school early to come here. But no, it would have to be winter. I'm still sixteen, as a draft of winter hulks under the dressing room door when someone comes into the store, or leaves. It is winter because Tom is still here, integral to my time.

And because it is winter, we can get away with stealing a good portion of the clothes I want, stuffed into the arms of our puffed jackets. I put some of the clothes I want to buy back on the racks: "Too short, what was I thinking?" I say, as Tom holds on to my elbow. We buy the blue shirt. Eyes, thank-yous, a faceless "*Salut*."

We leave the nameless store and shore into our huge coats again, jeans stuffed against biceps, shirts balled in inside pockets.

"*Mon garçon*," Tom says, climbing blind into the driver's seat, into the dull lingered heat of Del's car.

I'm sitting beside him, farther on the drive toward home now. He's still wearing his blind man shades as he unzips his coat and pulls out the clothes. The heat of the car feels like the tickles of the house's radiator. Tom hands me clothes, clothes that must exist but that I can't see. They are just empty insinuations until they take the shape of Mother's clothes, in the armoire. I'm gripping them in the seat, the music on the radio waning, gripping them so hard, as if worried that if I let them go, then I'll forget who I am, forget who I want to be. Tom is whistling along, quieting down, looking over at me. His face isn't there but for his eyes. His eyes and those sunglasses.

The doors of the armoire close. Faceless Tom echoes away into wooden silence. I am standing in front of a closed armoire, Mother's hanger-shaped blouse in my hand.

Meeting Genny, falling in love with her, changed the order of things. As I got closer to her, I spent less time with Tom. I don't think he could get over the fact that I walked in on them, and I believe he would have preferred Genny to have disappeared from his life after that moment so he wouldn't be reminded of it. I understood. I was so much more embarrassed, back then, about anything that related to my body. I hated thinking about my body, hated acknowledging that it wasn't as malleable as I wanted it to be. I felt like I could never fully make a home in it, like I would always be trapped there. It was a classic teenage condition to have, only it was compounded for me by my gender trouble. I could never have the man's body or the woman's body I wanted. That hasn't changed, but I've realized over time that feeling like a prisoner in your body is what being human feels like. That you aren't your body, that you're not defined by it. But back then, I put a lot more names on all the different gender spaces I was feeling as a way of having a sense of agency. Of coherence. Of order.

With Genny around, though, things became a different kind of slurry. Parts of me began to connive, to get excited, and less and less was there the full sense of dread at waking up as someone who was myself but kiltered just enough not to feel very much like me. Genny's manner was quiet in a goading way; it created a silence different from the silences that Tom and I held. The silence between Genny and me was one I could spill more of myself into.

Soon, she was the one I'd run off with at night. And it became clear to me for the first time what it felt like to love someone you could communicate anything to, instead of someone you could be anything with. My many disparate bits started to rally, commingle, and coalesce into fewer, more sizable parts. The shifts I felt were more dramatic but less strange. I knew those parts of me, and they were all tied together in that they were all in pure love with her.

During the time—when I was tailing out of my junior year, when I was considering dropping out, and Genny was graduating with honours—Mother, I think, started to suspect something had changed in my life. Reeds had grown from the seeds of my secret life, and the wind in the house hinted at it. In the middle of the night, my key started to hit the lock different. The front door opened with a new creak. I showed up earlier sometimes, and walked with a different weight of my feet. I even stayed home some nights, and used the phone in the living room—the only phone in the house. Slowly, my routine broke. She saw me, Mother.

I spent half my nights at home, ate there for the first time in what felt like years. When one of us made dinner, we started to consider the other mouth in the house. We began to account for each other again. Sometimes Mother would even ask my opinion on photographs. She would hand me a sheet of film and a magnifying glass, and I'd lean against the window in the living room, as the last hours of the day's light were leaving, and tell her which of them I thought looked the best. She didn't know then that I, too, was taking pictures. That I ran off with one of her cameras every now and again, when she was out working, and shot rolls and rolls. That sometimes I would skip school and come back home when she was doing a shoot or visiting Asha's for a lesson, and work in the darkroom. We spoke every now and again, not too deeply or with too many words, but we did.

We were aware of each other, and I was aware of myself in relation to her. We were in some ways overlapping again, as we hadn't in years.

And that was why I had to leave.

I don't know why I chose Hamburg exactly, but I know why I left Minneapolis: I found Genny's letter.

I woke up the day after—on the mattress I was intending to abandon but had left in the corner of the collective's first tiny studio space downtown, above our little gallery—and it seemed like the time to go. The darkness had found me, had got its hands on me, pushing. I had no control over myself, and I just had to go. The girl that comes to pack our bags came, helped me dress. From a phone booth, we called the airport and asked them when the first available flight was to Hamburg. They told us—me—that there was a flight that night, a red-eye, that still had a few seats. I went back to the studio, took off my clothes, and pulled my camera out of my bag, Mother's camera. I set up the small travel tripod, screwed the extra-long cable release into the shutter button, and stood against the blank white wall, naked, with my hands pointed from my groin. In the shot, I'm looking down and appear to be grieving. I don't know why. At the time, I didn't really know who I was, who I'd become after reading the letter.

While the shutter was open, for a long second, Darius sprinted across my legs to paw after a moth that was fluttering low against the wall. His running smeared the frame with a soft Persian white that almost made it look like I was levitating, or the photo was fading from the bottom up.

There were reasons why Hamburg made sense, mostly because I wanted to see that monument, the Monument against Fascism, which was at the midpoint of its vanishing. I also wanted to go to Germany, since that was where Mother came from, and where I was born. The closest I'd ever come since then was when my face was inlaid in my German passport. Mother had been vehement about renewing them, just in case she ever wanted to go back. She talked about doing that fairly often—before Selkirk, before she didn't talk about it ever again.

After I took the photos, I was running on a kind of autopilot, not really knowing what I was doing. All I knew was what I wasn't doing— like telling Genny where I was going. I left a note in the studio asking Karen to watch over my things, and to be safe, I didn't tell her, either.

I took a taxi to the airport, paid for my ticket, and flew. When I finally developed a contact sheet of that roll of film in Germany, a year later, the photo I'd taken of myself before leaving Minneapolis was right beside a photo I'd taken of Genny while she was drinking a glass of red wine beside her window. I'd somehow missed and focused on the tree some ten feet outside the window. The photo of me wasn't out of focus, but I'd moved, so my form was soft. We both lacked definition.

The whole time I was in Germany, I never called Tom. When I finally came back to Minneapolis, I found out that the phone number I always reached him on—his mother's—was dead. I decided that this was a sign, that I shouldn't try to find him. Tom had been so formative for me, for the way I carried myself when I was a man, but at that distance I realized how much I'd failed him. How much I'd always depended on him. I didn't think I had anything to offer him, and I didn't want to take anything more from him. There was too much guilt piled up between us, and I felt the least I could do was let him go on without me.

As I pull the vacuum out of the closet under the stairs, I keep the dark-room's door in the corner of my eye. Mother's camera is on the other side, pulling its limbs out in the dark.

I vacuum up the new wave of dead bugs. My body is tired from the fever, but I float through the house. I vacuum the hallway. I vacuum the living room. I vacuum the kitchen. I vacuum the hallway again on my way to the stairs. There aren't as many bugs as there were when I got here, but there are many in places I've already removed them.

I get to the stairs and find more dead flies in the shadows. I lie down and get close enough to one to notice that, no, it isn't exactly dead. It is still twitching.

As I make it up to the armoire, to the bathroom, to outside the studio I don't open, I imagine the dead bugs and the dust shaking free of the rags and the trash bags and splaying back to their places over the windowsills, the furniture, the banister, the stairs.

I stop for a second, just outside my room, to close my eyes and see the palace, smouldering and char black. I open my eyes. I drag the vacuum into the room, vacuuming everything but a skirt of dust around the old pry bar sitting in the corner.

When I'm done I put the vacuum in the closet downstairs, and then go back up to my bed and collapse. I turned all the lights off behind me. I don't want to see any of it happening, the dust and the dead reclaiming their place.

My bedroom door is open, because I am afraid that if I close it, some phantom will show up with a chair to stick under the knob to lock me in. I hear the quiet creaks of the cat, in the house, moving. I want to warn them about this place. I try not to think about anything, so I think about the ceiling. I look over at the vent above the loft bed, stare at it. My eyes get heavy as the blue ekes in at the edges.

The sun climbs into the window, and I'm sweating from the cranked radiator heat, but I can almost breathe again. Getting up from my old bed, dislocated, I find three dead flies on the windowsill I vacuumed last night. As I go downstairs I hear the cat skittering across the hardwood floors. I pull the vacuum back out of the closet and go through the whole house again.

When I get back to my bedroom, the pry bar is still sitting by the window. I pick it up for the first time in twenty-seven years. It feels so much lighter than it did that night, when the door was closed and I had to do everything I could to escape from that life.

But as I hold the pry bar, its weight gradually increases until it drops onto the floor, clanging over toward the middle of the room. I can hear the sound of it falling echo through the house, my head, my memory palace.

And I can hear the darkroom scratching at the door.

7

MEMORY TRIPPING

You try not to notice it, but you trip a lot, on things you don't remember until you do—things that are cluttering the memory palace. You stub your toes on them. You pierce the un-callused pads of your feet. No matter how often you come in here, the bottoms of your feet are always nubile and vulnerable. Always susceptible to the past breaking in, getting you to notice it, which you do despite yourself, despite your attempts to make the tour of the palace clean and easy and simple.

Sometimes you hit a patch of rogue memories so cluttered you fall over, memories stacking into drifts where they shouldn't be, memories that you didn't curate into the palace, but they rise up from between the seams of the floorboards. Sometimes there's rubble so high it obstructs all forward movements; pathways are blocked and the order you remember is wrong. You circumvent your usual sequence and go through some of the rooms backwards. You go through others partway, before quitting or circling back to try again, building up the palace by rote. At times you can't reach the warm door of the darkroom, where you pretend to know what it holds. At other times the door isn't there. Despite your having curated the palace to avoid the clutter of memories, they crop up. Dim sensations and half images, contextless clips of time looping in the back of your eyes.

But mostly you try and pretend to be graceful. Pretend that only what you meant to remember is in here, in the palace, and that there's no dust and no dead flies and none of Tom's leftover clothes, that Mother's clothes do not let their own phantoms storm your walls. But they do. They reach up from the floor and grab your ankle. They slip out of the ceiling and tickle your scalp. They pile themselves against doorways and windows and other memories so thick you can't hope to make it through. Not without remembering them, which you don't want to do.

Sometimes you can't make it inside the palace at all because of all the wreckage of memories piled up in front of the door. Sensations half recalled, busted-up bits of conversations ... "ever again, I will" ... "me be frank: I can't tell you" ... "whenever it happens—" "Whenever what?" ... muddle up the lawn. *The lawn is not part of the palace*, you tell yourself, always, as you make your way to the door. If the door is blocked, you try and move the contradictions: the things that are on the lawn because they cannot fit, the things that you are able, most of the time, to keep out. Things you are able to mostly ignore into forgetting until they flare back up and break into the rest of your life. Into the life you want to try and preserve.

No matter how hard you stand there, atop the mess piled at the door, you cannot clear the path. You want to get to the door so you don't have to stand so close to the little mailbox. But you just fight against the dimness, populated with the half phantoms of your life, before you open your eyes, stop your hands from shaking, and get up from the bed or the couch or the stair where you were sitting and go to the kitchen for a glass of water. Or whiskey. Whatever you have to do to make the world pretend to stop fraying.

For the first week I was in Hamburg, I wrote letters to everyone—letters without envelopes, without postage. I wrote them on cardboard and card stock and between the lines of days-old German newspapers: to Tom, to Mother, to Karen, to myself, to Darius—purring on my lap—and of course, to Genny. They were the things I would say if I could say what I wanted to. They were fearless. I considered sending them to the States so that I'd have something to come back to, but I had no address to send them. I wrote those letters knowing that I had no place to come back to, though when I was in Germany I didn't actually know that I'd ever leave. I spent those first evenings in my little room, at my little table, writing sprawling letters that capped off my previous life. I went days without speaking, walking and biking around the city, not yet understanding much of anything that was being said.

I was trying to locate myself in those letters by talking to everyone, telling everyone what I thought, of them and of myself. Every letter felt like it was written by someone different. Some were furious. Some were abstract, insane, written illegibly, left-handed. I used the distance as an excuse to be honest with everyone without having to actually communicate anything to anyone beyond the versions of them in my head.

Eventually, I felt like everything had been said, squared away, and for a while I was quiet inside. Life moved forward with less hindrance. The letters stayed a pile of pages in the corner of the room. I didn't reread them, and I didn't throw them out. I thought I ought to save them, just in case. You never know when you might find it useful to have an artifact from a cavalcade of ghosts.

It's a day.

I open the door of the memory palace and bloody my foot on the frame on the landing that I couldn't make out for the layer of ash from the fire. It's hard to breathe as I walk the endless hallway to the place in the wall where the closet should be. I put my hands through the coated wall and pull out the vacuum. The one Mother used to have. I can't find a plug in the palace, for all the ash, so I plug it into my chest. I start to vacuum up ash from the walls, the ceiling, the floor squelching with the blood from my foot.

I make it down the hall, to the darkroom door, through the kitchen. I leave the places in the palace I can reach with the vacuum spotless and make my way to the living room. I suck away the ash coating all the memories playing in the frames, on the floor, the wall, the ceiling—the looping memories of Germany and Minneapolis, of Genny and Tom, of Erwin and Mother. With Mother still looming in every single one.

Only now, after the fire, I discover she isn't standing there like she usually does. She's lying on the ground, on the floor, on surfaces of water—wherever there is space for her.

No, I know she is not doing yoga. I can't trick myself into thinking that, but I try so hard. Her hands and legs are stretching bently into the sky, coming together, twitching. She rocks back along the curve of her back. In every single memory I clean, the scene blurs and she gets tack sharp in a far truer corpse pose. Wingless. She looks as if she is falling through the sky, her heavy heart falling fastest.

And no matter how hard I try, sticking the vacuum to the memories —through them—only frees them of her for a second. Then she comes right back up, slowly fading back into too much sharpness.

I open my eyes out of the palace and prove I can still move my body, creaking from room to room toward the bath.

After writing the letters in Hamburg I started venturing out more, away from my little room where Darius was not yet comfortable, going out to galleries and sitting in parks with Mother's camera around my neck.

One afternoon I was at a tiny gallery looking at some portrait photographs, of pairs of people and single people, old and young juxtaposed—classically composed but expertly shot—and Erwin Egger came up to me. He had grey hair receding at the sides of his widow's peak, his body thin and wizened. The photograph I was in front of was of him. He walked over to me with one thumb in his belt loop and the other pointing at the old Leica III. He asked me, in German, if I took photos—"*Machst du Fotos?*" I, a little guarded, said, "Yes."

He put out his hand to me. "I am Erwin Egger. I took these," he said, tipping over into English and gesturing to the photo on the wall, him staring out unsmiling. I shook his hand. "Well, not this. Since it is of me, someone else had to hit the button."

He didn't ask me my name. First, he asked me what sort of photos I did, and I told him mostly self-portraiture. "Finding someone else to hit the shutter is a challenge," I said.

"I am doing a project now, with photos of myself," he said. "I am not quite happy with this one. Are you here long in Hamburg? Are you by chance looking for some work?"

"I am, and I am."

"*Wunderbar.*"

Before I left, I got his card. As I stood in the door, he called back to me, "Wait, I never asked your name."

"Sofia," I said, without thinking, remembering one of the names the old woman at the hotel said while walking down the halls with the room keys, a name down another hallway, a name that was both here and far away at once.

Erwin smiled; he did not disbelieve me.

But then again, neither did I.

It's a morning.

I pick up the pry bar from the floor in my bedroom, and then there's nothing in the room—in the whole world—but the window and the dark outside it, nothing but the window and a rope made of knotted clothes, a rope with one end tied to the bag of things I've packed to take and the other to the steel pipe of the radiator. The rest of the radiator doesn't exist, along with everything else in the room, everything that makes as much difference now as it did back then. Now. Whenever for whoever. I can't see my reflection in the window, but I do see me—them—in flashes from my perspective standing behind in the empty dark. My hair is growing out from the buzz I'd done that January, and I'm slipping the bar into the gaps in the boards that hold in the window.

Outside the window is the world. The sun is out, but it is also the middle of the night. Neither contradicts the other. My hand pushes against the bar, slow, quietly wrenching the house apart.

I pry one board loose, then another. I can't look back because I know what is there. To look back would be to lose, to lose momentum and then everything else. It would be to lose Genny and fall through the sky on melting wings.

On the last board, across the bottom of the window frame, I struggle. I put all my weight into it but still fail. I feel things closing in on me, and I want to cry and scream and make every noise, until there they are, the hands atop mine on the pry bar with me.

We push one more time and the board comes up, easy. I'm sweating, holding the pry bar and watching the window slowly pull out from its place. I watch the rope lower the bag from the window toward the ground, watch me as I look down out the window, and then slowly lift my leg and climb out.

And I don't look back into the room; my eyes follow the rope down into the night, into the new world.

The sun makes hard shadows. I am not in the window—there's new glass there now, panes that you could open up and slip through. It is not midnight and the pry bar is in my hand.

I kneel down to the light the window cuts on the floor. I set a hand there, then set the pry bar in the centre of it. I go downstairs to the darkroom, swing open the door, pick up Mother's camera, and go back. The camera is empty, I know, but I take a photo of the pry bar anyway. I open my head to gobble up its light.

On the day of the first shoot I was to help Erwin Egger with in Hamburg, I left Darius alone in my little room and went downstairs to the office. I knocked and the woman with the keys around her neck answered. I pointed to the phone inside near the door. She let me in but didn't leave the room as I dialled his number. She walked over to a chair in the corner and sat, the keys clittering.

"I will come and pick you up, Sofia. Do bring your camera, too, if you can. I will be out to you soon."

I thanked the woman and went out to the curb in the heat of that late-summer morning, with Mother's camera around my neck, to wait as the occasional breeze blew over the city from far over the harbour, from the sea. I looked up at the windows of the old building that stood out in the neighbourhood like a sore thumb. As I itched the ankle Darius had dug his claws into two days before, I counted up the windows to the floor that held him.

Erwin showed up in his truck, smiling, and I climbed inside next to him. He drove and told me about the project. He wanted to re-create photos he'd taken so many years ago. Photos of himself, his best friend, and the girl they'd both loved. Two people the war had taken from him.

"I destroyed those photos, not long after getting back from being in the war prison. I was not happy, then, and I was afraid of photos, particularly those. So I want to make them again, now, how I remember them." He made a turn, slowing. "I will destroy them again, by bringing them back how I want them to be."

Erwin pulled up to a little house, where two boys a few years younger than me were sitting on the porch, listening to music on a little boom box. Erwin's son, Georg, and Georg's best friend.

"One of my models has cancelled," Erwin said, putting the truck into neutral. "The one who would play the girl. Do you think you could be a model for me, as well as help shoot?"

I thought about it—Sofia did. I didn't want to admit it, but I was so hungry to feel loved again. I wanted to come back to all that pain. "That would be just fine."

"Do not worry," he said, honking at Georg and his friend, who put the stereo back into the house and came toward the truck. "I will pay more for it."

It's an afternoon.

I have been trying to make it out of the house for days now. I have gotten to the door, I have opened the door, I have walked to the edge of the property, to the opening in the little fence. I am standing there now, here, but the tension of the hold this house has on me is too much. I'm afraid to lift my legs and try another step because I'm afraid I will be dragged back in. I want to be anchored; I want to pull away.

Mother is so far from these walls, even though she is storming through them. I can see her, bones in fabric, hair and skin, sitting up in the bed. I grab hold of the fence, and my hand touches paper.

The mailbox.

Pain, like thunder, reaches you differently depending on your distance from its source. There I am, coming back out the front door of the house without shutting it behind me. It is daylight, though there was a cloudy half moon on that night. This one. On my way through the fence, having stepped through a coldness, I stop at the mailbox. I lift envelopes to the dim light from the sky, from the street light on the corner, take a few important notices addressed to Mother, and the one letter addressed to me. What I think is a paycheque from the job I haven't been to since I told Mother I was leaving with Genny and she locked me in my room. I put everything in the bag and walk down the street. I keep walking but slip out of myself, to this place behind the fence, still in reach of the mailbox, my fingers digging into the once-soaked, now-crackly flyers. That night flickers in for a moment, then it is light again. It is a sunny day in the once-wet city.

"Burn the letters!" I yell, as the night flickers in and away for good. And before bodies can come to their windows and see me, before people can turn their heads, I surrender myself to the black-hole gravity of the house, remembering those words pretending to be a paycheque, remembering them blasting through me.

The darkroom is open, hungry. It has things it wants me to see.

The head—the mind—is a labyrinth, and we—who we are, when we are dissociated, distinctly nobody—are the Minotaur. Our many identities, which we acquire and wear throughout life, are the identities of the little people running through, feeling along the smooth walls of the dark, trying to make their way to the port at our circle's centre. We, the Minotaur, who have mastered the dark and are hungry to be someone, hunt these identities through the cool halls, and when we find one—a sweet femme thing, a barnacle of a man—we chase them down until they're exhausted, tripping, and then we stomp them into stasis and gore them on the rough spit of our time-stained horns.

And so we walk through the halls, for a time, wearing these corpses as our crowns, their blood covering us as we look down and believe that we are them. Someone. We believe it until their bodies begin to lose their integrity and fall to the ground in pieces, until their blood turns to red dust and blows away from our skin. As they're falling to bits, blowing back into nobody, we chase down others in order to continue the cycle: spearing and smearing them across the reflective nothing of our hide. Stacking one identity on the heels of another to avoid the vacant moment between.

Sometimes the identities fight back. Sometimes they win, for a moment, and the transformation doesn't take. Sometimes they chase Ariadne's thread to the centre of the labyrinth and escape, to wherever that escape gets them. Wounded and unsuccessful, we slip out into the phase of nothingness, of suspension, until we—desperate—find the next us to gore and shroud around our lack, our next me to wallow through.

That's what it feels like to be someone: a temporary opening, a drooling coat. It's nothing but slipping along a slow restless cycle, where we must always be moving through the labyrinths of our minds, vigilant, to be sure that no identity gets a chance to escape without us killing and wearing it. Because what would happen if we took a rest, a short nap, and they—all of those they who we want to be—all crowded out into the light at the centre?

What would we do then? Who would we be?

In the photographs Erwin was reinventing, he had his son Georg play the young version of himself, and Georg's best friend play Erwin's former best friend. Georg's friend was lanky and reminded me of Tom, of myself. Erwin had me—Sofia—play the younger girl they had both once loved, despite my being a few years older than them both.

Erna, Erwin's wife, always prepared some small meal, a collection of some sort of wurst, bread, and cheese, for us when we went out on a shoot. She'd bring it in a small picnic basket, usually with a canteen of coffee. Erna was a small woman, a good deal younger than Erwin, who had once been a stage actress in West Berlin before moving to Hamburg to marry him. Erwin had met her when he was in West Berlin to show a selection of self-portraits he'd taken thirty years after he'd been released from prison, thirty years after he'd given his testimony at Nuremberg concerning his commanding officers and atrocities he'd witnessed in Crete. The portraits didn't show anything but Erwin—then in his fifties—sitting on a lit chair in the middle of a dark room, cropped to around the elbow.

If you followed the trail of his eyes in those portraits, you could tell that he was looking just about a foot away from the lens, which was where prints of the photos he had taken in the war, mostly in

Crete, were being held up for him for the first time since. Erwin's expressions in the photos are mostly the same: a blank, tired, aged face, with hints of shame and guilt and anger. Some affect him more than others, but it's not possible to know which photographs he is responding to because they aren't contained within the frame; only his reactions are. The show was called *Negativ (nach 30 Jahren)— Negative (after 30 years)*. Erwin showed me a small hand-bound book of the show, and in it was an essay, which he roughly translated for me, talking about how the negative is itself art's reaction to the world, despite it being seen as an objective representation. For Erwin, art was the point where a moment in the world met an artist's decision to save it. To clip its light into a box.

Erwin's son, Georg, was quiet, just like him, and he seemed so young. It was shocking to think that Erwin was that young, seventeen or eighteen, when he went to fight in the war. I was maybe five years older than Georg and knew quite well that even at that age I was completely unprepared for anything as serious as that. Georg joked with his friend on the shoots in a German tongue I was beginning to understand, though I could still hardly speak it. They joked about innocent, silly things: girls, the toils of school, their shared joyous moments while drinking alongside the canals of Hamburg.

Once, all five of us took a car down to the town of Ansbach, west of Nuremberg. Erna sat in the back between the boys, jabbering along with them. There was a bench that Erwin wanted to find and re-create a photo at. A friend of his who lived near the town and had told him that the bench was still there. We drove nearly a full day to get there, as the light of the day was perfection.

"It was reaching twilight that time," Erwin said to me in the passenger seat. He was so excited he was shaking a little.

When we got there, the bench, of course, was gone. His friend had misinterpreted his directions. We all stood next to the car while Erwin walked circles, head down, around the street lamp that had replaced it, pulling at the remains of his hair. There was a bench a block away that we suggested we use, but Erwin did not want that. He wanted as few simulations as possible, as few built-in doubts.

Instead, he had us sit on the ground where the bench had once been. He arranged the composition as the sun shot its last hour of beautiful shadows. I sat with the pole blocking me from the camera. Erwin directed the boys to look at me, with affection, which they did, after laughing about it. When the photo was ready to be taken, Erwin stood in the background, beyond the focus field, and stared straight into the camera. Erna hit the shutter.

It's a night.

I'm at the bottom of the stairs, looking straight into the dark, my eyes wide so as to brighten the darkness with attention. I am opening myself up to its small collection of light. The darkness of the darkroom stares back into me. There is the wind, cascading across my throat, cradling it like a voice, like a noose.

The cat comes out of the living room and into the hallway, stands between the darkness and me. Looks through the open darkroom door and then at me. I break the room's gaze to look at them. Grey.

"I wish I had your eyes," I say, and sit down on the floor, my back against the front door. The cat doesn't run, but they turn their head and take a step back.

"No, don't go, no," I say, pushing my back against the door hard as the cat disappears from view.

There is nothing between the dark and me but the light fixture on the wall. I want to have the power to run upstairs, turn my phone back on, and call Genny and tell her I'm trapped. But I can't. Because it's too late. Because at the end of the hall, the dark has set its hands on the darkroom's jamb, the dark is pulling itself out of the room and dragging itself here. The light on the wall is gobbled up by its fist. The knob of the front door is a distance too far. The wind is pushing hard against me, so hard, and my body starts to shake as the dark comes to me, puts its huge lips around my face. It is an incubus of light. It is a gorgon. It is a great and mortal distance, falling back into yourself like this.

But like nothing, the cat mews at the other end of the hall, and the dark yanks its teeth out of me and recedes. As it snakes back into the darkroom, the cat swipes at it. The light takes back the space; the cat stares into the darkroom with those eyes. It's so hard to live a life with such darkness. To be diurnal while living through the absolute night.

The cat turns back to me, starts to boil away some of the dark that leaked inside.

Sometimes you are walking through the memory palace and you remember the sinking Monument against Fascism in Hamburg, and it rises up from the floorboards in front of you, rises up in that moment when you held the stylus at the end of its tether, tip nearly touching the monument's skin. Standing there, not knowing who you were, thinking everything made so very little sense to you. You went to the monument that day because you thought you could find yourself there. With the stylus in your hand and the demand of your participation, you could filter yourself through the conviction of that act. But you just stood there, not moving, seeing bare lead ready and hungry to hold your name: nameless. A woman scratched at another flat side of the near-obelisk. A kid stood behind you, chomping gum, muttering to his dad. You thought of a bunch of names that passed over you. Your hand shivered and the tip of the stylus dug into the monument, deeper in slow scratches. You let the hand shake out an impression of you onto the monument. With your free hand, you grabbed at the flesh of your cheek, and eventually, you stopped. You breathed. You looked at the little figment scratched into the monument. The father standing behind you takes a step beside you, from the past into the palace, walled in. There is nothing but the two of you, his hand on your shoulder. "It's okay. We all lose people."

It is morning: Friday.

I'm sitting by the landline, listening to the house transcribe the cat, listening to the cat come down the stairs, down the stairs until they stand in the doorway and look over at me, greyly. My hand is wrapped in the phone's cord, but I can't get to the phone to pick it up. It is ivy, holding me down.

There are so many numbers on this little sheet of paper I want to call.

Life on a quiet, sunny morning in Winnipeg in May is an emergency situation.

So I just sit here and watch the cat recede into the house's noise. I watch a slow, dark fog skirt across the hardwood, seeking.

When I told Mother I was going to leave with Genny, to follow her as she went off to school, she lost her mind. She started to shake. She told me no, I wasn't allowed to go. I told her because I wanted her to know that I wasn't leaving because I didn't love her, because I didn't love her less. But what I couldn't say was that living with her was killing me. Genny had proven that, given me a dependable outlet, a two-way mirror, a kind of relief I hadn't known I'd ever wanted or needed. I could trust her, then. With Genny it was a ground I could stumble over, and with Mother it was all crags and clouds I couldn't stop falling through, breaking myself on.

So she stuck a chair under the doorknob to lock me in my bedroom. I'd gone in to escape her and she snagged me with a bang. As soon as I pulled on the door and failed to get out, I started yelling at her through the wall. She yelled at me, too, and the closed door translated. I wanted out, but I had nowhere to go. I loved her so much then that I could have easily killed her if that door hadn't been locked. I could have pulled every blink from her eyes, put her heart in my chest and carried her to the edge and leapt. But the door wouldn't open. I imagined Genny waiting for me to tell her how it went. I heard the phone ring in the evening, a sure sign. Mother picked it up. In a minute, I heard her put it back down.

I looked out the window to the backyard. I packed and unpacked, dressed and undressed, revised and reviewed my way of moving forward as I paced circles in that room. Al would break down the door. Annie would start a fire on her bed and sit through it to death in protest. Allie's hair would be cut off. Someone would break the window and jump feet first to tumble. Another would jump out neck first to snap. Alice would defy herself and rob Mother, or I would hug her, or gut her. I was an unbreakable force. An unbridgeable chasm. I was going to be left behind. As I looked out the window to the back lane, to the trees in the neighbours' yards, I imagined Ovid's Pyramus and Thisbe nearly making it to one another alive but arriving instead to die of misinformation.

Mother quietly pushed a few slices of cheese under the door on a sheet of blank paper. I didn't move to devour them until I was certain she'd left, until I heard the house creak away under her retreating steps.

Eventually, I was a version of ready. Mother had removed the chair, but it was too late. I had locked the door from inside and tied the rope of blankets and clothes. I don't know whose idea that was; just all of a sudden, it was there. I had the little pry bar Tom gave me and, slowly, with great ceremony, removed the windowpane from its socket. It was August, but a cool fresh wind came in through the window, through which I lowered the knotted rope. That rope took me a whole day to make, to decide on, to start then quit, then start up again, to finish. Someone knew that they had to keep knotting it up, that it was either that or I was going to be stuck in this house, this world, forever. And at the end of all that buildup and second-guessing, climbing down that rope, forgetting my pry bar propped in the corner of the room, took all of nine seconds.

Once I'd made it around to the front lawn, the house leered at me. Its blank, dark eyes followed me as I went to the front door with my key. I went to Mother's darkroom, turned on the red safety light, and found the old empty film canisters where I knew she hid money. I took everything, including all the film.

I also took her earliest archive of negatives, three-ring binders filled with sheets of them, the ones most likely to include the most of me.

I hadn't planned to steal her Leica, but it stared at me through the red. I hadn't planned to loop the strap around my neck and leave the darkroom for the front door, heading down the real hallway that felt infinite then, and then turn back to stare through the dark, creaky house. But I did all of that. It must have been around five a.m., only a few minutes since I'd gone down the rope. I stood there long enough to hear every closed door in the house: mine, the bathroom, the studio, Mother's. The removal of the window caused a pressure shift that made the doors slam in their frames. The house was ticking, like a sequence of horizons stacking, about to be shuffled up. Readying to explode.

I had to burn all the love I was feeling for Mother in that moment for fuel. I had to fill myself full of hate for her, just to be able to turn the knob and take another step into the night and not run up the stairs, open her bedroom door, and apologize with every word I knew, tell her that I would never leave her, and then go into my bedroom, pull up the rope, and hang myself.

Steam billowed through my limbs; the front door opened and then closed behind me. On the other side, I locked the door and kept the key. I shouldered my bags and wandered down the street toward Genny's, moving like a janky automaton, hoping she hadn't left without me.

But before I left I opened the mailbox, and there was the pay-cheque I didn't know was actually a letter. I looked through the living room window where Mother had always sat and waited up for me. The house was glowing red from the safety light I'd left on in the darkroom. Mother's favourite camera was heavy on my neck.

When I got to Genny's place her car was still there, so I left my bags in the dark, climbed up to her window, and knocked.

It's still Friday morning and I have made some coffee and am sitting by the landline again. The house has gone quiet. The cat is not moving. It feels much less strange, being here, now that I've gotten it to look more like the memory palace.

My phone is open to my contacts. I dial the number on the land-line, the number I'd saved.

I let the phone ring once.

It is ringing again.

I let it ring a third time, and finally it connects. The voice says hello.

I take a breath. The sun pops in through the window and comes over to lean into my chest. I don't look down at it, because I know exactly what the sun will look like.

"Hi," I say. "My name is Hedwig Baum and I'd like to sell my house."

8

THE TOP OF THE STAIRS

You get to the top of the stairs. Blank walls and doors—four of them. It is almost serene, a breath of fresh air. Nothing but closed doors and the armoire.

You are always worried by this part of the memory palace, because it belies what is to come. It is the essence of the calm feeling before being pushed from a tall place, thrust into exile—the tranquillity before the peace of terminal velocity is interrupted by solid ground. The top of the stairs is the precursor to a new level of memories, the memories you've kept up here because you don't really want to remember them, not often, but you know you must keep them.

What is in these rooms are not so much memories, exactly, but a preservation of sensations that have wrapped themselves deeply and darkly in the bundling of your nerves. Sensations that if excised from your memory, might dismantle the whole shaky logic of your life.

When I get off the phone with the realtor, I take an inventory of the house. I go upstairs and grab a pile of blank paper from my luggage and start to walk through the whole house, deciding what is still here. I keep my eyes open as much as possible, so as to not let slip in the furnishings of the memory palace.

I mark everything. I go through every cupboard in the kitchen, account for every item in the living room, the dark of the darkroom, the closet under the stairs. Everything on the walls. I go up the stairs, to the bathroom, account for the towels and an old owl carving sitting on the windowsill. In my bedroom is the bed, the loft bed, and the pry bar. I scratch at the sheet of paper, doing my best to account for it all. The unlined paper is unruly, and my lists waver and wave across the pages.

On a fresh sheet, I note every piece of furniture in Mother's room. The mirror, the empty hangers in her tiny closet. On the floor in the closet is an enlarger, one that is newer than the one she used to have, safely stored from the accumulation of dust under a sheet, sitting next to a little bag filled with accessories. I rifle through the bag and write everything down, including one red bulb (safety light), then go back out into the hall and stare at the armoire.

I flip onto a new page and write across the whole of it: *armoire (old, maple wood, handmade in Manitoba, decent condition, just too huge)*. I do a new page for the armoire, for the leftover clothes in it, so that it feels like the contents of the house take up more space than they do. Despite the house's emptiness, I want to feel like there's more that could be carried away from it. I want to fill up this pile of too many pages.

Every door is wide open but the studio. I go to the door, the door in the expiring house, and I open it in the palace, then slam it shut before the memory can begin to play. Mother's body coils around in my head. I don't open the door in the house because I can't. The studio feels like a Pandora too far.

Instead, I go back into Mother's room, into her closet, grab the safety bulb, and go downstairs. I stretch my body long as I screw it into the darkroom's sky. The light comes on—deep red—and my fingers slowly warm. I keep them there until it's too hot. I leave the door of the darkroom open when I go.

I go to the page that accounts for the darkroom's darkness and cross the darkness out. In the red light, I look through the rest of the things I've written down. Shocked by how much you can find if you make a point to notice absolutely everything, and at the same time sad about how little that still is. How much paper is left over.

Yet even though I surveyed the whole house so closely, every room besides Mother's studio, I didn't see the cat. I don't write them down.

Maybe two months after I came to Hamburg, after I'd started working with Erwin, Darius ran away. When I went out I'd left the door of the little room ajar, hoping to let out some of the boiling late-summer air. I'd looped a piece of string between a light fixture just inside the door and the doorknob outside, to keep it from opening wide enough for Darius to get out. I wasn't worried about anything or anyone getting in.

But when I got back that night—from shooting a few posed photos outside the city from Erwin's time in Crete—the door had blown wide open and broken the string. Darius was gone.

I went into a frenzy. I looked through every floor that day, knocking on doors, and walked the neighbourhood for nearly two weeks, asking everyone, "*Persische Katze? Persische Katze?*" I printed photos of Darius and pasted them around the streets, carried them with me. For weeks

I left my door open, enough that he could squeeze back in. When I wasn't out working, I sat in the room, afraid and quiet. I didn't say a word there, besides *nein*, to the old woman with the keys who knocked softly at my door every few days to ask if I'd found him yet.

Eventually, one day in late September, I thought I saw him. There was a white cat walking along the short flat roof of a warehouse, maybe two blocks away. I was frozen in the window watching, wanting nothing more than to open the window and literally fly to him, grab him, and throttle him with my belated, angry love. But I couldn't do that. I couldn't do that.

Because it wasn't until he was outside of that tiny room that I realized that living in that boiling coffin was cruel. I saw that he was alive—alive outside the life I'd been forcing upon him. So I didn't fly to him. I unfroze. I let the boundaries of my life widen a little.

I started to take some food out, every now and again, to the alley behind the warehouse. Three times he visited me and his bowl. When he came, mewing, I moved away from him as he tried to head-butt his love to me. On the third visit I realized that Darius was happy, no longer slashing at me, and he wasn't hungry. He was no longer himself. I stopped going to visit him, and I never touched him again.

With the darkroom a red-lit skull, I feel Mother's studio floor creaking upstairs, reaching out for me, and I use the sound to leave the property—to open the door and walk out past the fence to the sidewalk and away from the house into the cool, bright day. As I make it away, toward Portage, I smell smoke but don't turn around. I know what is after me.

I'm riled up, but I'm in motion. I flutter in and out, from midnight then back to midday now. I make it to Vimy Ridge Park, and it is midnight in a different park, and Genny is with me, and I'm a man again. We are breaking into the Assiniboine Park Zoo, through a secret flaw in the perimeter that only Genny's friend Jack knows about. He has brought a boy, and once we get in, we splinter off into pairs of shadows, toward the enclosures, eyes open for anyone still here. We go to the gibbons and I bend Genny over the railing and slip a hand up her dress.

"Pardon me," someone says, and it is sunny, and I step from the middle of the path, step off to the edge and keep walking and watching myself and Genny in the zoo. I feel sick.

I remember how far I felt from my body that night, how deep I hid in my body to let such crudeness happen. How far sex can alienate me from my skin. The gibbons were asleep, but I remember making eye contact with one who came to the little window to inspect us: little eyes, little hands, at the edge of the light.

I remember how far apart and incompatible Genny and I felt then, how quiet we were, how unintimate our touching was. How I knew Genny was aroused by him—me—but that she also wanted him not to be the way I was wearing my body. How I refused to let her touch me back, because I felt so far from being the man I was. How I felt that her touch would shatter what little certainty I held. How our bodies got along while our hearts were hiding, deep and silent. How we didn't talk, until I asked her to let me sneak into her room and sleep with her, and she told me no. I remember, two nights later, how she picked me up from Mother's house and only drove three blocks before she pulled over and started to cry. How I rubbed her back, and then tried to slip my hand down her pants, and she told me, tears taking over her face, to get out of her car. Oh, how she'd yelled at me. Oh, how I'd earned it.

I open my eyes, and open them again, at the other side of Vimy Ridge Park, in the light. I take a few seconds to anchor myself in the present and then jaywalk across Portage avenue like an old pro, as I had done so many nights with Tom, waiting on the median and hoping none of the headlights marooning us there were cops.

The gas station. I walk inside and turn around to the closing door and another night, a few weeks later. Genny's car is parked at the pump: I'm in the passenger seat, and she's filling up. I'm looking down at my chest, my hands, the strap of Mother's camera around my neck. I put my hand to my chest and I'm here, inside the station, touching the binder, grazing down to my belly. I watch myself in the car, watch myself lift the camera and look directly into its lens, and I think that nobody will ever see me like that. Full of a sad and naive hope. And then Genny gets back in the car.

"Excuse me?"

Genny pulls away with me, pulls away with me and that letter in my luggage, pulls away from this city for a promised forever, and the sun fills in after our absence. Nobody is at the pump.

"Sorry," I say, as I walk over to the counter, reaching into my back pocket for my wallet.

"Can I help you?" the attendant asks.

"Yes. Please. I'd like a gas can. And gas for it."

During those few months when Darius was missing, when I left my door open, two mice began to explore my room. After I found Darius, they would squeeze their gaunt little bodies under the door in the evenings, just after dinner. One after the other, the mice would cram themselves in, their ears flapping out from their heads when they peeked out the other side, noses wriggling. Then I returned from a work trip down south to find they had moved permanently into a near-empty coffee filter can.

The building I'd been staying in—the hotel—had somehow been spared the destruction of the Allied bombing of Hamburg in 1943 for Operation Gomorrah—a horror I had no knowledge of before I came to Germany. I'd been surprised when I flew into the city at dawn almost half a year before to see some districts still with rubble from the bombing. All the buildings around mine were new, with bigger apartments, because after the bombs there were fewer tenants to fill them. Erwin showed me a photograph of the area from 1948, when he came to Hamburg from Berlin, three years after he'd given his testimony at Nuremberg against the commander he'd served under in Crete in 1941.

In the photo Erwin showed me of Hamburg, the destruction was widespread to the point of being sublime. Erwin was shocked that I hadn't known about it, about the near fifty thousand civilians killed almost overnight. He was surprised how little information about atrocities the Allied powers perpetrated actually reached their public, whereas the German people were reminded of nothing more regularly than their complicity in the cruelty of the war.

Erwin had come to Hamburg to help clean up and rebuild the city. While working, he picked up a camera for the first time in five years, to help document the state of the city and track the progress of the cleanup. Even in 1948 they were still finding bodies, unidentifiable through both time and fire. Erwin told me that seeing the dead only became more difficult the more he did it.

"The expected is what destroys you," he said, looking down at the photograph where my little apartment building stood out as a towering strip in the waste. His fingers traced the glossy print, smudging it. "When you know you're going to find something, something horrible, and then you find it, you're still in no way prepared."

I still remember what Erwin said, as Erna was singing in the other room and Georg was clomping down the stairs with German music popping from the Walkman strapped to his head. Georg stopped to stare at us sitting quietly in the little circle of the lamp's light. I couldn't see Erwin's face in the dark, so I looked up at Georg's, at his young doppel.

"It's a rare and horrible thing, Sofia, when the world becomes exactly what you think it is."

I lived in that tiny room for another five months after seeing that photo, living on the small salary I got for assisting Erwin and whatever extra I made from my freelance work for the German press and foreign and domestic fashion magazines. That whole time, the air felt explosive. Volatile. Yet that little room, with the mice who slept in a coffee can, that room felt holy. The apartment was a sepulchre surrounded by death and danger but not filled up with it. It was surrounded by places that were haunted and replaced by the foundations of the dead.

When I moved out, to the extra room in Erwin's house, I put the lid on the coffee can and poked holes in it. The mice had babies in there with them by then, the mother nursing them. Erwin drove me down to the Elbe, to a natural green patch at the edges of the city. I walked down toward the riverbank with the can, opened it, and placed it in the shadow of a cool grassy mound. I'd heard the little squeaking on the drive there, but now, in the wild, they were silent. I didn't wait to see the mice emerge, twitching, from the shelter. I went back to the car and we went home.

A few cars pass me as I'm trying to find the best way to get the nozzle of the gas can into the tank of my car, as the fumes circulate through me. A man has been squinting out at me from a window of the house I'm parked in front of. I'm trying to forget he's there.

I am back in the moment of the car, set upon by memories with claws. Genny and I are pulling away from the city in her car, and she is also pulling away from dropping me off after the zoo and leaving me in the exhaust, and she is also sitting on her bed as I climb up to her window, and I am also at her front door, a few days after she yelled at me in the car, after she drove away from me, and I am knocking. I don't care if her mother is home, or her sister; I am here and I need to talk to her. I'm in a dress. My knuckles are reddening. I am not a man. Not that one. She should be able to see that.

Her car is the only one in the driveway. There are lights on in the house. If I were to look behind me, I'd see my car and me fuelling up. Him. Me trying hard to feel at home in my inflexible body.

But she doesn't come to the door. There is the smell of gas. There are eyes in the windows, looking at me. I am sure that the whole neighbourhood is watching, and I'm sure that this is what clued in Genny's mother, what got us tied up and away from one another when our escape was most imminent, when being in touch mattered most.

When Genny wrote that letter.

Someone honks at me and I'm out of the dress and in my body, feeling naked and off target. The passenger-side window of a truck rolls down: "Al! More car troubles?"

It's Blaine. He is smiling at me, and I try so hard to be here and now and polite.

"Different car, different troubles," I say, lowering the can that has been empty for who knows how long.

"One of those weeks?"

I just smile at him.

"How's your mother doing? In Ste. Agathe, right?"

I can hear her voice, calling out to me, but I pretend that I can't, that I'm here. "She's well. You know how it goes."

Blaine checks his mirrors and notices that a car has turned down onto Ethelbert, coming our way. I remember the squinting man and want to run away. "I do know. You need any help?"

I notice the blond dog hair covering the empty passenger seat, which has several shadeless, bulbless lamps sitting on it. I count five.

"She was just a little thirsty," I say, closing the tank and putting my hand on the car's roof, falling back, as somewhere I'm turning around to Mother's car, and it is too cold tonight for this dress. I don't know how Mother found me here, at Genny's. Genny hasn't answered the door, but Mother's here, with her car idling. She is looking right at me, calling to me: "You, come on, let's leave."

My car door opens, and I get inside. Blaine is gone, down the street, turning onto Wolseley. I am her, Hedy, and I turn on the car and pull away from the house, without looking at the front window.

There I am, sitting beside me, in a dress and quietly crying. Hair to my ears. Made up but alone. I put my hand on the centre console, which doesn't exist in my car, and I reach out and take my hand. We hold it as we drive, keeping our eyes on the road ahead.

As much as you appreciate the blankness at the top of the stairs, the blankness almost hurts the most. It is in blankness that intensity lies: the emotional blanknesses in your censored past, the years of quiet between yourself and Mother, the years of silence between yourself and yourself. Though the blankness lets you breathe, it also removes from you any tangible excuse for why you would choose to breathe at all. Sometimes when you come up here, the doors of the armoire open and close a little, like lungs. Sometimes you walk up the stairs and the armoire turns to you, seemingly staring. Once, it bull-rushed you, and you leapt up out of the memory palace.

Here, all the absence trembles. The doors judder in their jambs. Sometimes the armoire does not breathe but begins, slowly, to spit up clothes onto the floor. Those are the times when you walk through the palace far too aware of the blankness of your own body, and you want nothing else but to wear something. But what the armoire spits up is all the things that you don't want, that don't suit you, and as soon as you realize this the armoire explodes into cottons, synthetics, hosiery—whatever is least suitable. You begin to be pulled under, toques and tops grasping at your feet while nylon stockings wrap themselves around your throat. Nothing can stop them, and you can't even make your way out of the palace until they've got you under their surf. Until you're deep enough to not see the light. Until you're deep enough to give up on air, and your lungs are a furious pair of empty canvases in empty frames.

Only then can you open your eyes to the real world, to your little darkroom in Minneapolis, or the dimly lit living room of Mother's house at night. Only then can you open yourself up to knowing how unpopulated your numb world still is to you. How a heartbeat can pummel you forward, further into more blank time, and horror.

I didn't drive back to the house. I turned away, toward the Neighbourhood Bookstore & Café on Ruby. I disappeared from the passenger seat as I turned right instead of left on Wolseley. Before I got out of the car, without privacy, I pulled the binder down onto my belly. I breathed. I let my hair fall down, grabbed the purse I keep under the passenger seat, went inside, and bought a coffee—this coffee—and sat down here.

The walls are coated with shelves of used books. I've got my phone out, logged in to the free Wi-Fi, the pile of list-filled papers in front of me. Without a bra, I feel visible and comical.

The shelves of used non-fiction beside me seem to loom like some kind of blatant symbol. An emptied-out body, well worn, or a bandage covered in dry blood. A wedding ring bought from a pawn shop. This list of things in Mother's house.

The boy who sold me my coffee comes out from behind the counter and wipes a clean table with a dirty wet rag, smiling at me, each one of his lips half my age but together trying to add up, curving, to build a bridge to me. My chest is obvious in the tight black shirt, but it's me. I smile without teeth.

He's at that lonely age, that lonely age I feel like I've been a hundred times.

On my phone I try to ignore the wave of email notifications from the last week as I open the browser and check out Craigslist, Kijiji, the online classifieds of local newspapers—anywhere someone might request things: wanted, needed. Nobody is looking for most of the things in Mother's house. There's a radio behind the counter, transitioning from music to talk, but I can hardly hear it. The boy gives up on me, goes back there, and switches between stations until it's music again. He sits there, looks down at his phone, sighing. I look up between swipes of my own.

I wonder how old he is. I swipe and swipe, past pages looking for information about missing people and pages looking subtly—and unsubtly—for sex. Then hit a few that I save the phone numbers for:

a father asking for a twin bed for his growing family, a group of artists looking for any sort of spare, old art-making equipment. I look up and the boy, blond hair ruffled, short, is almost eating his fingers as he sits perched behind the counter, scrolling through his phone, like a breathing Rodin.

I get up with my emptying cup, walk along the shelved spines of fiction, as he switches radio stations again at a new pop song he didn't want to hear. At the CBC public station he pauses for a few seconds, and the voices seems to be talking about the body found in the river again. As I get to the counter, the boy has his back to me, rapt, until he notices me standing behind him and switches back to music.

I hold out my cup to him. "How old are you?"

He almost jumps at the question. "Sixteen," he says, pouring the coffee and not looking up at me, face going flush. Seeming so sixteen, so completely sixteen. The ages of both his lips actually adding up only to two-thirds of me. The boy hands me the coffee and looks over at the cakes and sandwiches in the glass case beside him. He doesn't look me in the eye; he looks from the case to my hands. "Would you like anything else?"

I want to tell him to turn the radio station back, but I don't. He switched it off for a reason I've no right to question. "No," I say. "Thank you." He smiles in my direction as the bell on the door pings.

Back at my table, the shelves full of doctored versions of real life turn their backs to me. I finish the coffee, repack my purse, and get up. I look at the bookshelf, but no titles make it into my head. The front door itches at me. I turn to the boy at the counter, and the boy is gone.

I get out the door. The wind hits me and I shoulder my purse and move toward my car. I get inside and turn away from the house—yet again—before circling back. I park in front, run inside to grab Mother's old Leica, and run back out. There is a huge cloud of smoke coming for me, I know, rolling down the stairs like a boulder.

I get back in the car and drive, turning away from the house, only this time I am turning toward Mother.

Time—time away, time unknown—can do strange things. A bright moment can wait and, in waiting, become inconsequential. A blip can become a blimp as time bloats it forth. A smile can be re-evaluated, depending on the day, the week, and any meaningless action can either be lost completely in the fog of yester or amass meaning, furious and new.

Genny wrote the letter for me when we were still in Winnipeg, at the end of the summer of 1987, when she was leaving for school in Minneapolis and I was going to ditch my senior year to join her. She wrote the letter when our plans to leave for Minneapolis together became known to our mothers—hers a domineering Christian zealot, mine depressed and alone and without any comforting ideology—and we'd been imprisoned from one another, boxed in. We could not reach one another, so Genny sent me the letter disguised as a paycheque from my summer job at the used camera store on Portage.

In the letter, Genny left me.

She said that she had to move forward with life, had to move forward with life without me. She said that she loved me, but I was too immature and she was too desperate. That she was too busted by her parents splitting up, by her life tumbling out of her control, that she had clung to my beautiful chaos. That perhaps this inconvenience was all for the best. That being separated gave her a moment to think, and she didn't think we could work out.

She also wrote that, a month or so earlier, she had fucked another guy. She said she didn't know why she'd done it, besides to spite me—him: Al. She said that a night a few days before she'd fucked him, when we had broken into the zoo, he had—*I* had—made her feel so incredibly far away from me. So something took hold of her and she just went to this boy she knew liked her and that was that. It happened like nothing and led to nothing.

I didn't open the letter posing as the paycheque until a few years after taking it from the mailbox and packing it away. I'd forgotten about it, just carried it with me from place to place, bundled up with the other mail I stole from Mother that night. The thing that scared me, then, was that so soon after she wrote it, I was breaking out of my window and scrambling up to hers, that so soon after, I crawled into her bedroom and we merged. I had chosen the love I was going to commit myself to. After she wrote me that letter—even though I hadn't read it—we did not break up but instead ran off together, and because of that one night of concentric rebellions we became insep-arable, and soon became so complicit in each other's lives that they were nearly impossible to untangle. What scared me was how hard the following years were, trying to get by in the new, strange world, and achieving a sort of stable mayhem in our love. How hard we worked for that—yet the whole time, there was this message folded in a piece of pasted paper cornered with a stamp, this moment capped in a bottle lurching wave over wave to me, to when I was the least waterlogged, to when I was most willing to concede that life could be worth living.

I discovered the letter—gutted from its gorged camera store envelope—while I was packing up to move out of my apartment and into the collective's studio for a week before I could sign the lease on a new apartment of my own. While I sat there looking down at the letter, Darius was scheming with a low mew after a moth on the other side of the room. It was to be my first nice, solitary place. It was to be the beginning of a real life.

It's shocking how an unknown thing can suddenly pop up fully formed in brilliant sharpness on our horizon. How a dead, inert thing can simply saunter in and manipulate history with its old injuries. This letter had sat at the side of our relationship, had walked alongside us, yet I'd never known it or seen its shadow. How long had it been there, hiding in the bundle of old papers in a drawer, behind the teeth of her kiss, swirling in the slow drain of the tub or ghosting through the strands of my hair? How it must have been pulling at things, inhibiting actions, lubricating thoughts between us without my ever knowing. How stupid and innocent and stupid I'd been.

It was a thing Genny had thought insignificant when I called her after reading it, frantic, screaming. Which was almost worse: her minimizing a maximized moment of our past. The shrug-off of a potentially enormous leaving. How she had almost murdered me. So I called her awful names—Annie did—and then we hung up on her.

A part of me was missing, after that letter struck me. Some of me had stopped walking with us, fallen down in the pack and been trampled, and I found myself thrown into the imbalance that would lead me to run away. Again.

The girl who packs our bags and leaves came by, to the collective's studio, and helped throw us together into another departure. To Hamburg. A land that ran through my blood, though my heart had never really pumped it over every edge of me.

I drive toward the home and I don't turn around. The gas light is on, but I don't want to stop. I have more than enough to reach her. The beeping is steady and seldom and oddly comforting. The current of the traffic carries me, and eventually, I reach the patch on the shore of this river of machines where it sits: the home. Mother.

I park in the lot. The whole drive her camera around my neck has been staring up at me, at my chin, as if trying to focus and understand me, which has always been its function.

The only film in the camera is the roll I shot when I got to the house. It is rolled up and ready, but I haven't taken it out yet, even though there are no frames left.

I keep the camera on my neck when I go in. The nurse—the same nurse—recognizes me and calls me Miss. I tell her I've been busy and ask her how Mother is.

"Oh, she's about the same," she says.

The thought of Mother being the same seems like worsening. A static level of hell never feels the same day after day—you lose your resilience to it.

I go to the room. The paper on the door with Mother's name has been re-taped. It's still yellowing, but it's flatter. It reminds me of a placard in a museum: *Hedwig Baum (1931) Mixed media (depression and used non-fiction).*

I do not know who has made her.

She is sitting up on the bed with a newspaper spread out across the sheets. I walk into the room and watch her finger the headlines, flip through the sections. Sports, entertainment—all bullshit. This was her domain. Her photos once dotted these pages, images she clipped out from a world and fixed here, in exclusion from it.

I sit beside her. She looks up at me. Her hands dance on the paper without needing the guidance of her empty head. Her eyes look at my shoulders, my chest, lead down the straps to the camera.

They stop.

I lift it over my head, and she stares at it as it stares into her. I put it down on the bed, atop the newspapers, weeks old. I place the camera near her eager, pink, scarred hands.

"This was your camera," I say, picking up one of her hands and rubbing it along the old Leica's smooth brushed-metal surface.

Mother stares down at it. At her hands. At their joining. She looks at the camera and her hands as if she doesn't recognize either. Her face doesn't change.

I watch her and forget why we breathe. My heart bounds against my chest, wanting nothing but to force my arms to take Mother by the shoulder and shake her out of it, the silence and the weakness she recovered from so many times, so many years ago. But my heart knows that Mother has reached the other end of an unbridgeable distance. That she can no longer be loved into speaking.

I remember the I-35W bridge—only a minute after I decided to take the 10th Avenue Bridge that ran parallel to the south instead—twisting and falling while Genny giggled on the phone in my ear.

I don't cry. But my eyes do.

The thing about degenerative diseases is that they never stop, never start regenerating things again. They only move one way. They rip out bad boards from the boat as it floats but don't replace them with anything better. They just tear the boat to bits until you forget what it's called. Forget the reason why it ever set sail. Forget what buoyancy means. Just forget.

Mother looks away from her hands and the camera they are feeling. She looks down at the newspaper and over at me. Her eyes have lost their lustre.

But while her head spins away from me, and the moment, her hands on the camera, weak as they are, try and try and try to remember how to grip it.

Before Pyramus and Thisbe were lifted by Shakespeare and dropped into Verona, they were taken up by Ovid for his *Metamorphoses*, and even he didn't create them so much as borrow them for his own use. The pair died tragically before Ovid, and they haven't stopped since. They just wake back up in their bedrooms, separated and so deeply in love—ready to let its foolish depth slaughter them again and again.

In Ovid, the two lovers are neighbours kept at bay by their fathers' unexplained ban, their love described as a mutual fire burning without an intermediary to communicate through. They are like two trapped infernos at opposite sides of a wall shared by their houses, as if they live in ancient tenements, in which their love illuminates a fissure they can whisper through. Every night, one crackles on its side of the wall and fuels the other, infernos swelling in that unconfined yet trapped way that only first love allows.

Ovid's pair blame the jealous wall for thwarting them, for not opening up for them to exchange more than words. But they also praise it for allowing so much to pass between them. It is the architecture, the structure—the house—and not the unexplained rigidity of their looming fathers keeping them at bay.

There are no mentions of mothers. Mothers are not important in every story.

From here, the story is well known: They agree to meet—to escape their lives, to coincide—one night beneath a tree. A tree where there will be a dire misinterpretation. A tree that will be the last mulberry to have born snow-white fruit.

Thisbe shows up under the tree first, and while she waits for Pyramus, a lioness arrives from the forest, her snout red from a recent kill. Thisbe runs away to a dark cave nearby, dropping her shawl as she goes—because in myths, as in life, something is always left behind in our leaving. The lioness takes the shawl in her bloody mouth, biting and pulling at it like a ball of yarn, before getting bored and leaving.

Pyramus arrives, finds the bloodied shawl, sees the beast's prints, and—of course—believes that Thisbe has been killed and eaten.

After a melodramatic speech, Pyramus sinks his sword into his side and falls down under the mulberry, dying, his jilted blood fountaining the air and blotting the boughs of the tree. As he is on the ground, twitching and flailing in his throes, Thisbe comes back and finds him there: "Paler than boxwood, shivering as the sea / Shivers beneath a sliding breeze." She falls to him, tears mingling with blood, and says his name.

He looks at her and recognizes her for one brief moment, before his head falls dead.

And before Thisbe stabs herself, transforming into another pricked can of bloody spray paint, she bids the mulberry's pure whiteness remember them by making its "fruit funereal." With those words, the pair's blood blots the white fruit forever purple.

We always feel dread when we hear people tell the stories of their first loves, because we know how they end: misunderstanding and massacre, or at the very least, some sort of metamorphosis. A sort of metaphysical Rubicon crossing.

At some point, each of us tries to reach someone through a too-small fissure. We make bold plans that could never work in a world larger than our skulls. Some aspect of ourselves runs from a lion encountered in a place where no lion should be, while another aspect always bleeds out under a tree.

Surviving a first love like that is metamorphosing into the mulberry. Into its ever-purple fruits.

I fuel up the car on the way back from the home and pull into Mother's space in the back. As I get out, I look up at the window, the small, simple shape through which the most seismic action of my life took place. A decision I could never excise from me, because it is me. I am the window, the frame, its replacement.

I unlock the back door and come in through the kitchen, and while I do, the landline is ringing. I walk over to it and remember the doctor calling. I don't want to hear more about Mother, about how far away she is, how unreachable.

I was just there. I have seen it.

The phone rings again and again, never ending, and I know that it can't be the doctor. My bones know it. I have heard phones ring like this before.

As I pick it up, I am already saying that I'm sorry, that this has all been horrible, that this has been one long and never-ending mess. I tell her about Mother, the word "aphasia," the look of her now. She breathes on the other end. She can't tell I'm crying because I'm an expert at hiding.

"Should I come, then?"

"No," I say, and before the air can stop coming out, before I feel like I might just stop talking altogether and quietly fall so deep into all of this too-much, I keep my voice moving: "I'm going to bring it all back. I'm going to bring all the Winnipeg back that I need to, and you can help me deal with it then."

"I'm sorry, too," she says. "I just—I remembered when you left before. I didn't—"

"I know, I know, listen: I can't talk. I can, but not now. I'll be back soon, okay? I won't stay any longer than I need to, but I do need to stay longer. But I will come back, okay? I promise. Don't worry."

"I'll be here," she says, and she always is.

"I love you, but I have to go. I'm sorry. See you soon," I say, and stop listening.

I put the phone back down into the cradle. I take out the pile of paper, the list, and a pen. I go into the hall, and there is a face at the bottom of the stairs, a face in a deep grey cloud of smoke. It stares at me blankly and recedes as I approach, as I climb the stairs, looking straight into my face as I do. I can smell it—fire, so much paper burning. I get to the top of the stairs and follow the face to the studio door. I get a blank page ready, fresh, for a new room.

I train my eyes on the floor and open the door. As the seal breaks, the face disappears back into the walls of the house.

The floor is a bare film of dust blotted with dead bugs that I haven't come in here to clean. I keep my eyes away from the walls, the windows, and write down dead flies and dead ladybugs and start to tally them. By the time I am shaking and weak, by the time I feel like I need to get out of the studio, get out of this whole life, I've got twenty-seven flies and thirteen ladybugs. Dead feet stroking the dead air.

Staring down at the floor, I imagine Mother's body coiling behind the bars of the vent in my mind, and I see myself standing there, with her, still invisible to her. That's a vision too far, so my eyes instinctually break from the floor and find themselves staring at the place on the wall where the wallpaper burnt off to the old wood planks beneath. It radiates up from the place on the floor where the fire started. My hands—instinctually—reach for the place, and my hands are Mother's, bubbled up with scars.

The house is creaking under me, watching me. I can't stand to look at the scars anymore, so I look away, to the ceiling, where half at least is blotted a deep ash black. I stare at it and feel heat come in at my fingers and look down, thankful to find that it's just light coming in from the window, this time.

Then I feel the dark grey rubbing along my ankle and freeze.

But no, the grey is purring, not billowing. It's simply the cat, marking me with their scent.

NOW

The girl who takes me into the basement of the old house off Ellice Avenue is gorgeous: long haired, pierced, and named something I didn't exactly catch. She is shorter than me and young, probably in her mid-twenties. She does not look like I did when I was in my mid-twenties. None of me. Instead, she reminds me of Raya in her air of intensity. The biggest difference is that this girl smiles more.

The basement isn't musty or dark, but it's almost too low for me to stand up in, so I hunch a little, which is easy with Mother's enlarger in my arms. It's nearly thirty years old, and a pound for every year. It isn't the one she had when I left; it's much better, and I've never used it before.

The girl brings me to the darkroom under the stairs. She opens the door to the dark and turns on the light.

"Hudson built this here over the winter," the girl says, touching the sanded wood of the jamb, pointing to a clear spot in the back corner. I go past her and put down the enlarger. She hands me the bag with the lenses and the extra bulbs, and I put them beside it. "It's small, but it's cozy."

"So long as it's dark," I say, unhunching for a moment. I feel the ceiling at the top of my hair, tied tight at the back of my head.

"We're really happy you responded to the ad," she says. "We've been hoping to get some more photographers involved with the house."

The ad said they were attempting to create a new community of art making and crafting in the city. They wanted to try and keep things like painting, sculpture, photography, textiles, carpentry, and music alive in a too-modern world.

I look at her little hand on the wood frame. I count all five of her fingers. Every other one with a ring on it.

"I may be a bit too old for you guys," I say. "And I'm not in the city very long. I'm just trying to get my mother's house ready to sell."

She smiles at me again, flashing just a tiny hint of a gap tooth that drives me deep into my skin. She's half my age and she's alive and I don't know her name.

"Oh sheesh," she says, pointing to Mother's camera, which is slung under my right arm so I could carry the enlarger. I'm bound up and feel constricted. Allie. "That thing is probably five times as old as you are."

Part of me wants to blush. Another wants to roll his eyes. Some me, in another reality, has fainted. I look down at Mother's camera and touch its smooth, coated brass. Still filmless. I remember her hands on it, just the other day, fingering its ignorant knobs. I lift the camera away from my side and then let it fall back, with a huge, splintering thud. I look up to the girl, who is looking up at the ceiling.

"Hudson must be at work again." Another thick hit. "Wanna meet him?"

I say yes, so we climb back up out of the basement, back into the cramped house with the art all over the walls: A mounted bull moose head with mobiles hanging from his antlers. Photographs. Paintings. Wire sculptures hanging from light fixtures. There's not a place in the house that's empty. In every room we walk through someone is sitting, reading, drinking coffee, or on their phone, smiling. The girl, whose name I still don't know, tells me they switch out the art in the house like exhibits because there's only so much space. They have no room for things to go stale. She points to a wall covered in abstract carvings of bone and says they're hers. We stop and look at them.

"I make them from bones I get from people. I put an ad on Craigslist every now and then asking for bones and people bring them to me. Sometimes I meet them and sometimes they just drop them off outside. I don't know what half the bones are from. There's an anthill in the backyard where I put the ones that are still stinky. Sometimes people just leave roadkill on my lawn."

The whole wall feels like some sort of bizarre collaboration. I take it in, then she taps me on the shoulder and we continue. We get to the back door, which can't open more than halfway, and somehow cram through. Everything in the house is tiny and quirky.

In the backyard there is a small concrete porch where a man in a stained undershirt, his long hair tied back in a sweat-drenched bun, is swinging a huge wooden mallet at wedges in a section of huge, freshly cut log, trying to split the log in two.

The girl and I stand there, watching him as he takes up the axe and swings it into the edge of the rift he's made in the log. Once the axe is in, he hits it deeper with the mallet. When it won't go in any farther, he turns to pick up one of the wedges from the pile beside him and finally notices us. Blue eyes, bare face, glasses laced with sweat and particles of wood, surprised.

"Helena," he says, pronouncing her into being.

She scurries up to him and kisses him, without touching him. He doesn't touch her either; they just meet at the lips for a beat, nothing but energetic air between them. Then Hudson takes a handkerchief from his back pocket and wipes his face dry.

"This is Hedy," Helena says, gesturing to me. I'm Hedy. I forgot I'd said that when I called, responding to the ad. "She's a photographer. She brought us a new enlarger!"

"Lovely," Hudson says, putting down the huge wooden mallet and picking up one of the wedges. He is maybe thirty. He plays with the wedge in his hands and sits on the huge log.

Helena goes inside to grab us a few beers, to cut the rare late-spring heat, and Hudson asks me about what I'm working on right now. I tell him I'm doing something about my mother, but I'm not sure yet what it's going to be exactly. This feels like a lie wrapped in truth. He is quiet and easy to speak to because I can tell he is listening. I tell him that all I know is that I might call it *Shadows of the Prison House*. The name comes from a line from the first page of a book Genny had, which stuck with me more than the title. I did not know I intended to call something that until I said it. Hudson sits there, listening, and when the beers come, we drink them.

I've got the roll of undeveloped film in my pocket, the one I shot when I first got to Mother's house. After we chat for a bit, Hudson gets up and goes back to splitting the log and Helena takes me back down to the darkroom. She wants to be there while I develop the roll.

In the complete dark I can hear her breathing. I open up the roll and pull out the long strip. I string it onto the spool of the developing tank. Hudson's mallet is thudding at a regular rhythm again, like a bass line. I turn on the light, pour the chemicals into the dark tank, and start to agitate it. I agitate it in time to his beats. Every six hits. I can sense the moment of the light being set in the film. Helena is leaning against the door, watching me. I glance over at her and her mouth is half-open. She is concentrating.

Hudson hits and hits and hits, big beats of an old wood heart, far off. Once the roll has had its time, I stop the developing and wash the chemicals from the roll in the sink. I decide to take it back to Mother's house wet.

"Don't be a stranger," Helena says from the doorway as I go out toward my car.

I smile at her and wave. Instead of saying what I want to, that I will always be a stranger, I say "I won't."

9

THE UPSTAIRS BATHROOM

You take a step, then another, and soon you're going past the bath-room. The door is closed; it's always closed. There is light coming out from under it. You always pretend you're going to skip the bathroom, but every time you get here you still knock on the door, lightly, and every time you do nobody answers. So you put your ear to the door and you hear it, the breathing, similar but different from the sound of the darkroom ventilation's sucking and blowing. You listen and you think, *It's Mother, isn't it?* You believe. You go to the door and put your hand on the knob and it isn't locked, of course.

You open the door and look inside. Inside is Mother, sitting on the toilet, crying, as you yourself—whoever you are when you get to this part of the tour—are sprouting from the top of her head. You are almost completely out, but it seems like your foot is stuck. Neither see you at the door. Mother is crying and you are crying and they are both breathing. You can stand the crying, but the breathing—Mother's breathing, and yours in sync—is too much. You step back slow through molasses and close the bathroom door before you can catch the tears from your own eyes rivering toward you.

When Genny and I escaped Winnipeg, escaped our mothers, mine moved out of my life and into my skull, and along with her came—integral to Mother and me—the expanse between us. My heart was easy with love for Genny, but my head unfolded into leagues of absence. Sometimes the closest inch of my life felt like it was at the end of a very long tunnel. Sometimes I tried to look myself in the eye in a mirror and could not see myself but for a blip, deep in far-off eyes.

I was obsessed with Mother and Winnipeg as soon as I left. The act of leaving this city and her behind with the vow of never return-ing made them both stiff and unmoving in me. Static. The streets of Minneapolis paved over Winnipeg's, were renamed, but I knew that Winnipeg's were there, always just under the surface. I felt, moving through my new city, the surge of Portage and Pembina, and all of Wolseley's little veins. I could close my eyes and see them. Hear them.

I became afraid of construction sites, of potholes, because I thought that if I looked into them I would fall back here, to this city.

When I ran away to Hamburg, those streets were paved over Minneapolis's streets which were still over Winnipeg's. Though the canals of Hamburg seemed a strange novelty, they seemed to be thick with a mixed swill of the memories of elsewhere. They were tiny versions of the Red and the Assiniboine and the Mississippi, repeating themselves inescapably across my new landscape.

Mother lived at the corner of my eye. She wandered the streets under the streets.

Everything was thick with a reminiscence of home, yet I pretended it was pure freedom. I pretended that I'd escaped it, that I'd moved past that life, even though in leaving it I'd only ensured the permanence of its hold on me. It was a sort of preservation of it. I was just pushing it along with me, up the hill.

The further I got away from things, the wider my head could get, and while I grew more and more capable of taking measures to zoom into the reality of my life, into where I was, there was no escaping those moments of vanishing, those moments when it felt like I was falling from the lip of my eyes all the way to the back of my skull.

It felt like I'd been holding onto the edges of a cliff until someone came over and stomped on my fingers, making me fall deep into the dark chasm of myself.

I didn't head back to Mother's house after meeting Helena. I came here, to Cousins Deli on Sherbrook, a table in the corner. I'm meeting Dorothea in person for the first time.

She comes into the deli, picks up her food, and walks straight over to me. Sits down and puts her hands on my hands on the table.

"I can't believe it's you," she says. "You have her exact eyes."

Dorothea is maybe fifty-five or sixty years old, stout and smiley. She has a beer, a local Half Pints IPA, with her sandwich. I'm drinking tea and mostly I just want to hear her talk. If she has anything to say about Mother, I'll hear it. I will let myself—or make myself—hear it.

Dorothea tells me about some of the heartbreaking minutiae that led her to think that Mother may need full-time care: emptying the cans of soup from the pantry into the bathtub; screaming at Dorothea the times she arrived a few minutes late, or without knocking first, or on time; filling all the small plates with water and putting them in the closet, under furniture, on the stairs, for the fish, she explained, who were looking for a home. Despite it being a cold April day, Mother had opened all the windows in the house to let them in. One of the plates of water on the windowsill in the kitchen, Dorothea said, was covered with a very thin layer of ice when she got there.

When Dorothea refers to Mother she calls her by her full name: "Hedwig forgot my name a lot. I would sometimes, while dusting or cooking her breakfast, sing my name throughout the house. 'Dorothea! Dorothea!' And once, when I got there in the morning and let myself in, I met Hedwig coming down the stairs, and she looked at me and sang, 'Dorothea!' It was very touching. But in a few more weeks, she started falling."

At this, Dorothea finishes her beer. The sandwich is already done. "Then, of course, there was the fire."

But Dorothea talks past that, because we talked about it enough years ago. Instead, she small-talks about some of the other clients she's already seen today. I half listen and wonder if she knew that Mother, when she was around Dorothea's age, before turning to photography, did exactly what she's doing, with Ilsa, with other elderly people around the neighbourhood. But I don't tell her that. I don't want her to imagine herself in Mother's shoes. I'm not finished with her shoes.

She stops talking, so I stop listening. We get up together and go to the counter, and I pay for everything. I thank her, and she hugs me. It feels like a century passes by the time she lets go.

"Give my love to Hedwig," she says.

When I get back to the house, I park in Mother's spot again, carry the negatives I developed this morning at Helena's up to my bedroom, string them out atop my empty little bed, and go downstairs to call the realtor.

She says yes, she will be coming over today.

I put the phone down and realize that Mother's old Leica is still around my neck, lens-capped and collapsed into the body, realize that it has been there all day, maybe longer. Filmless.

For a moment, I do not remember it ever being anywhere else.

For a moment, I wonder if it's still a camera if it doesn't have film inside? If it doesn't have the capacity to hold on to things?

In Germany I began to shoot photos that abstracted the body in a more constructed, material way—where the shots were more complex than just my body meeting light. I incorporated sculpture, painting, anything that inspired me. I lifted the limits. I had a shot where a friend of Erwin's painted my own face offset onto my actual face—my eyes on my cheek, mouth on my chin—so that I looked like a double-exposed portrait. I had a shot where I held a mirror, hinged at my abdomen, to reflect myself into a kind of four-legged, double-vagina'd aberration.

My favourite shoot was one where I built a scaled diorama of the blue-collar mall surroundings of the Monument against Fascism. I stepped into the role of the monument in the shoot. I painted my body fully black, greased my hair jet black, and scrawled on my body in silver paint and splashes of graffiti colour—just as the monument was, at that time. I set up small wire-framed figures, some drawing on me, others considering me from farther back, as I stood, for the first shot, belly button up, bare and monolithically tight, my eyes looking down at the figures beneath me with an air of statuesque judgment, if not slight worry—as if challenging them to prove they were not the monsters that humans very often are.

For the second shot, I was lower, my breasts scrawled over and drooping across the ground, my face more furious. The third showed only my neck and head. The last seemed flat but for the crown of my head and my fingers snaking overtop.

That was one of the few shoots where Erwin used his Polaroid to show me the compositions before I committed them to film. He helped me with a lot of my shoots, as he was intrigued by my use of the body as a tool of abstraction, and felt guilty he couldn't pay me more for my help. For Erwin, the bodies he used didn't abstract so much as refract his scenes through their presence. They were like magnets, interrupting a story. His bodies were about the artificiality of art meeting reality, about how the act of looking back colours and off-sets the past. In mine, the body almost always abstracted an object or idea. Bodies in my photos were inconvenient; they got in the way. His haunted in a way that clarified his vision, while mine just obscured any sense of a vision. By making the body an object, I was trying to erase both the body and whatever the body stood for. What was left was the very material of absence.

The moment he took the Polaroid of the first composition of me as the monument, the composition that would become the best image from the roll, I saw him pause, as if struck by the power of the image. He didn't bother to show me the Polaroid first. He didn't want me to break from whatever moment he'd captured. He told me to stay as I was. Then he looked through Mother's camera and took the shot.

I go up to the bedroom where the negatives are lying out, snoozing in one huge string, on the bed I grew up sleeping on. The sun is slicing in through the little window—this life I sliced my way out of so long ago. I pick up the string of negatives and carry it toward the light, doubled over and slung across my arms like a body. I hold them against the cool glass and look closely as the light comes through the film, through where the darkness would be printed. My mind reinterprets them, develops them, as I slowly draw the string of them up, spilling over my turned head.

The images are as expected: blurry, underexposed. If they are printed, they will be expressions of darkness. The negatives themselves, though, are bright and nearly transparent. By the end of the string, I am seeing spots from looking into the sunlight. Darkness balancing the eye where the brightness once was.

As I step back from the light, I notice the pry bar on the floor. I pick it up like it's nothing, like it hasn't been waiting, and take the string of negatives and wrap it around the bar, bottom to top, permanently scratching them, permanently ruining the chance of making a clean print. The negatives wind up the whole shaft, to the start of the crook.

I carry the bar wrapped in the negatives downstairs to the kitchen and crudely tape each end. I go and stand at the big living room window and stare out at the street. I lift the little bar above my head in both hands and hear a mew in the doorway. The cat is standing there.

For the last few days I've felt them at the edges of my life; I've heard the house's pulse change as they moved through it. They have gotten brave, finally willing to approach me. I stand still.

When they reach my ankles, they sniff me. Sniff again. Then, they press their little grey skull against me. I crouch down, and they back away but not out of reach. I put the pry bar on the floor, wondering if I will ever be able to pick it up again or if it will have to live here. I stretch my hand out toward the thin little cat, and they sniff the air and don't run. They let me trace my fingers along the top of their skull.

I try to ignore the faces coming out of the walls. The smell of smoke. The whispering I can't unravel.

When you get up to the top of the stairs, before you make your way toward the bathroom—before you try to get past it—you always look at the four closed doors. If you want to get out quick, you skip straight to your bedroom, because once you open any of the other three doors you'll have no choice but to remember the whole thing before you can leave. But if you decide to leave without going through the rest of the rooms, to go directly to your bedroom, you don't get to actually go through the door. You touch the knob, and then you are out of the memory palace. You can breathe again, but you are filled with a sunken feeling of defeat. You've let the palace overwhelm you. You have let yourself go.

Even though you can skip the rest of the rooms, getting out of the palace from the second floor is difficult. You always try—at this point—to turn back, to recede down the stairs, but the stairs either disappear or end up leading you back here. You can't escape, not like that, just like you can't *not* try to. This is your palace; this is your life. But that doesn't mean that you don't have to follow the rules. They're built right into your brain.

After the realtor called to push our appointment later in the day, the cat transformed back into a sound in the house.

I hung up the phone and tried to look out the window, but the smoke was obscuring the space. I could only really see the light of the outside world through the holes of its open eyes staring back through me. I wanted to pick up the pry bar and swing it at the cloud like a sword.

Now, I am sitting on a blank, shallow counter in the red—the darkroom. The door is very closed. I've kept the fan off, because I don't want to suck anything outside in.

I have my cellphone out, to watch the time. The realtor won't be here for another forty minutes. I pull up the emails on my phone. Minutes from the collective's board meeting. An email advertising some talk at the university that they want me to help share. A YouTube link from Archer. A string of emails from some of the grad students I'm advising, including Ess. Things to look at, things to sign. A few emails from Mother's home, about social events.

I feel suspended from time, as I always do when I'm in a darkroom. Everything in the room is red from the light. There is so much space where Mother's equipment used to sit. Where Mother used to bring lived moments back to life in stillness.

I think of Helena, Hudson, their darkroom. I think about my darkroom in Minneapolis, in my little house across the street from Genny's. I want to open the door and come out somewhere different. I want to be able to pull things back that have slipped away.

I put my hand on the door, on the doorknob, and try to turn and push my way out. But I can't. Because I'm in the memory palace. Because I'm on the other side of the door, aren't I?

Before I came back to see Mother I was beginning to lose myself in the lack of drive to do my work. My life had turned consumptive, based purely on the detached external. I started to drink over my dosage from my Mnemosyne flask, to go to more shows, movies. I gave myself into the criticisms I offered to Ess and the rest of my students, others I advised whose long summers of intense work had just begun, or whose years of suffering had finally finished and loosed them into the terrifying post-grad life. I wandered out into the streets more, did more planning for the collective, booked shows for other artists, helped draw lines from one to another.

I also stopped looking at myself in the mirror. And I've stopped doing that again.

I couldn't create. I was jamstuck with an uncertainty of conviction stemming from an uncertainty of who I was. I didn't look in the mirror because I didn't know who I'd see, and I got sick thinking about pointing a camera at myself again, to try and get that sort of distance. Why waste the frames documenting a mundane absence?

Despite all my movement, despite all my chatter, I'd lost my voice.

I spent more time with Genny and Karen and my other friends. I turned inside out: charming, a vacant social shape. I circumvented the darkroom in my house, my darkroom that is across the hall from my bedroom, as well as the cabinet where I keep all my equipment. I left Mother's camera on the shelf, quiet, only getting near it when I went into my bedroom to sleep.

There's a sweet spot to doing art: when you're a bit uncertain of yourself but not so uncertain that you're not sure you're anyone at all. The best place you can be is on the brink, negotiating the details of your existence while still believing in its intrinsic presence. You need to be able to believe that your body is your body, your life your life, despite feeling a bit of a stranger in them.

Just before I got the call from the doctor, I was starting to think that it was too late to regain my voice. My drive. But when Mother stopped speaking, that girl knocked on the side of my head and climbed behind the wheel and we just went. We felt a sort of communal effort in returning to her, to Mother, and with that found a semblance of conviction. We were so ready for it, and came together over how disconnected we each were from Mother. Face-to-face with the absence of her, the steady and predictable and terrible lack of her, we somewhat filled up. We turned back inside. The wind, through the gaps in us, sang from floor to floor. We heard it.

We picked up the camera from our chest as soon as we entered the house, and we began to re-insinuate our presence here. Her presence here. And despite the lack of Mother, the house was all here waiting for me. For us.

I leave the darkroom and head up to my bedroom, leaving the door open and the red safety light on, because I don't want that toothed darkness to come back. The smoke finds me, gusts from room to room, creaking, obscuring all movements, rustling the house into a wooden wail at me. I close my eyes and cut through the memory palace, the relative peacefulness of its chaos, until I get to my bedroom door. I open the door and my eyes at the same time, and as I fall out of the palace, I am inside my real room, rifling through my luggage for a pair of scissors and one of the extra rolls of film I'd packed: ISO 400 Tri-X, black and white. I put the film in my pocket and keep the pair of nail scissors I find in my fist. I grab the packer and the binder, and when I turn to leave the room, there it is—the cloud of smoke, of dark stone-grey ash—staring at me. I wonder if its face is mine and I just haven't been able to recognize it. I wonder if it's Mother's. All I know for sure is I feel stronger with the scissors in my fist.

So I walk through it, heart pounding. Walk through the real house as its dark swims around me, showing off so many different faces, so many faces I don't want to see. I hold my breath until I make it downstairs, until I make it to the red light spilling from the darkroom. It does not follow me in, and I leave the door open. I stand at one of the counters, take Mother's camera off my neck, open the bottom, and pull the film from my pocket. I open the canister, pull a few inches of the film out, and trim the lead longer before I can wind it onto the spool—an accommodation for old mechanics.

I realize that this moment is symmetrical to the night I left this place: door open, red light on, Mother's camera sitting and waiting to be filled. Only I didn't; I just walked out of the house, out of this life. Now I tip Mother's camera upside down and gently slip the film inside.

When Mother was doing photography full time, she would disappear into this darkroom for hours on end. I'd often stand outside the door, when I was little, and listen to the ventilation sucking chemical fumes and blowing fresh air, to the sink turning off and on. When I was little and wanted to talk to her, when we were talking so often, about small things—like nothing would ever change—I'd always have to wait.

There is a sound at the top of the stairs, cushioned.

One summer, when I was nine, I broke my wrist, because I'd thought it would a fun to slide down the stairs on a pile of my clothes, like sledding down a snowy hill, like I'd done once or twice the winter before at Garbage Hill.

I hear feet above me, a short sprint, and a brief moment of hang time, followed by a whimpering tumble.

The clothes went with me for about four stairs—until they didn't—when I rolled the rest of my way down, knocking my nose to blood, scuffing up my limbs, and—luckily—only breaking my left wrist.

At the end of the hall, at the bottom of the stairs, in a canopy of the grey cloud, is me: crying. The sounds of the darkroom are blaring—though I don't have the fan turned on, though I don't have the sink running, their sounds are here. I start to crawl toward me on three limbs, down the hall, down the so-long hall, out of breath from crying, mouth moving in a shape, a sound I can't hear. But I know. I can feel it in my throat: *Mother, Mother.*

I look around the darkroom and I'm all alone. Then I am on the ground, outside, sitting up and pawing at the place where the door should be. I can't see the cloud around me, because the cloud is not there. Blood drips from my nose. I can't tell if the safety light is on, or if Mother is inside in complete darkness. I just put my good hand on the door and try to knock, try to say her name between sobs. The door flickers in and out. I flicker to either side of the jamb where a door could close the world out.

She doesn't hear. Eventually, I'm sitting up against the wall, my shirt covered in dry blood rivered from my nose, exhausted and hoarse and shivering and holding my swelling wrist, and I hear the fan go off, and the light switch on, and the door open outward.

Three bodies walk out from the dark: Mother's carrying prints, mine following her with the camera in my hands, and another composed of the grey, smouldering and widening.

When Mother sees me she throws the prints onto the floor, kneels down beside me, apologizing, probably. I can't hear, standing behind her, watching me hold up my little wrist to her, face so pale, blood snaking down lip and neck and chest.

All I can hear is the wind howling. Mother puts the small human in her arms and carries them out of the house. And I can't follow them, can't move, can't go along to see the quiet intensity Mother had at that time, as she put me in the car and drove, that quiet intensity that seemed so cold and efficient but I later realized was actually silent adrenalin. Passion. Because I came out to the waiting room with the cast and the lollipop, and there she was: waiting and inconsolable, a two-seat buffer of discomfort around her.

I stand here, unmoving, with Mother's camera ready at my chest, until the smoky arms unwrap themselves from my shoulders, and the grey wind stops howling. Silence fills the hole, and the cat comes down the stairs. The grey dissipates through the gaps in the walls, the empty places where so much used to be, as the cat sits down a few feet ahead of me. The cat meows, a soft, breaking sound.

But all I want is the voice of that grey again. That noise, that inflected, meaningful nothing.

As soon as you see yourself emerging from Mother's head in the upstairs bathroom you've set the sequence of these memories in motion. There's no getting out now, and there's no changing the order. Things focus in and the experience loses its breadth of possibilities, trading variation for intensity. Instead of the lack of control you have on the first floor of the memory palace, where things sometimes happen one way or another, here you have a deeper lack of control. No matter what, as soon as you choose not to surrender by reaching out to the door of your old bedroom first, you can't take the rooms in any form other than as they are. You know exactly what is coming, and the dread of the inevitable is enough to ruin you. Because who said remembering is easy? Who said that you should be able to waltz through life nodding to the things you've passed by? No. That's not what remembering is. Remembering is being dragged through the waist-deep rubble of the whole of your life—what you've lived and what you are living—without being able to get free. Or turn around. It's seeing what's already happened, all that reality that you can't do anything about but watch pass.

The cat evaporates back into the creaky and whispering wood of the house. Before I open the door for the realtor, I adjust myself in my shirt. From the top of the neck, cleavage shows, and I'm not sure what I was thinking.

The realtor is a middle-aged woman in an electric-blue, knee-length skirt and a blazer. She is carrying an umbrella and the sky is clear. I introduce myself, correcting her assumption that I'm Hedwig.

"I'm her daughter," I say, even though I don't feel like it. I do not say what I want to say: *I am her son, and she is no longer with us.*

I show her the house. She steps over the pry bar wrapped in the negatives on the floor in front of the living room window, makes notes, and tells me what the great features of the house are, and what we would want to change. The darkroom should be brightened up. The living room should lose the old, dusty furniture that makes the room feel like it's stuck in the eighties. The kitchen and the cabinets should be updated with fresh paint. I don't take notes myself. I'm overwhelmed and envious of the coldness with which she surveys and prescribes for the house. My eyes get tight, edging.

I take her through every room, the same way that I would take her through the memory palace. A few times I want to point to the place on the walls where we've set up the photos but catch myself. She would not be able to see them, and if she did, she wouldn't be able to care. As I take her through the house with a sort of natural order, I wonder what she is placing there. What her own life, maybe only ten or fifteen years longer than mine, would look like superimposed here.

I take her upstairs and try not to imagine all the people cluttering the steps. She marvels at the charming old sounds the house makes as we move and marks that down. I take her past the armoire, past the litter box and the food and water dishes that sit on the bare floor beside it, through Mother's bedroom—where I avoid at all costs making eye contact with the mirror, where I don't want to see myself trapped—and finally arrive in the doorway of the dusty studio. We step inside.

The realtor stops breathing, staring at the huge scar blackening the floor, the burnt-through wallpaper, and the ceiling in an expanding darkness. I stand behind her, looking at the hair on the back of her head, sprinting out in every thin direction from her part at the crown.

"What happened here?" she asks.

"An accident," I say, not looking. The statement reinterprets and rearranges reality, and I try to believe in it. "A candle kicked over into a trash can. The power was out."

She walks up to the wall, her hand over her mouth, as if she is shushing the whole house. The house doesn't listen. It creaks at her feet the whole time she walks. I imagine the candle, the trash can, the fire eating away the dark, trying to confuse the walls, the floor. The realtor doesn't seem to notice the house getting louder and louder and louder.

"This," she says, stepping nearer to the wall and opening her arms to it. "This will have to be fixed."

After the realtor leaves I sit down in the chair at the phone table. The number she quoted me for the house is nothing but digits. I think about Mother in the home, and all the digits involved in keeping her there. This is an exercise in practicality, a concession to the end of something.

The cat comes back, stands in the opening to the kitchen. They are rough and dusty from rubbing up and nestling into the places in the house they've been hiding, their fur a mat of weird clumps, a pointy collection of grey directions pinned to a skeleton. They stare at me and I stare at them, into them, into their nameless dark eyes.

I get up from the chair and the cat doesn't run away, so I take a few steps toward them. I kneel and they let me pet them. I pet the grey cat and try to think of a name for them. I'm not sure that I've ever named another living thing since Darius. The cat begins to purr under my shallow rubbing, shallow in my hesitance to scare them away. They put their paw on my hand beside them on the floor and clench. No claws come out. I stop petting them and I grab their little paw and squeeze it.

I think of all the walking I've done around the neighbourhood since finding the cat and do not recall any posters looking for them. A few times, walking around here, I've noticed the poster for the missing teenager, the one I noticed on my first night here and thought might have been me—a girl. The one I haven't been able to look at for long, because the picture on it is a black-and-white photo of a painting. The idea that a girl has disappeared before she was photographed is too much. The world is a horror, and it is coagulating in this city, in this house.

I let go of the cat's paw as their nose edges toward my hand because I don't want them to bite me. The cat is bones—curves and angles. Jagged. I do not have a name for them. The cat looks up at me, and then I go to the stairs, and up.

Outside the house is air. Inside the house is old layers of time. I dream in coats of paint and re-upholstered lives.

In Mother's bedroom I don't look in the mirror, not right away, but eventually I do. I see myself, in stride toward leaving the room, head and feet cut off from the frame. In the middle is paused movement, a genderless intention to put myself back into motion. I cannot tell who I am in the mirror, but whoever I am, they look ready to move in a decided direction.

The middle in the mirror looks determined.

10

MOTHER'S ROOM

This is the end of the beginning of the end of the tour, where the order and construction of the rooms are firmly set. The mirror is sitting in the corner of the room, and in the mirror you can see yourself in the bed, but when you look over to the bed itself you see Mother—younger, as she was once; sitting in bed, as she is now. But she is looking you straight in the eye, a gaze you can't hold for long, until you look back to the mirror, where the you in the bed is meeting your gaze. Lenses breech the walls, tearing the wallpaper, lenses of different cameras—taking lenses, viewing lenses, large format lenses, and little Leica lenses just like Mother's Summar. You can feel them focus, hear the faint buzz of a thousand shutterclicks and five hundred mirror flaps, the combination of which sounds like bugs scratching through the walls. Everywhere is the gleam of light crossing glass. You look back and forth between the mirror and the bed. You don't look into the lenses.

Quite frankly, you don't know what you even remember here. Every time, you're unsure; you have no words to shape its importance. Instead of tangibility, this room stands more as a place where you go and feel shame, all that shame that has built up after years and years of pushing it away, of keeping it behind the camera instead of pulling it out front—where it should be—where it could go to be expressed and maybe, somewhat, silenced. Or at least understood.

The room gets louder and louder. Mother looks deeper and deeper into your eyes and you—in the bed in the mirror—begin to grimace. You find it harder to hold that bounced gaze than it is to hold Mother's, though you keep looking back, and there you are, fuming, inverted, furious, deadly. You don't want to look, but you've got no choice. This is you in your memory, not you in your life. A firm hand is on your head, turning you, curating the experience, and all you want is out.

Mother starts to look sorry for you; she starts to cry. You start screaming on the bed, and even when you're looking at Mother, you can hear her, them, him. Your head is overcrowded. You want out and you want out and you want out—and you don't get it, do you, the point of all this? You can't know it. *This is why you're here!* you scream at yourself from the mirrored bed. You can hear the spit flying from your fucking mouth, can't you?

You can. You feel it—swelling like an island collapsing in on itself. The walls shake. The house creaks. Mother can't stand the sight of you anymore, so she stops meeting your gaze. You want it back because you don't want to be forced to look in the mirror. You scream for it: *Look at me!* you scream. *Look at me!*

And so you do, look at you, in the mirror. The bed is empty. The mirror turns to face you, but as it turns, you realize that the doorway is empty, too.

Leaning against the jamb of the darkroom's door, my shoes on, my coat over my arm, I use my cell to call the number the realtor gave me for a friend of hers who often does last-minute fix-up work for her clients, and he tells me that, from the sounds of it, it would take him four days to do the job: paint the kitchen, paint the darkroom, and replace the wallpaper in the studio.

"I just had a job sniped from me. Could start as early as tomorrow."

I thank him and give him the address, the numbers for both my cell and the landline, and the name of the paint the realtor suggested for the kitchen: Moonstone.

I do not tell him about the smoke, billowing room to room. I do not tell him that the house has grown so loud. That there is a cat, slipping in and out of view. I do not say any of that. I thank him again and hang up.

I can feel the house stalking me, eyes on me as I leave the red light and head to the back door in the kitchen, the kitchen that will not be this old yellow much longer.

I've got Mother's camera around my neck, still. There is film inside it, and the lens cap is off. This has been dissuading the house from showing itself, from allowing the grey to seep around the corner into a room I'm in. The house has become the sound, instead. Creaking, knocking, coiling around me.

I put on my shoes and go—get in my car and drive.

Life seems almost peaceful: the cars move quiet through the morning, the sun is half-blocked by clouds, the music playing on the radio is not as objectionable as I expect. The city is coming back to life after long winter. I stop and start, keep my windows shut because I don't want the world to feel fresh, don't want to feel the wind on my face. Not wind but air, coming at you fast because you're going fast. It's different. It's friction.

At the home, the nurse at the desk tells me that Mother is finishing breakfast in her room.

"Would you like to go in, or wait?"

"I'll wait," I say, going over to the seat with the silent televisions, not playing the news anymore but sitcoms, where the comedic timing of the captions doesn't work. I dig my phone from my pocket and join the home's guest Wi-Fi.

Seven emails, the most recent from Helena, replying to my response from Craigslist: "RE: RE: RE: RE: Winnipeg Artists and Creators, Join Us!" I click it.

> *Hedwig!*
> *Are you still in wpg?? Our darkroom is lonesome!*
> *There is a cool new show in the Exchange I've been meaning to check out. Lemme know if you'd like to come along.*
> *—HV*

Helena included her phone number in a PS at the end, so I add it to my contacts and text her. I do not read any of the unread texts on my phone.

—*Hey this is Hedwig. Still in wpg. What show?*

I wait, in this room built for it. I think about Mother eating, about how the last time I remember looking in her mouth was when I was holding the flashlight and making sure she'd swallowed her medication after Selkirk. How dark and deep Mother seemed then. I remember wishing I could climb inside and see it all, understand all that pain.

—*Hi! It is called stitches or sutures or something like that? Not sure tbh. Supposed to be cool. Busy this afternoon?*

"Your mother's finished her breakfast, if you'd like to go in."

I put my phone away and go to Mother's door, rest my hand on its jamb, and look at her. She is in the chair again, in the light, looking out the window into the building's little green courtyard.

I turn back, toward the nurse's station. "Can I get into the court-yard?" I ask her.

She smiles at me as she turns and points over her shoulder, to a little hall. "You'll need to buzz to be let out, but you can go out there. Do you want to take your mother?"

"No," I say, looking toward the hall. "I just want to surprise her." I wave a hand to the nurse without turning back because I know she'll just be wearing that hospital smile again. I have seen enough of those.

I go outside and count down the windows to hers, the first with open blinds on her wing. I walk down the little brick path, past the little bird bath, past the benches and the handrails and the planters filled with flowers still far from budding.

I climb over the handrail toward her. She looks down toward me. She is a pinhole camera. She just needs to look at me a long time, and then she will be able to see me. Lick by slow lick, I will finally burn back into her head.

I look at her face—still her face—looking out the window but not quite seeing me. The sky, the sun, blinks on and off. This is how I remember us: me looking in, being able to see her, and her looking out, only able to see the reflection of herself in the mirror of mid-night's window. Stone, slipping away.

She doesn't know me. I hold up her camera and she doesn't seem to recognize it. I extend the lens. I adjust the settings. I put the camera to one eye and stare at her. I put her into focus.

I don't see her, either. Because what do I even really know about her?

I don't take the photo. Mother looks away. I let the camera fall to my chest, turn around and climb over the handrail, lie on a bench gripping the camera and feeling those eyes behind me: blind, blown-out searchlights.

I look into the sky and a grey cloud stares down at me. It is the size of the world. I wipe my face and sit up and take out my phone. I don't look back.

—*No*

When Mother was doing work that didn't require her to turn in her negatives, she would often make small, unnecessary modifications to her shots in the darkroom. She would remove birds from the sky in the background of a portrait and add those same birds to the empty sky of another. She would remove shrubbery, street lights, and bracelets and add tiny freckles to the shoulders of brides. Sometimes, she would print old photographs and add whole new aspects that were not there before—people or objects she shot decades after those old photos.

Whatever she saw through the camera at that moment was hardly ever what she wanted to help bring into the world. She wanted to take what she had clipped out of the decided reality and add something to it, fix it, or just tweak it in some way that contained her intention. Her. She wanted, I think, to control the world. To be a witness but with some say in it.

She hated the world. She hates it, I mean. Or maybe she doesn't hate it anymore.

The photograph I remember best is the one of me digging in the backyard. It's the photograph that is most often framed and set on the landing of my memory palace, the photo that I haven't found anywhere in the house. Not that I expected to.

In the centre of the photograph is me, my body pointing toward the camera, throwing dirt over my right shoulder with a gardening trowel. I'm looking down at the hole I'm making between my knees, and the definition of my face is softened by small adjustments of the head because Mother set the shutter speed slow, probably around one-thirtieth of a second. Because of the speed of my digging, the trowel in my hand is blurred into my arms, becoming part of my body. In the background, there are holes from my other digs.

I don't remember Mother taking this picture, but she must have taken it through the kitchen window, despite the fact that the photo seems too clean to have been shot through glass. The windows of the house were probably cleaner back then.

But when Mother printed the photo, she printed the negative inverted, which I noticed because it feels more natural that I would throw dirt over my left shoulder than my right.

Looking at the photo in the memory palace feels like staring into a mirror, except that in the sky above me, Mother added a black, jagged sun.

I honk and here comes Helena—long jean shorts and a white V-neck T and her hair in a wild bundle at the top of her head—slipping out the door of the little house toward my car. I try to see her just as she is, not as the ghosts she reminds me of, but I can't. Not that I even know which ghosts those are.

My hand is on Mother's camera around my neck, and it seems that I left the home so fast I forgot to put on my seat belt. I leave it off. Helena opens the door and slides inside. She has brought nothing with her but a smile and a small sketch pad.

"You got here so quick!" she says, earrings dangling.

"Where to?"

"North, 'til McDermot." She points.

We go. She compliments me on my hair, my car, asks me how I've been.

"Alive," I say, and I can feel her roll her eyes.

"Come on, Hedwig," she says.

I keep my eyes on the road, the intersections, thinking of Mother staring out the window and through me. I keep driving as Helena talks until it's time to park. As I turn off the ignition, she puts two fingers on my forearm; I don't know what she's been saying. I don't move. I don't want to scare the fingers off.

"It's okay," she says.

We sit there, parked along McDermot, the day slowly decreasing. The air in the car disappears. The world crumbles into large, vital parts. Then—slowly—it comes back. Everything. I lift the neck of my shirt to my forehead and dry my face on the inside of it, feel its wetness as I let it go, lingering above the binder.

"Do you wanna see the show?"

"Yes," I say, putting my hand on the door and looking over at her, trying to look right at her and not at any of the car's mirrors, reflecting a darkening sky that I know she can't see. I look right at her face, diving directly into her beauty. "Absolutely."

She smiles. We get out of the car and walk to the gallery. Mother's camera knocks against my belly. My head is light, my limbs unheard of.

I found the print Mother made of me trowelling when I was maybe thirteen years old. I was wearing baggy hand-me-down clothes Mother got from Asha's son, who had moved to Alberta to go to university a year before. My body had split open by then, and I wore his clothes with an intense desperation.

I'd just gotten back from school, and I had a deep bruise on my arm from being pinched by a girl named Sylvia. I was looking through Mother's things for some money—I wanted nothing but to go down to the corner store and buy bars and bars of chocolate. I wanted to eat so much I'd die.

I was looking through the box in Mother's studio, the box that once held wine, the box filled with envelopes from letters in German and pictures she'd printed, the box that was the only thing in Mother's studio besides the small mat where she did her yoga.

A box that I had carried home, empty.

I rifled through, ignoring all the letters, all that information I'd never know, my body desperate for some sort of relief. I looked and looked, and there was nothing, no cash. Just paper: folded-up letters and prints of photographs I couldn't be bothered to memorize, photographs completely blank now in my mind.

But then I found that photo of me, and I was transfixed. Because of that sun. It was black as the page would go, round, with licking black flame. And the shadows were so stark and sharp and below me that it must have been noon when Mother took it. I sat there, looking down at the print, feeling a warmth in my body, and decided to walk to a gas station farther off and try to shoplift the chocolate. Then, I put the print back in the box, replaced the lid, and left the studio. Like it had been nothing to be in there, to have my hands inside Mother's private life.

But since finding that photo, I have seen it. That sun. I have seen it rising, slower, farther down the sky. Sometimes it comes out at night. It has been known to change its speed, to catch up with the real sun and eclipse it for days, for weeks, for much, much longer. Sometimes I wake up and it is there, in the wall, rays of a darkness so thick you could swim in them if they didn't burn you. It is a sun that is a problem even if you don't look up.

We pay the person at the desk, get our hands stamped, and make our way inside the gallery. A panel on the wall announces the exhibition:

THESE SUTURES:
Michael Wynne//
//Cathryn Logan

I recognize Cathryn Logan as the name I wrote to when I was trying to get a teaching job at the university here.

Life is a circle. Or an egg that needs to be smashed to its yolk.

Helena puts her hand on my shoulder and ushers me into the first room, which is very small, and where we are confronted in the middle by the single, long, dead face of a moose. A cow moose, or a bull without antlers. It is the head of a moose added onto the body of what must be a wolf. Along its back, large black wings, its legs wrapped in fish skin.

"The Canadian griffin," Helena says, kneeling at the placard at its side, eyes glimmering in the lights. She reads: "Moose, timber wolf, muskellunge, and turkey vulture." She stands up and comes back to my side. She doesn't open the sketchbook. "How bizarre."

"Yes," I say, and we eventually move forward, into a bigger room filled with more of Wynne's monsters, each one made from North American animals—versions of all sorts of classic folk monsters, as well as creatures of his own making, titled things like *The Thing I Saw Last Winter on the Ice of Ramsey Lake*, or *One of the Many Things I Saw When My Boyfriend Kissed Me in My Neighbourhood for the First Time*. A panel on a wall describes Wynne's work as a form of transrealism, merging the natural with the imagined, where Wynne's imagined, subjective world is constructed with well-documented natural creatures stitched together.

On the other side of the gallery Helena closes her sketchbook with a slap and I look over. "You know there's a sinkhole just a few streets up. On Princess. There have been a few this spring so far."

"I didn't know that."

"Did you know that I grew up in a place called Gameland in northwestern Ontario? And that every morning, until I was too old for the school I went to, I had to walk five minutes to the house where the bus driver lived at the corner? And that when I moved away to Winnipeg my parents couldn't stop crying whenever I called them on the phone?"

"I didn't know."

"And that when I brought Hudson home when we first started dating, when I was twenty-two and he was twenty-six, and my dad answered the door, he looked at us and told me he wasn't going to let dykes into the house and just closed the door? And that it was already getting late, but we just turned around and drove back, not talking on the four-hour drive except to the border agents?"

"I'm sorry."

"We went back for the first time since then a few months ago, after Hudson and I got married, which we did in a little warming station on the Red. Just me, Hudson, and our friend who was marrying us. The day after we did that, I called my parents for the first time since that night and told them I was married now, to a man named Hudson. He wasn't going by Hudson when we went the last time. He named himself after that polar bear at the zoo. And when we went back, my dad didn't recognize him at all. He smiled at us and shook Hudson's hand. Then he stepped aside and let us walk through the door."

I don't know what to say. I think of Hudson, splitting logs. I think of that sinkhole, blocks away, a hole in the fabric that needs to be stitched up.

"We didn't tell them that we were the same two people, that we both knew the whole story that they refused to acknowledge had happened at all. We were there, trying to be welcomed home, after being abandoned on the other side of the door." She pulls a piece of paper from the sketch pad and wipes her face with it.

"What I mean to say, Hedwig, is that everyone's childhood home is haunted. And everyone goes back." She folds the paper and puts it in her pocket. A mobile of chipmunks with fruit-bat wings hangs above her, looking down at her, looking a little scared of something. "And it always sucks."

She smiles at me again, surveys the room. "Now let's see some more art, and hopefully the rest isn't so interested in watching us cry."

Every time you open Mother's bedroom door, you want something else to happen. You even want there to be something worse, if only for a change. But there's no escaping. Every beat is the same, precisely, every surprise is so surprisingly unsurprising. It all hits you harder because it hits you in all the same places. The sore spots. There's no way out there's no way out there's no way out, you could say, about your life. From the moment you walk into the bedroom you want nothing more than to be free, to not be forced to confront the aches of another life which, in terms of proximity, dangles far off on the sinews of yourself. But the past mishandles everybody, forces everyone's present to be tinged in its dragging of the past along with them. Life is a string of photos on a roll of negatives, not a single frame. You're a pile of your life's prints, fading in the thunder of the moodless sun.

Just before I left Germany I started a suite of photos called *Shavasana*, based on Mother. While I was in Hamburg, I thought about her more than I ever had since leaving Winnipeg, wondered at each step whether I was walking in her shadow, or casting my own ahead of her. I allowed myself to begin to wonder about Mother: what she was doing, how she coped, what she coped with. Why she did what she did.

Why.

Perhaps this was all because I was going by the name Sofia. Perhaps I had more of a distance from which to view and to judge. The experience of living a life under another name in Germany was probably also how I learned to accept Alani—as much as I have. I learned that, sometimes, I felt proud to be misunderstood. To be convoluted and conflicted felt most honest. I realized that a name is a word, not a thing, and that a thing cannot be properly named because a word cannot smile or weep or fade. But I was still a stranger, so when I looked back at Mother as Sofia, I didn't feel the same guilt, pity, or anger. I just thought about a person who had, at one time, made impressions upon me—Alani, her only kid.

Perhaps what I was feeling was respect, if not the dimness of calm love.

Shavasana was originally an attempt to mimic Mother through her obsession with yoga—with her own silence and the tightness of stasis. I was going to take images of myself attempting—poorly, though not for lack of trying—these poses, shot with very tight lighting on a dark, unreflective background, to try and isolate the figure, which I would then—ideally—double expose onto images that Mother had taken over the years. I would use that binder of her negatives that I'd stolen when I left Winnipeg—not out of preparation but out of spite. They were the negatives I was in most. I took them because I wanted her to feel their absence.

In the beginning with *Shavasana*, I wanted to have my body, and my failure to control it, mapped onto her compositions, in juxtaposition to the scenes—many of which were the B sides of family portraits, or weddings, or—sometimes—me: in the backyard or in the street with a cardboard box on my head or posing naked as Mother tried to get the lighting right. I wanted to impress my artistic vision onto hers, and show my poor attempt to imitate her.

When I came back to Minneapolis, I finished the project. Sixteen poses over sixteen of Mother's photos, ending, of course, with Shavasana —corpse pose.

A friend of mine framed the prints, and I submitted them to a gallery that accepted them after seeing only half. People came to the gallery and read the artist's statement and went through the exhibition. Some wept; many told me it was gorgeous, that it was gothically haunting. The reviews compared me to Sally Mann, who was beginning to get more attention, and to Henri Cartier-Bresson. The latter comparison, of course, had nothing to do with my work but was because of Mother's ability—much like Erwin's—to catch that decisive moment, that moment that bridged both the moment before and the moment after.

I was interviewed for magazines and the exhibition was extended. It went to Chicago and then New York, a mid-sized gallery in Manhattan where the likes of Richard Avedon had once exhibited. With the recognition I got a teaching job—despite my having never finished high school—at the University of Minnesota's fine arts program. After a year, all the prints had sold, twenty-five copies each at a very good price. With the money, I bought my house across the street from Genny's and invested in a bigger, better studio for the collective, with an attached gallery for our exhibitions.

Eventually, I stopped. I started denying interviews and secluding myself, because I'd begun to feel an intense shame, the kind of shame that only an artist can feel when they believe they've succeeded while misrepresenting something that, albeit invisible to others, makes them feel like they violently obscured a kind of personal, intrinsic truth.

The project, as most are, was a failure. In Germany, *Shavasana* was a project of ideals, of optimism, and perhaps even of wish fulfillment. It was naive. But in the end, the images seemed to blur over the complications between myself and Mother. There was a sentimentality to them, which I had intended but wasn't true to our relationship. But worse, I had put my images over the bare shots of Mother's negatives, whereas she was an obsessive revisionist in the darkroom. She never let a print get past her without some sort of modification, however small, but here I'd shown her direct, unfiltered vision, which was, in fact, not her vision at all. I don't think she ever believed in the truth of the thing being as it seems, and by showing the raw image—because I could not modify as she had—I showed the false one that she would have formed into a kind of truth. I'd completely, utterly, painfully rejected and demolished every aesthetic vision that Mother had in her work.

So I sold off the remaining reprints to buyers as far away as I could find and donated my negatives to the University of Minnesota. I mailed Mother's negatives back to her, with a letter. I didn't tell her about the exhibition, didn't tell her about the money I'd made stealing her work. I just said I was sorry I'd taken them, and she should have them back.

The return address on the envelope was her own.

Helena wraps her arm around mine and we walk into the next room in the gallery, dedicated to Logan's work, which feels like walking into a traumatized vision. Along all the walls are huge paintings in an abstract expressionist style. The paintings are slaps and splashes, the painter's gestures swiftly mapped onto canvas, but the canvases are deeply busted, slashed, broken apart, and stitched back together crudely with thick gut, wire, and nails. Some are in such bad shape that I can't make sense of the paint for all the seams.

"I took a class with her once," Helena says, as we wash up in front of one of the huge paintings. "She builds these canvases in her house, which she uses as her studio, and if she has to show them somewhere, she has to cut them into pieces so that she can take them out the door. Every time a painting is in a show, she cuts it apart and puts it back together. Some of them have been taken apart so many times," she says, pointing to a painting that seems to be almost nothing but seams, "that you can't even tell what it's supposed to be anymore. It's all worn out."

We walk around and eventually find ourselves in one last, small room. In the middle is a small painting, busted to pieces, with a small hatchet tethered to a table nearby. A girl in a vest waves to us and comes over with a clipboard. On the placard screwed to the table is nothing but the title: *Unfinished Portrait of an Unfinished Portrait of a Dead Girl (Finish It).*

The girl shows us the clipboard. "If you'd like to contribute to the piece," she says, lifting the hatchet from the table and wiggling it in the air, "you just have to sign this little waiver."

"Shall I?" I ask Helena, at my arm.

"Absolutely," she says, taking Mother's camera from around my neck. I feel a sudden shift in the weight of the world and think of Genny. I miss her.

I sign the waiver with Mother's name, pick up the hatchet, and look down at the mess and then over at the girl, who nods to me. Helena stands beside her, eyes a little puffy, smiling.

I kneel down to the wreckage and raise the hatchet and start chopping at it, wood splintering off, canvas tearing. I wonder what the portrait looked like before it got destroyed. I think of the painting of the missing girl on the poster, the girl who may never have been photographed in her life, and then I stop thinking about that because I'm chopping at it, at the portrait that does not look like a portrait, that doesn't seem like it ever looked like a portrait, that never could have, but how can I tell? I chop, thinking of dead girls. And the dead boy in the Red. And Helena getting married on it. And Mother and me walking along and atop it. And Mother now existing farther north but still near it.

Finally, I stop, stand, put the hatchet back on the table, and look down at the mess I've contributed to. I can't really tell what I've added or taken away—it still looks about the same—but I can feel the hitting take residence in the muscles of my arm. I can feel it setting into a real ache in my flesh.

Then I realize there is a line behind me, that I might have been at this for far too long.

"There's no fixing that," I tell the girl with the clipboard, as I massage my arm and join Helena, who puts her ringed hand on my aching shoulder—the truest medium.

The girl with the clipboard smiles at me as we go. "There never was."

I look at her until we're through the door. My mind is a clean slate.

Two months before I left Germany, I called Genny. She'd moved since then, so I didn't have her number or her address, but eventually I got to her through the University of Minnesota, where she'd been working before I left. I kept asking for her—Genny Ford—and people kept sending me to other people in different departments they thought might know her. At the end of it, I paid the Eggers's phone bill for that month because it became an excessive list of long-distance charges.

Finally, there was someone who knew Genny, who said that she could give Genny my number, who said she didn't feel comfortable giving hers to me. She hadn't heard of anyone named Alani from her conversations with Genny. That hurt, and I luxuriated in that hurt. I gave her Erwin's number, explaining that I was in Germany, explaining country codes and international dialling.

Then I sat by the phone for three days straight. I hardly ate. I dragged the phone from the hall into my room sometimes. Sometimes I'd sit with my back to the door, the phone cable snaking under, quietly crying. I answered all the calls, because I didn't want the Eggers to get to Genny first, not merely because I'd become so desperate for her—because I had suddenly and once again hinged myself on her—but also because I knew she was going to ask for Alani, and that wasn't who I was. I had been Sofia for so long that I didn't think I could come clean about it—Sofia would be who I remained to them.

It went on like that for those three days until I thought I couldn't handle it anymore. Then, when I was about to give in and give up, and felt myself open up to actions I didn't want to fathom, Genny called, around three a.m.—eight p.m. for her. The phone barely had the chance to ring.

For the entirety of that call, I covered my eyes with my free hand in the pitch-black dark—to isolate the senses, maybe, or because I didn't believe that we were talking, not after so long. Her voice tremored into my ear, unlocking doors, closing windows. The many stagnant pieces of me began to move again like tectonics. I reactivated.

"When are you coming home?" she asked.

At that moment, and for the first time in the longest time, I realized that she was right: Germany was not home. Germany was a ghost whose back I'd climbed. Germany was shadows, a crowd of foggy idealisms. I realized that if I stayed, it would get too easy to live there and become Sofia.

I knew I had to go back.

I told her, "Soon." I told her I'd call her. I told her not to call me, and if she did—ask for Sofia. "Long story," I said, tears streaming down my face because I knew that I would tell it to her.

For that first call, we pretended that nothing had happened. We pretended that I'd never found her letter, that I'd never used it as reason to run away, without telling anyone where I was going. We ignored the terrible things I'd called her when I found out. I just told her how hard my depression was back, how it was disconnecting me from myself, how I was again feeling as I'd once felt, how recklessness was going to take over, the kind of recklessness that's so hard to survive. I just told her that, above all else, I fucking missed her.

"Don't worry, Al," she said then.

I couldn't breathe, and I lifted the hand away from my face enough to let the wave of tears I'd been cupping make their way down. I told Genny I'd call her again, the following day, at a more humane hour.

She laughed and said, "Okay."

After we hung up, I sat there for a little while, the phone on my lap, my eyes and my mind drying out, and I just stopped worrying.

After dropping Helena off at her house, after hugging her in the middle of her street for what felt like a long while, I thought about going to the sinkhole. But I drove past it, around it, and came back here: the home.

I get out of the car, then go back for my phone, where I left it while Helena and I were in the gallery. There are four missed calls. They are from the home, so I don't shut the door of the car, don't let the waiting room slow me down, and crash into the front desk.

The nurse jumps in her scrubs and puts her hands up, recognizing me. "Don't worry," she says. "Your mom is fine. The doctor is with her."

"What happened?"

"She fell from her bed an hour or so ago and hit her head." She is standing up behind the desk, her warm hand on mine. "We think she probably figured out the buckle and wanted to get back to the chair. We found her on the floor, crawling toward it. We tried to call," she says.

"I know," I say. "Is she okay?"

"She's fine, just has a cut above her eye, on the brow. The doctor is just giving her a few stitches."

"I'm her son. Can't I see her?" I say.

She stands back and puts her hands on the desk and looks down the hall. This place is more hospital than home. "Of course you can see her."

I follow her as she walks calmly down the hall to a little room that does not seem to want to deceive anyone into thinking it is not a hospital room. The doctor has his back to us, standing over Mother sitting up on the bed. All I can see are her hands beside her.

The nurse taps the doctor's shoulder. "Her son is here," she says, gesturing to me with a sympathetic smile.

He looks over his shoulder and is confused for a second, and I hate him, and also float in the brief pleasure of feeling so confusing.

"Good afternoon," he says, turning back to Mother. "Just finishing up."

The nurse tells me to let her know if I need anything and leaves. I look over the doctor's shoulder at Mother as he is cutting off the end of the stitches he has done on her right brow.

"Just going to clean her off and put a bandage on this and she should be good," he says.

Her face is covered in smears of dark blood, the tips of her short white hair rusted up with it, and she is staring through the doctor's chest. She seems unfazed. The doctor gets an antiseptic wipe and starts to clean her face. I sit in a chair by the bed and take her hand in both of mine. I don't say anything to her.

Mother's hand moves around in mine, but she doesn't look at me.

The doctor puts a bandage on Mother's face, says something about how there's little chance she's gotten a concussion considering the placement of the hurt, but they will keep an eye on her.

I almost want to say, "So you can watch her fall next time?" but my mouth is too dry.

Finally, he leaves and the nurse comes back with a wheelchair. I help the nurse lower Mother into the wheelchair, even though she weighs nothing and the nurse is strong. I push her back to her room, following the nurse in her slow, salmon scrubs.

Mother's room smells intensely of cleaning products. The green curtains are closed, casting a grassy light across the tiles. There is a new belt across the bed.

The nurse picks Mother up from the chair and puts her back into the bed, pulls the covers up to her chest, locks the belt with a key, and leaves.

I sit down on the edge of the bed and hold Mother's scarred hands. I run my fingers along them and can't tell which parts are scars and which are wrinkles. Which come from pain and which come from time, as if there is a difference, as if one isn't the other, just stretched out more.

"Why did you do it?" I ask. "Why did I do it?"

She looks at me, holds her eyes on me. Her camera is still around my neck, I realize, and I put it back in her hands. She looks down at it and then puts her fingers on the shutter button, and when it makes its tiny sound, she flinches.

I take the camera back. I put my hands on her face, swollen a little from the fall, and look her in the eyes. She returns the look, but I know that she doesn't know who I am, that nobody really knows anyone because we spend so much goddamned time trying to figure ourselves out. That if she knows anything about me at all, she'll know less tomorrow. And the next day. And so on.

I kiss her on the forehead, far from her new bandaged wound, put her camera around my neck, and go. I don't look up, but I can feel that some part of the sky is pocked by a dark sun.

When I was younger than the boy they found in the river—maybe ten years old—Mother and I took a long walk down the clear path on the Red. It was the tail end of winter and the ice was thick. Mother had let the pinned legs of my snow pants down twice already. I remember coming down for breakfast and finding her winding a scarf around her neck—overtop the old Leica—and looking up at me.

"Come, kid, get your clothes on. You're old now."

She smiled, then. Smiled so hard.

It was March, my birthday. Yes, I was turning ten and it was a weekday, but she didn't take me to school. She helped tie my scarf and tightened my boots and took me out, for pancakes first, and then to the river.

I don't remember much of what we talked about that day, because so little sound between us remains, but I remember being near Mother. I remember laughing and pointing and huddling together to warm up. I remember feeling special, feeling happy that I did not have to go to school, where I felt so different. I remember walking through snow to our knees to get down to the cleared path on the thick ice of the Assiniboine, heading toward the Red. It was windy, but I trusted the rivers then. We walked all the way to the Forks, bought foot-long hot dogs and hot chocolates at the market.

"Where next, Alani?" Mother asked, and I pointed north, toward the bridge that someone would find a body pinned to thirty-four years later, the bridge that so many other bodies have probably passed under, unnoticed. A river hitting a brick wall, a sequence of photos unfinished because no more film remained on the roll.

Mother took three photos of me that day. The first was of me standing on the house's snowy stoop, bundled up beyond recognition. The second was of me sitting in the market, coat open, toque-less and toque-haired, with the hot dog buried in relish. Smiling, at her.

The third photo she took of me was under that railway bridge, with a train trundling along overhead. I was standing with my arms up. She captured the train right as its CN-marked engine was nearly overtop of me, creating a wonderful visual tension—on a different plane of existence, it would have hit me.

I remember her taking that last photo. I remember taking off my gloves and using Mother's light meter to get a reading for her, even though I don't think she needed it. I remember Mother hearing the train and looking over at it coming, pushing soft at my shoulder and telling me, "Hurry!" as I sprinted down the half-cleared path to the bridge. I remember the sound of the train when I turned and raised my arms. I remember seeing her, sixty feet away, looking through the camera, her knees clamped together to hold her mittens between her thighs.

All the while, the water moved deep under the ice.

That day on the river with Mother, I realized exactly what it meant to love her. We stopped under every bridge we passed to huddle together for warmth away from the wind. The same bridges I would wander under years later with Genny, who would be obsessed with them in the same way that I would be obsessed with her. There was something about bridges that would hold Genny's attention, draw her eye into circles that on every rotation still marvelled, trying to figure out exactly why. For most of my life, I've been trying to do this with

Genny, with Mother, with myself: figure out what exactly fascinates me. I haven't figured it out, but I keep trying.

That day with Mother, that good day—whose contrast created our worst days together, my worst days alone, days filled with personal and impersonal tragedies—seemed to have the brightest sun. The few photos Mother took that day showed otherwise. I can tell the amount of ambient light from the depth of field of those images, under those bridges, on that ice path, that ice path where we shared a mitten because we wanted to hold hands without freezing, where she took the photo of the man who called, "Passing on your left!" while he speed-walked past. In the photo, he seems to be sauntering into the future—a procession of blurring, dark-swaddled bodies. But in my head, that day was brilliant.

This incongruence of our memory of light has something to do with the amount we can hold our eyes open, I think. When we are young, dumb, energetic, naive—before our minds start to inseminate our pain with some invented narrative—we can keep them open wider, less sensitive to sucking in more light at once. But as we age, and break down, and fix up, and stop reading books in school and start reading stories in newspapers—about murders, about suicides, about international atrocities, about how big the world really is but how tiny gestures of either violence or kindness can still shake it—we start to squint. The darkening is us, stacking up dense filter upon dense filter, trying to keep what's bad out and hold what good we still have in, in. We start to see the world go to shade, lose its saturation, vignette our lives into a tunnel.

That day in my memory is brilliant, and from there the dimming started.

I don't want to remember that day on the river with Mother anymore. I can't handle it, how it insinuates that if nothing had changed, if that day was exposed onto every one of our other days, we would have had a perfect, perfect life. Mother would have smiled. I would have run toward her. I would not have put a pry bar to a window and demolished a house, a life.

On the way back to Mother's house, I take a detour to the sinkhole, barricaded by pylons and tape, an oblong darkness inset into the pavement. I look down into its maw, and it looks straight down into me.

At the bottom of the sinkhole: all that I really know about Mother.

11

MOTHER'S STUDIO

After you've disappeared from the doorway of Mother's bedroom, you find yourself in the doorway of Mother's studio, where there's nothing but a cardboard box. The ash is not on the studio's ceilings and walls in the memory palace. There is no smell. Once the door is closed behind you, you open the box and look inside. You pull out an empty cardboard box, followed by another—more and more until the whole room is filled with them. Once, these boxes held wine or bourbon or gin. You can't get to the bottom of them. Every time you make it into the studio, you try and try and try and try to get to the bottom of them, and you never do. You just try. You look inside each of them to try and find the things Mother put inside them, the things Mother now and again transferred from them into brand-new boxes, but all you find is more and more corrugated lack.

When you're in the studio, gutting the box of all the other boxes, trying to reach the bottom, you do not remember the fire. You were not here for the fire. If the fire were allowed into the palace, perhaps all the missing pieces would make sense. The full box that slipped away. The last straw that led Mother into the home, into being locked down for her own safety. Into receding from being at all.

The room is nothing but the boxes, and you swim desperately through them, abandoning the first box and looking inside the rest, knocking on each like the empty skulls they are. On and on. The room is dead quiet. The boxes do not relinquish any sound when you move among them. You can only hear yourself breathing.

You want out, and eventually, just as you think you'll never find the door, there you are, outside the studio. You breathe. You breathe again, even though the air doesn't help.

There is only one room left: your bedroom. All the other pathways have disappeared, and it is just you and the door.

At this point, you always feel flammable. You take a step.

I wake up in my little bed, in my old bedroom, with Mother's camera still around my neck, strangling me. At the other side of the room, on top of the creaky loft bed, is the cat. They are staring at me. I can hear the rest of the house storming with the grey, the grey with its many faces.

I slowly climb up to where the cat is sitting, looking at me, clawlessly pawing at the stiff foam mattress crumbling under the fabric.

The bed feels like it's going to collapse. But it always has.

The cat comes to me. They rub their head along my bare hip.

I look through the vent, into Mother's studio, and feel a gust of wind and ash blow through me, into me. I remember the smell of air moving, and Mother is there again, young, in the middle of the room. I don't move, not wanting the bed's creaking to give me away, to break her meditation.

She is breathing in and out, bending her body into shapes my bones have never been able to comprehend, despite the months of classes I've taken. She is nude to her undergarments, sweating. Sweating so hard, because just a few feet from her—pushed up against the wall—is a cardboard box filled with fire.

The wall is burning, and there she is—in the middle of the room— twisting. I can smell the smoke as it vibrates in the walls of the house. I can feel its eyes as sound, no longer afraid of the camera, since once again it is emptied of its film. Mother continues folding and unfolding herself, like an anxious jackknife, trying to pick out its tool. Eventually, her body chooses to become nothing. Lies in the middle of the room. Shavasana. Only she's not breathing and the cat is pawing at my leg with no claws and she's still not breathing.

I remember all her photos that I stole onto which I exposed my own body—trying to be hers. It still didn't help me find peace in my body.

I can't move. The fire doesn't spread, but it seems to get brighter and brighter. Flecks of burnt paper flutter through the sky like snow, begin to vortex around Mother's body in the middle of the floor until the body gets up, still not breathing, and goes toward the fire. I am watching as Mother slowly places her hands inside the box and pulls out the fire. I watch her hold it in her hands, watch them scarring over. As she holds the fire, the vortex of ash and smoke increases the room's opacity, and I watch her body fade, grow old, watch her beautiful long hair go white and suck up short into her head.

Then I watch her put the fire back into the box, almost tenderly, stand up, take a step, and fold herself slowly into the flames. As she disappears into the fire, one of the boards of the loft bed snaps under me, and I fall flat to the mattress. Flat in fear. As I look to see if the bed is falling, I watch the cat sprint through the door and down the stairs. But the bed stays up.

I turn over onto my back. Bright light shoots through the vent onto the ceiling of my room. Then the world darkens a bit.

On the ceiling, in a widening circle: the burnt sun is blooming.

Everything. Everything must go.

It's warm, and I sit on the stoop flicking away email notifications on my phone: from Ess about revisions for hir thesis essay, from other students asking me for advice on putting together their portfolios. The house is closed up behind me, and the painters are coming by today, and Hudson is coming over, too. Because I called and asked him to help me dismantle the darkroom.

—*I'll be there in 20, H*, Hudson sent, twenty-six minutes ago. Either signing off or addressing me: Hedwig.

I'm starting to think he's not going to show up, but of course, just as I think that, there's a little flat-nosed Toyota truck pulling into an open space a few houses down. The passenger side opens and Hudson steps out, in open flannel over a black T, jeans, and steel-toed boots. He waves to me as he grabs a rusty tool box from the truck bed. I wave back.

I get up and go toward him, try to ignore the eyes of the house following me. The tendrils trying to yank me back in. As I reach the truck, I can see he is alone, and the truck is right-hand drive.

"Didn't know what I'd need," Hudson says, smiling, then putting a hand out to shake, because he's a stranger still, isn't he? "That sundress looks great. Been a while since I've seen a sundress." He gestures to the sky, as if that sky were not steadily darkening from a black, widening aperture.

"Thank you," I say, and we walk to the house.

I want to tell him that the house is on fire. We walk in and I want to ask him if he can smell the fire, if he can hear the house wriggling in its skin.

"You can leave your boots on, of course," I say, and direct him straight down the hall to the red-headed darkroom. He goes and starts inspecting all the ways the counters have been attached to the walls.

"I just want to get these removed so that it can get painted this afternoon. I'm also hoping we can get that toilet up and running again."

"Easy," he says, putting down the tools and looking up at the red light hot in the sky. "And maybe a new light?"

"That's an idea," I say, remembering the shadow birthing from that room and dragging itself to me. Sinking its teeth into my shoulder, which is still sore from the hatcheting at the gallery.

I leave Hudson to work, go upstairs to my bedroom, get out one more roll of film, snip its lead to size, and spool it into Mother's camera. I put it around my neck again; there's no getting away from it.

Shadows of the Prison House.

Light is spilling into the window and I walk over and look through it. I think of Mother burning in the next room. I think of taking every single thing from the house and taking photos of the places they leave behind—their shadows but without the shapes to cast them. I want to rub it in, to prove the place I knew is gone, even though it isn't. To trick myself into thinking that even our shadows have left the building.

A gentle knock pulls me back, and Hudson is there. Behind him, the cat is crawling up the stairs and looking at me, scared.

"Sorry to startle you. The painters are here. I let them in. They're waiting in the kitchen. Bathroom is all fixed up, too."

"Already?" I say, walking past him. He follows; the cat is gone again.

"It doesn't take long to unscrew a few things from the walls."

I turn down the hall and see the darkroom open, its landscapes reshaped. The red light is off.

"And the toilet?" I ask, standing there, paralyzed.

"Seems to work just fine," Hudson says, walking past me into the room and flushing it. "Just had to turn on the water."

I try not to panic at the idea of the dark rallying around him, possessing him and trapping him here forever. As he walks out, I reach into the darkroom, turn the red light back on, and close the door.

I make my way to the kitchen. The two painters have stepladders, paint cans, and paint-speckled white shirts.

"Hi," I say. "Thanks for coming."

I hold on to Mother's camera and feel the house getting furious.

When I came back to Minneapolis from Hamburg, I stayed with Karen. She'd finally gotten a place to herself—a tiny place with the most finicky radiator in the city, but her own place. She was finally doing okay. She was still working at the café, but she'd gotten a small local grant for her performance art, which broadened her network in the art world, which also increased her ability to sell drugs—mostly pot and elementary hallucinogens, but she could get you anything you wanted. While I'd been away, she helped Genny get heroin for a dying friend.

I felt the lack of Darius in my life when I got off the plane and met Genny by the baggage carousel. I didn't even have a checked bag to grab, but we held each other while it spun, slowly spitting out the things other people brought from one side of an ocean to the other.

I didn't move in with Genny, despite the fact that with Darius gone there was nothing keeping me from living with her and her dog,

Hamm. Instead, I worked on *Shavasana* while crashing on Karen's couch, and eventually, I moved in with Archer, who'd just had top surgery and needed some help with paying rent and living life while they recovered. I sat on the side of the bed, made them food, brought them their guitar, listened to them pluck out a new sonata in chaos with the instrument nestled at a weird distance so as to not hit the stitches. We shared Archer's double bed and I wandered around the apartment feeling oddly electric in their presence. I was in the room when the bandages came off, and we stared at the beautiful coils of the swollen, stitched scars, which I've always wanted, and not wanted, my body not agreeing with itself long enough to commit to any permanent modifications. I considered getting scars like Archer's tattooed under the overhang of my breasts, so that I might be able to cup them in the mirror and believe them gone when I needed to. But whenever I walk by a tattoo parlor and think of it, I fear that it could throw me into a new imbalance, and imbalances like that have historically led to me disappearing.

Once *Shavasana* was done and Archer was working again, I bought my tiny house kitty-corner to Genny's. My excuse for not moving in with her was that she didn't have enough room for me and a darkroom, that it was my dream to live with one.

A soft truth with a sharp lie in the middle.

I didn't tell her that I also felt obligated to cloister myself from the intimacy of living a life with her, the happiness and the comfort that could allow. I felt an obligation to be alone in a house with a darkroom and my thoughts, thoughts of Mother and all my other darknesses. The pain Genny had inflicted on me and the pain I had inflicted on her. On Mother. On Tom. I felt that she would not make room for my demons in her house, so we kept dating, spending all our excess time together but living separately, albeit only across the street. I felt like I owed it to the world to be miserable, and I wanted to feel pain every morning, wanted pain to absolve me of all my guilt. A wound that must forever stay open.

The street between our houses felt like a river bisecting my life. I've always felt like I have to cross so much turbulence to reach anyone.

After coming back from Hamburg without Darius, life in Minneapolis felt simpler than it had been, less strict. I could leave home for days or weeks and nobody would tear my house to pieces while I was gone—in Brooklyn or Chicago, or wherever it was I was dragged to for this conference or that talk or the workshops and residencies and shoots on location. The house would be fine, alive, still watching Genny's across the street. Nothing was pissed on or torn apart. There was just a little dust, a few dead bugs to vacuum away—a few little reminders of how time was coagulating.

When I came back to the house, I felt like it had missed me, instead of resenting me for leaving.

Without Darius, though, I sat around quiet. I could no longer pretend that someone could hear me, so I stopped chatting with myself. Some nights I sat in the living room and looked out across the street to Genny's house. Some nights I ran over desperately and knocked on the door and spent the night. Sometimes I invited Archer or Karen to stay with me, after fetching a few bottles of booze. And some nights I was carried up alone to my darkroom—which I'd made in the bathroom on the second floor—and got locked in with all my demons. Transported, strangled.

I used my darkroom to teleport to Mother's house, long before it had become my memory palace. I would feel myself sitting beside her on the couch, looking out the wide front window and waiting, as the demons—both our demons—took up their siege engines to remove the front door. We were quiet. We didn't look at one another. Eventually, I felt their hands on me, trying to drown me in the riverine gaps, as they finally broke into the house. They billowed. They bared the shadows of their teeth.

After Mother was diagnosed and her house finally became the memory palace, all the demons trying to reach me wore the many faces of myself.

After Hudson leaves, waving, with the wood he'd reclaimed from the darkroom stacked in the back of his little Toyota, I leave the painters to their work and go back upstairs to find the cat. I can see their paw slipping under the closed bathroom door, and I kneel and hold on to their paw for a moment. They don't pull away, until they do, and I open the door and slip inside. I sit down in the tub and call to them, and they come to me and we sit like that, while the painters bury the old walls downstairs. In the tub, grasping the stone-grey cat, I feel like we're hiding from a shooter, or a tornado. The house makes its noises. Mother's camera is still around my neck.

The cat jumps out of my hands and stands on the edge of the tub before falling out of view. I look around at everything in the bathroom and imagine a crowd of people coming to carry it all away. I imagine myself picking up every single thing in the house and putting it somewhere else.

In the tub, I think about all the things that are in the house, all the things I could move, all the things I could document.

Shadows of the Prison House; or, These Photos Are Too Late.

I start to list the things off in my head, trying to come up with enough frames to fill the last roll of film: the phone, the couches, the loft bed, the mailbox, the armoire.

The studio's scar.

The cat somehow loses themselves in the bathroom. We are very similar, us two—we can be locked in a closet with a mirror and still lose sight of ourselves. I lie back in the dry tub and close my eyes. I think of the house emptying out, imagine myself picking it up and turning it over and knocking it empty like a glass bottle of ketchup. I imagine myself leaving it bare, removing everything that the house could ever possess and persist through. Everything.

I imagine folding myself into a box and being mailed back to Genny. Imagine scrawling on the outside of the box: *FLAMMABLE*.

With my eyes closed, I end up slipping into the palace, and there's the cat, at the door of the darkroom. I cut my feet on the memory on the landing and walk down the hallway and it takes so, so, so long. By the time I reach them, the cat is so old, but they are reaching their little clawless paw under the door again. I put my hand on the knob and the darkroom—which never opens in the palace—opens.

So much comes out, so many shadowed bodies walk past me and push me and crawl around me. They are palpable darknesses. The cat goes into the room and turns around and looks at me, through so many dark limbs, as if they are asking why I haven't made it into the room yet. And so I do. I swim through the bodies and make it into the darkroom.

I turn on the light and, as the dark figures are annihilated, they are replaced with wind. Throughout the house the doors in their jambs start to shake and knock, and I am pushed into the darkroom with the cat, and I look down the hall and there she is—Mother—walking down the hallway toward the darkroom, aging a decade with every step, until she falls. Until her hands scar over with the fire. She crawls the rest of the way, toward the door. Her face is bleeding. Then she loses her face and she is just a surface with blood streaming down. Her details simplify, abstract, until she is just a suggestion of a face with a brushstroke of blood set into a rectangle, a frame of 35 mm film slowly fading clear. It reaches the door and the door slams and I come out of the palace coughing.

The house is quiet. The cat is sitting on the windowsill, looking down at me in the bathtub as I pull myself back.

The cat stays perched on the windowsill by the sink, staring out at the weak sky. I go downstairs. The smell of the house is different. The darkroom door is open, the light is off again, the back door in the kitchen is propped open, and the two bodies of the painters are looking around, pulling tape off the cabinets and the walls.

I stand among them, hands on the hips of the dress I found hanging in the armoire, looking around the walls of the kitchen like it's a gallery filled with pieces of art instead of just a newly skinned room.

Moonstone.

I remember walking to the liquor store just across Portage, on Burnell, with Mother when I was little, my hand burrowed in hers while we crossed the busy streets. First, she'd pick out a bottle of wine, always red. We'd walk through them all, quiet, until she found what she wanted. Once she had the bottle, she would grab a free, empty liquor box to carry home. Sometimes she'd carry it, but usually she gave it to me. I would drag it by the handle across the linoleum floors and stand behind her at the till while she paid.

As soon as we got outside I'd wear the box on my head, looking out through the hole for a handle on our walk home, hands clasping both the cardboard and her hand. As I got older, when I was still going with her, I grew more embarrassed, so I walked beside her, or a little behind, box under my arm, wondering why we didn't just take the car, wondering why the previous box wasn't good enough for her anymore. What was the point of keeping all those things, anyway?

But I never asked her anything about it, and she never told me.

When we got home, Mother would always go into the kitchen, open the wine, and carry the empty box up to her studio. She would sit on the yoga mat in the middle of the room and move things from the old box to the new one. She did this with the door closed, so I'd climb up to the loft bed and watch her through the vent.

I knew the ricketiness of the bed by heart. I knew how to climb it in a way that it made the least amount of noise. In my head, when I see Mother in the studio, there is always the knowledge that if I budge, my invisibility will be lost and our intimacy—which has almost always taken the form of surveillance—will shatter.

Through the vent I'd watch as she'd take each piece from the box, read along in quiet wisps, then place it in the new box, and drink. Mother didn't drink very often, not even when she was in a deeply depressive episode, but she always drank then. Whatever was at the top of one box would end up on the bottom of the other, such that she'd reacquaint herself each time with the contents—photos and documents—back to front. It was always the same. She did it slowly— as if she could only handle reliving it all at a certain speed without breaking.

Every time, I'd watch Mother take the empty box to the remains of the old coal barbecue near the corner of the fence, left over from the last owner. She'd put the old box in and burn it. By then it was always night. We were far enough downtown that the stars were invisible because of the city's upstretched radiance, but from that brief fire, smoke would billow up, obscuring the space between us, which had always been uncertain, bound only by blood and a sideways, ever-unspoken kind of love, wherein we both knew that we would never comprehend each other fully: Mother would never understand how I could swing between myself and myself and never get to firm ground, how there were so many dysphoric, duplicitous facets of myself that could never be fully known, even by me. And I would never understand whatever it was that she was—*is*.

After that last fire, after Mother was taken to the Misery—the closest hospital—with second- and third-degree burns, any paper that was left untouched was annihilated when Dorothea threw a soaked towel from the bathroom onto the box. Dorothea told me that while Mother was moaning at her hands in the hall, she stood in the middle of the studio, lancing the last cinders of the fire on the wall with the mop she had been using to clean the kitchen floor.

The ink of the pages ran. Dorothea, naturally, threw the box away.

After I show the painters the studio they're going to repaper, after they wow at the ashy burn that splits the room like a widening grin, after they leave and I close the front door behind them, I turn on the red light in the darkroom—it is a bathroom, now—and start to take the photographs.

I start in the living room, with the phone, which I unplug and set aside, so that all that is left on the tiny phone table is the untethered cable, a little lamp, and the list of emergency numbers. I turn the chair so that someone could be sitting at the table and frame up the shot, and as I do I realize I didn't bring a tripod, or the Leica's self-timer. And then I remember that this photo doesn't have any reason to have me in it. That it was never supposed to.

So I put my finger on the shutter, and so I push it down, and so the shot is made in one-thirtieth of a second. And that's it.

1. The Phone

I don't put the phone back. Instead, I put Mother's camera on the table and take the bulb from the lamp and drag the chair to the darkroom and open the door. I slip the sundress over my head and climb up the chair and use the dress to protect my hand from the heat of the bulb. I unscrew it as fast as I can and screw in the bulb from the lamp, and suddenly the room is lit up in incandescent yellow. I climb down, nearly naked, with a hot bulb cradled like an egg in the dress in my hand. I go and screw the red safety light into the lamp.

I leave the dress off, go to the bright darkroom-bathroom, pull out the chair, and take a photo of the room.

2. The Darkroom

Suddenly, my head is filled with newspapers, Mother's hands running along them. So once I've put the dress back on, I use my phone to see if there's an archive of the paper she worked with online. I can feel the house closing in on me a little—coming after my edges—and look up to see the grey faces floating around in the corners of the room, watching me. I try to ignore them, look back to the phone, which is telling me that the archives for the dates I want are not available online, but there are archives downtown. I open Google and it tells me that the 10 bus will take me right there.

I pick up Mother's camera and go upstairs for my wallet, my purse—where I put the list of all the things in the house, as well as my previously soaked transit tickets. The faces pop up throughout the house as I do, drag alongside me like bones against sandpaper, watching me, looking so much like me. But I don't let them slow me down, even though, yes, I'm afraid of them.

They know too much.

I walk across the street from the bus stop and into the Manitoba Archives Building. I head to the guard at the table to sign in, tell them I'm here to look into some personal history.

"My mother used to work for the paper," I say, writing down my own name, looking down at Mother's camera around my neck. "She was a photographer."

The guard hands me a sticker to wear. "That's interesting. We close up in forty minutes, you know?"

"Of course," I say, and head straight for the desk and ask the archivist if they can help me search the newspaper's database, from around 1980 to 1984, the years when Mother did the most work for them, when I was still here.

The archives are empty but for us, it seems, and an old man hunched over a microfiche machine. The archivist takes me to a computer that might have been brand-new five years ago, logs me in to the database on a browser, and shows me the search.

"Here's how you can look up by date, and the text of the papers should mostly be searchable," the archivist says, pointing.

"Thank you," my voice says, and as they leave, my fingers go mad with typing: her name first, and I find nothing, of course. Because she didn't get credit for most of the shots she took; that wasn't how things worked.

So the words that come out of my hands are "Assiniboia Downs," because that's the only newspaper job I remember going with her.

Pages with horses come up, pages of jockeys looking down and a horse running a nose ahead of a few others, bodies of beast and jockey trapped eternal in the motion of a few hundredths of a second. I realize as I flip through horse picture after horse picture, through sports sections from so many decades ago, that there's no telling them apart. I don't know which could even be hers.

But then there is a photo of a jockey on a horse, wreathed, the owner holding its reins, while the jockey looks candid down at a little kid at the horse's side, a kid who is feeling the wet, shivering flesh of the horse's hip and looking directly into the camera. Their hair is short, their body in an overlong shirt. Happy.

Me.

I hit print, bring it to the archivist, and ask if there's a way to get a better version. The archivist helps me figure out how to download it as a pdf. I thank them and log in to my email, ignore all my unread messages, and email the pdf to myself. I check the time and, with the twelve minutes I've got left, go back to scrounging, page after page, year after year.

1982. 1983. 1984.

And then it's there—a small story squashed beside an almost full-page ad for a spring sale at Eaton's department store, the headline, the words I searched for highlighted:

Psychotic Woman Stopped as She Tries to Climb Fence at the Assiniboia Downs, Stops Races for Half Hour.

There is no picture, just a few short columns, which I start to read and then stop. I don't need to know any more about that. I know everything that matters. I was there for all the parts that did.

I mash the back button on the browser before I can change my mind, mash it until I'm at the home page, until it can't go back any further. I sit here, eyes closed, shaking a little and wanting not to be here. So I go to the memory palace, but I just stand outside and don't open the door. I decide to turn and give my back to the palace. I sit on the stoop and look down at my hands, and all that's there is the photo, of me and the horse that won the race. *Yesterday*—that's what the caption says is the horse's name.

Someone taps my shoulder.

"We're closing," the archivist says, ages away, it seems.

And then I am out the door and at the bus stop. And I can barely see to fish out another ticket to slip into the slot on the bus.

"Hello again," the driver says. And I zoom back into my body. "Did you try the microwave?" It's the same route.

"Of course," I lie. "The tickets only barely lit on fire."

"That's what I like to hear," he says, smiling.

The door closes behind me.

I didn't leave Germany as soon as I first started talking to Genny again because I wanted to help Erwin finish his project.

The middle of the days—as well as the entirety of our cloudy days—were little use for shooting, because of either the lack of light or the uninviting harshness of the shadows, so during those days and hours we took to separate darkrooms. During a block of rainy days, I got around to finally printing some old shots from rolls the girl who runs had brought with us from Minneapolis. Before talking to Genny, I'd refused to look at them, out of fear of deciding to destroy them.

Whenever I look back at these photos, photos of moments I remember so vividly, I find them bizarrely more comforting in their negative state. One is of Genny sitting on the hood of her car in the suburb of Minneapolis where we broke down, mercifully, at the end of our drive down from Winnipeg. Genny is doused in film grain and fatigue, leaning against the negative-black hood of the white car, the bright grass of the lawns a grey smudge across the frame. In another, of me and Genny in front of *Spoonbridge and Cherry* in the sculpture garden—shot in colour—the negative of the cherry on the end of the spoon is a strange blue orb looming in the bright orange sky above our heads. Then there's a photo of Genny and me, taken from a tripod, probably at her place, which was taken a week or two before I found the letter and ran away to Germany. In the negative of that photo we are sitting naked on the bed, bound up in each other, wrapped up in brilliant dark bodies, clutching each other in the folded bright. My back is to the camera, my face in Genny's neck, but she is looking straight into the lens, her pupils burning like little suns, one grey nipple peeking out from around the side of my binder and a cable-release in her hand to fire the shutter. Each of those shots in the negative feels so honest, while others look so lifeless until their print comes out of the bath.

I sometimes wonder if Erwin was ever comforted by photographs, either printed or in their negative. During those last weeks, I got the sense that he was deep in a well of remembering. The photos in his series were harshly felt, and sometimes he was so overwhelmed that we had to take breaks. It would be anywhere from ten minutes to an hour before he'd restart the process of posing us and framing the shot. Sometimes when he stopped I would stay sitting where he'd directed me to sit. There was something about occupying that space in the composition that felt both fragile and freeing. There was something about wearing the skin of an important stranger that was so entrapping.

For a few minutes at least, I would try to disappear into the abstraction I was pretending to be. I would just try to be beloved.

I get back to Mother's house, her old Leica uncapped, the photo of me and the horse rolled up in my purse. I come in, look down, and see the ratty welcome mat that has been in that space for years, that I never put in the memory palace and I don't really know that I've noticed until now.

I grab the welcome mat and throw it out onto the lawn. I raise Mother's camera to my eye, stand where the welcome mat was, and point it down at my feet. I focus, widen the aperture, and take the shot of my feet on bare floor.

3. *Standing on the Welcome Mat*

I start looking for more things I can photograph, small things, things I can carry. At the end of the hall, the darkroom's door is open and light is bathing out. I notice the Ansel Adams print hanging in the hallway, a landscape with a river oxbowing under the shadow of a mountain range. I pull it off its hook and there is the faintest outline of the frame on the wall. The empty hook stares out.

4. *Print of Ansel Adams's* Tetons and Snake River *on the Hallway Wall*

I take the print out to the lawn, to join the welcome mat.

I climb up the stairs to the bathroom, find the dusty, warped wood owl carving, and pull it off the windowsill. I take a picture of the dirty, fog-glassed window.

5. *Wooden Owl Carving against the Bathroom Window*

I wrap the carving in a dry old towel from the bathroom and carry it downstairs, add the telephone to it, grab my purse, take it all out to the yard, and unroll it for the Ansel Adams print, for the ratty welcome mat.

Before I roll the towel back up, I see the junk mail sticking out of the little old metal mailbox on the other side of the fence. I yank the mailbox from the deteriorating wood, put it down at my feet, raise

Mother's camera, and take the photo as wide open as I can, to force the house to be blurred out behind the fence. When I hit the shutter, I make a point to blink.

6. *The Mailbox*

I put the mailbox on the pile—the tiniest yard sale. I roll the towel over it all, go around the house to my car, put it all on the passenger seat, and back out.

None of these things will ever go back into the house.

I make it to the home and it's an hour before they are going to feed Mother dinner. I nod to the nurse with my arms full of the artifacts wrapped in the towel and carry them down the hall to her room.

Mother is sitting, locked into her bed, looking straight at the doorway when I come in.

"Hello," I say. I put the towel down on the bed and pull up a chair.

I want nothing more than to tell her what has happened in my life since I left her all those years ago. I want nothing but to tell her about why I've lived the exact way that I have, about which parts I blame her for and which I don't. But I can't say any of that because that information is so important to me, because I don't want to think of it disappearing as soon as it's written in her head. I don't want to torture her with any information she can't hold on to.

I hand Mother the owl carving. She holds it, looks at it, then puts it down. I decide to reintroduce the items to her. I say, "Here's your welcome mat," "Here's your mailbox," "Here's your Ansel Adams print from the hallway."

She rubs her hands on them, looks at them. When I give her the phone I put her hand on it, take the phone from its cradle so that she can grasp it, hold on to it longer. So that it might drag some noise out from the dark.

Then I remember the photo in my purse, from the archives, and take it out and unroll it. I look down into my happy face, then over at Mother, who is watching me.

As I roll the paper back up, without showing it to Mother, the nurse knocks on the open door and comes in.

"Sorry to barge in," she says, with a meal on a tray. "It's time for dinner."

"Oh, sorry," I say, standing up and putting everything back in the towel.

"Are those your mother's things?"

"Yes," I say, not wanting to look at the food.

"You know," the nurse says, setting the tray beside the bed and pulling up another chair. "You could also bring Hedwig back to the house if you like. We can arrange a visit for you, if you think it would help. You could just show her around all the old things."

I slip the page into my purse. "I didn't know that was an option," I say, forgetting that I pay for her to be here, that Mother pays to be here, that the door is open if I want to carry her out.

"Just give us a day's notice and we can probably arrange it," the nurse says, picking up a bowl of something from the tray and a spoon.

I make for the door, trying to imagine what it must be like to know what you're going to do that far in advance, to see a future worth making.

Driving back to the house, I remember Hamburg. A day before Erwin was to drive me to the airport I asked if he could take me out of the city. I had something to do.

This is a memory that I hate that I have. The symmetry of this memory scares me to my core, because it is how I know that I'm far too similar to Mother.

Erwin drove me an hour out into the country, near where we let those mice go, upstream on the Elbe. It was broad daylight, and we pulled over near a place where one could launch a boat from a trailer.

"I'll just be a minute," I said. "Honk if you see someone coming and want us to go."

I took out the paper bag of letters I'd written when I first got to Germany, the many letters that said all the things I had needed to say. Things that had spilled out. I took the bag down next to the water, poured a whole can of lighter fluid into it, and then dropped a lit match inside. The bag went up like nothing, huge flecks of paper, huge flecks of who I'd been, rising in the hot air. A boat slowly trolled along the far shore.

I didn't want to bring them back with me. I didn't want to be able to look at and remember all that leaving, the permanence and resolve of that decision.

I watched the bag of paper burn down into nothing. Into a fluttering bloom of ash. Which I kicked into the water as it was smouldering out. All that pain, all that life no longer worth keeping hold of. I was finished with all of it.

But of course that wasn't the end of all of that. Much of the wound that act was trying to forgive has been bleeding ever since then. Will always be bleeding, no matter how hard I might try to cauterize it.

I hate this memory because it means that Mother probably didn't get past anything by lighting her box on fire in the studio, either. She just got rid of the proof, and whatever wanted to stay probably just migrated into her head, where it would have started living a life, changing itself to her new shapes, floating atop the current of her mind without any concrete thing to haunt.

I stop at a red light and remember climbing into the passenger seat, beside Erwin, remember the quiet drive home. Erwin told me that when he got rid of the photos that we were re-creating, instead of burning them, he dropped them in a heavy box in the Elbe.

"The same way you stop a vampire," he said, smiling at me, and I smiled back.

Back then, I still thought that what I had done would work. Even though Erwin was sitting there, driving along, the smiling proof that it didn't. He was trying to drag the lost past back into the material present, so that it could be stuffed into a drawer rather than be held in the grey folds of his mind. But I didn't think about any of that yet. I just smiled.

Stopped at a red light, I look over at the passenger seat and see me, at twenty-three, smiling back at me. And sitting on their lap, me at ten, smiling, as if I have a hand on a horse's flank.

I look away and grip the wheel hard. I can feel the past climbing up onto the back of the car, into the wheel wells. I can feel the sun getting slapped around by the black. I can feel the whole city turning in on me. I grow terrified that the light will never go green.

I grow terrified that no matter how hard and how long I drive, I will only ever end up here.

But then the light goes green, and I start moving again.

The next morning, Helena drops Hudson off in their little Japanese truck. She idles out front, her side of the truck nearest us. I come over to the window and she puts her hand on my bare arm as Hudson pulls his tools from the back. Drills and screwdrivers and saws and all. All those things I should be able to handle on my own. He hoists them with his deceptively strong body and carries them into the house as Helena pulls away.

Hudson is wearing overalls and a clean white shirt this time. As soon as he comes through the door I hear the cat scurrying around the hardwood, hiding from the stranger. I show Hudson to my old bedroom, to the loft bed. I can hear the cat moving slowly in the house, coming up the stairs.

Hudson's eyes behind his glasses study the way the bed is constructed. "It's actually pretty nice wood," he says. "It's mostly the parts holding it together that are making it dangerous."

I carry the thin remains of the flat mattress downstairs and stuff it into a garbage bag. I don't catch sight of the cat on my way, and I figure they've slipped into the memory palace. I hear Hudson moving around upstairs. I carry the bag outside and stand at the curb, not wanting to go back into the house. I close my eyes and see the palace from outside, feel the sink of flesh at my feet, like a wet lawn. Or quicksand.

I open my eyes and stare the house down, think about Hudson and Helena, wonder what it feels like to be driven around in a right-hand-drive car. It must feel strange to sit on the left and be without control, to have all the visual advantages but no ability to turn the wheel. To feel like you're marooned on the wrong continent. I try to picture the sensation of surrender. It comes naturally. I feel it.

When I get back upstairs, Hudson is bent over his tools, looking for something. The loft bed is on its side in the bedroom and he has already knocked most of the sagging supports for the mattress from the bed. He has a little sledgehammer in his hand.

"I forgot my claw hammer," he says, making a levering motion with his hand. "You wouldn't have one, would you?"

"You may be in luck," I say.

I go downstairs and look for it—in the closet with the vacuum, in the kitchen. I forget where I last saw it. I close my eyes and see all the photos on the wall of the living room and remember holding it above my head. Remember the realtor stepping over it. I open my eyes and it's there, on the floor, in the light: the little pry bar wrapped in negatives.

I go up and see Hudson crouched outside the room, stretching his hand out to the cat, who is licking it. The cat is a real cat, not just in my head.

I hand Hudson the pry bar. He looks at it, adjusting his glasses, questioning.

"Some art has its uses," I say.

The cat stays outside the room. They don't run away anymore. They're used to this world, my world, its people.

When Hudson finishes, I go downstairs and grab the vacuum and a pail from the closet. The same pail, presumably, Dorothea used to fight the fire. Hudson has turned the bed into long planks of unrecognizable wood that he carries downstairs. The house moans under the weight of the removal.

I clean the place, and then stand on the other side of the room, lift Mother's camera, set the exposure, and hit the shutter. It's that easy.

7. The Loft Bed

Hudson brings his tools downstairs and calls Helena to pick him up as I come down. As Helena begins to make her way to us, from whatever corner of the city she is driving the mirrored truck through, I take Hudson back upstairs one last time to look at the armoire. He puts his hand against the wood, just like he did with the loft bed. As he does, the cat crawls out from underneath it—a place that I had no idea could fit a living thing. The cat comes up to Hudson and rubs against him.

"They've really taken a liking to you," I say.

"What's their name?" he asks, reaching down to pet the cat.

"I don't know," I say, leaning against the wall, dwarfed by the armoire. "They haven't told me yet."

Helena knocks on the door, and we help Hudson get his tools and the wood into the back of the little truck. I try and give him more money, but he just says: "I can come the day after tomorrow and do the armoire."

In my old bed, I dream.

I have removed all the windows and doors from the house. All the city has come to the house, each person walking or flying inside, each person carrying a single piece out. The house is gutted and then dismantled, board by board, nail by nail. Eroded.

I wake up and can't move. It is an all-white room. I can feel smoke holding my body down, paralyzing me. And so it comes up to my face—its face—and looks into me.

I know I'm still dreaming, but I want to scream, but I don't want to, and I don't want to and I don't want to, and then just as I open my mouth, the smoke flies inside and I'm awake, breathing fast.

The cat is sitting beside me, looking at me. I try to move my arms, and they do. I scratch the cat's neck.

There is thunder but no rain, no lightning. A storm circling, but not entering, the city.

I close my eyes and there it is, yes, the storm pounding down on the memory palace.

I open my eyes and am on my bed, feeling the dark sun setting in the calm after anxiety has burnt you down. And then I get up from the bed, grab my purse filled with the loose paper containing the list of all the things in the house. I go downstairs and get a marker from a drawer. I turn one of the pages over, the page that reads: *armoire (old, maple wood, handmade in Manitoba, decent condition, just too huge)*, and on the back scrawl:

YARD SALE, SATURDAY MAY 24.
NAME YOUR PRICE!
EVERYTHING MUST GO!

Then I turn the paper back over and write, in small letters: *Especially me.*

WHEN

I stayed out pretty late yesterday. The day the painters came back to fix the studio, spreading a thin layer of plaster on the ceiling—because they figured that would stick better than paint—and tearing down and putting up new, simple wallpaper. We'd negotiated possibly removing the wood panels and replacing them with drywall, but I said no, because it sounded like it would extract too much from the house.

I don't really want the bones of the house to go; I just want it to be re-skinned.

I drove around Winnipeg, seeing how everything has changed: neighbourhoods going from cute to crowded, downtown getting taller and taller. I just drove, circling Assiniboine Park, hitting red lights on the one-ways of downtown to reach and lurch through the veins of the Exchange district. Even there, despite its preservation, feels different. Perhaps in juxtaposition with the construction zone of the looming downtown wannabe-scrapers, the old buildings, with fading advertisements painted on their sides half a century ago or more, feel *quaint.* Like the city is not so much upholding some tradition as it is clinging to nostalgia.

I've begun to think that the past is not worth keeping around simply because it actually happened.

When I grew sick of the stop-and-go of the heart of the city, I went to see Mother. The nurse let me have a bit of their lunch, but I lost my appetite while I watched her feed Mother in bed.

After the nurse left, I let Mother hold her camera again. She rubbed her hands on the coated brass skin, occasionally looked at it. I watched her hands move, thinking of the flaming box in her studio, thinking about the people working on that room at that exact moment. Then I picked up her camera and left.

I kept going north. I remembered the dead boy as I drove along the river. I thought how something occasionally singeing the fringes of one life must be an inferno in others. The nearness and farness of human suffering. How quiet it can be. I thought about bridges reaching out from one shore into a wet, ever-empty dark.

I kept going north until I got to Selkirk. It wasn't really my intention to go there, but I drove around, in and out of strange streets, until—around sunset—I found the red-bricked, sharp-roofed building. The thickly divided, probably barred white windows staring out and bouncing back the sun.

The mental health centre, where Mother went—years and years ago now—to be fixed.

I'd never seen it in person before, but it was far less jarring to stumble upon it in person than to stumble upon the idea of it in my head. It looked sort of like a nice old university campus, a collection of old dormitories. It looked like some of the aging buildings I'd lived in cheaply in my life, like the building in Hamburg with the tiny rooms, like some of the old buildings that still stand in the Exchange, in Osborne, in Wolseley.

It did not look like a place worth fearing.

I didn't stay very long. I couldn't. As uncompelling as it was, I couldn't stop imagining Mother being endlessly carried in and out of those buildings, even though she'd only been there once. I kept seeing horses rushing through the streets and Mother trying to throw herself under them, as if to become one with them, only to be stopped and dragged into more life. Into Hell.

I could not stay there long because I kept seeing myself breaking out of every single one of the windows, leaving her alone there, only to walk back in the front door, backpack filled with anchor and rope.

As I turned on the car and left, sun eking out its last wisps over the horizon, I felt sick. I'm tired of the forever trap I'm in, the guilt I'm shawled in from reacting to the world in the only possible way I could in order to survive it.

The world only ever told me to do one thing—run—and I've done it again and again.

I haven't called Genny in more than a week.

Before I made it back to Mother's house, parking in my spot in the back, where her car once was, I did a loop around the city via the perimeter highway. In the dark, Winnipeg was mostly just a dim glow. I drove all the way around, without stopping before passing the Downs, slowly getting a sense of the city's scope as if I were a snake gauging its size for possible consumption, and then I slipped back into it, south.

At Mother's house, I turned off the car and went in the back door. The kitchen walls—freshly repainted days before—shocked me. For a moment, I thought I had used my key to get into a different house.

Feeling displaced, I went up the stairs to the studio and saw for the first time in a long time—between the windows, in the middle of the night—blankness.

Then, I went through the house and started carrying everything downstairs. For the sale.

12

YOUR BEDROOM

At the end of the tour of your memory palace is your own bedroom, the bedroom you grew up in, where you watched Mother do yoga, where you lie awake at night trying to find steady ground for yourself.

In your room is turbulence. The turbulence gets in because the window in your room is gone. Whenever you imagine your room, you imagine the window being gone, even though you were only inside with it gone for a few minutes before you'd lowered yourself down the side of the house on the rope you tied of blankets and old shirts. The rope is still there, too, draping out the window, because that is how you always remember it. The turbulence of the room includes no pictures. It is not like the other rooms. Instead, it includes odours and bodies and screaming and names and smiles.

This is the room where history enters to be sorted; this is the room where you stand and let things enter and swirl and overcome you as you decide what to focus on, what to care for. You are pushed around by fragments of senses and selves and stories that knock into you, bruise and bolster you. When you walk into the room, the door closes because of the wind that is blowing all of this in, and now you can't open it to get out.

If you closed the window, this wouldn't be a problem, but then you would have never been able to escape.

This room is the gift shop you must always pass through. And when you are done with the room—where you take precious things from the swirl and place them in your pockets, which are openings in your chest because you are always naked when you go through the palace—what do you do? You go to the window and look out, out at the silt of the future coming toward you, pieces of sound knocking into other pieces of sound until they make up a word. Touches grabbing onto other touches, knocking into a familiar hand and reaching for yours. Reflections refracting on new ideas for old hunches. Staring into the slow progression reminds you of how whenever you stare into the night sky, at the stars, you are staring into the past. Only this time, you are the stars. You are the past staring into the now and into becoming.

So when you're done with the memory palace—which is really just a house in a different mouth—you let yourself down on the rope. You always remember the way that feels, that escaping. But at the end of the rope, you find nothing, because you never get to the end. You just pretend that you do, as you open your eyes, stand up, and shake yourself out of your vanishing.

I carry the last of the empty boxes, from the liquor store on Burnell, from my car into the house, into the living room, and start putting things inside them: cutlery, dishes, empty picture frames. Things for the sale.

The living room has everything in the house in it, everything but the armoire, the bed in Mother's room, and the bed in mine—since the person who posted the ad wanting a twin bed told me they didn't want one that was so old.

In the corner, again, is the mirror, reflecting the corner at itself. I carried it downstairs backwards this time so that I wouldn't be distracted by my reflection. Then I went upstairs, cleaned the spot in the corner where it had stood, lifted Mother's camera, and took a picture.

8. Self-Portrait of the Child in the Full-Length Mirror in Their Mother's Bedroom

When I carried the mirror, I imagined the house watching me going down the stairs and seeing only itself.

I don't want the house to see me in it anymore.

I grab one of the empty boxes and carry it upstairs, to the studio. I point Mother's camera into the box and take a shot.

9. All My Mother's Precious Things

Then I pick up the box, throw it out of the room, and take a photo of the repaired wall, between the windows.

10. Mother's Box of Things on Fire, the Wall on Fire, Her Hands on Fire, Too

The more I've gone back to see Mother at the home, the easier that act has started to become, because the more I go back, the more I realize that she isn't even there.

I walk into her room and the light—bright or grey—always spews across the tile floor, and I go over and I sit beside her and I look at the body obscuring her. There's almost nothing left that I can cling to, that can remind me of her. She hardly looks like her. She can barely move or operate herself, but when I look at her I don't see her struggling; I see someone else entirely.

She has started to get blurrier in my head. She has slowly whittled down the her that she was in my head. She has gotten easier to see because she has slipped away.

One of the clearest similarities left is the silence, but there's a difference to it. Before, when she was most quiet, she was always moving: around the house, in the darkroom, in her bedroom—in rooms that were closed off to me. The creaking house was a concerto of her, and I could not catch any glimpse of her in these moments except through the bars of the vent in my bedroom, where I watched her bend and pause and bend again. A regular, cyclical, methodical interpretation of pain.

Before, it felt like there was a tsunami ripping across the flood plains of her head. Now, it feels like she's got nothing to hide.

In the bed in the home she is a sort of revival of Mother, a stand-in to prove how dead she is. She simply lies there, abstract and uncompelling as concrete.

And when I am near her, when I am seen by her, I can tell that I'm dead, too. The I who she knew, who she loved and was so hurt by, the I who got away in the night because their Mother locked them up because she was afraid of them leaving her. When I'm with her, the I who digs in the lawn is dead, the I who puts their hand against a winning horse's thigh is dead, and I'm just a ghost, slipping along the never-gripping, unaddressable present.

I, as I am—as I have grown to be—am not alive in her at all.

The only place where Mother is still herself is in her hands. That's all she is now, the only part of her that's left. They flex lifelike, like daddy-long-legs limbs removed from the round body by a kid's fingernail. A kid could slice the legs off the body, hold them in their palm and watch them move, feel them tickle, maybe leave one leg on the body so it can push itself around.

Mother is her hands now, though they don't do much of anything but move. They live on for her, the her who is dead. Mother. They're living there, on the sheets, as her brain gets looser and looser. Her hands, pink-wrinkled with the firescar—perhaps the last significant action she ever took. Her head is free of them.

It's as if Mother's hands don't know she's dead. Or they don't believe it. They're waiting around, patiently. Her head is a gravestone, merely referring to her, but her hands don't know that. They're still there. She's still in them. Because if the hands knew, they'd stop attempting to grip.

When I hold them, their little old scarred warmths, I think they know that I'm dead. Sometimes I can feel them squeezing me just a little harder. I take the pulses of the muscles of her hands to be a kind of speech. The last living limbs of the dead speaking to the pure dead: me—her kid who loved her and left her because it was the only way they could survive.

Her hands comfort me, but not the me who is alive. The one who died with Mother's head. Those hands hold me, lovingly bury me, and don't know they're buried themselves.

I go to the Neighbourhood Bookstore & Café again, one last time, and the kid is still there, behind the counter. Mother's camera is still here, around my neck. He smiles at me, recognizing me despite the binder, despite my hair tied tight into a bun. I have the flyer, written out by hand and xeroxed onto blue paper, advertising my yard sale. I've plastered copies across the neighbourhood, covering out-of-date, sun-faded posters on lampposts and community corkboards. The sale is the day after tomorrow, a Saturday. *Everything Must Go*, the flyer says. It felt traditional and honest.

I hold the flyer up as the kid goes to pour me a coffee. "Can I put this up?"

"Sure," he says, putting down the cup and brushing hair from his eyes. "You can put it up on the doors if you want."

I thank him, put my coffee on my table, and go to the front door with my tape and one of the flyers. I wonder for a bit whether to put it facing out or in but decide that out would be best.

When I turn around the boy is out from behind the counter, taping another of the flyers onto the back door for me. I smile, and when he looks at me, I keep smiling.

"Thank you," I say.

I can feel a well of sensations bubbling up in me, and I sit down and try to drown them out with coffee. I go to Craigslist and Kijiji and any other sites I can think of and advertise the yard sale. I put my hand on Mother's camera, and when a few more people come into the café, I wipe my face and go.

Erwin didn't talk about the war, or what came before. He didn't tell the stories that were behind the pictures we were reshooting; he just made the pictures.

"It's not about sharing the memories," he said. "It's about getting them out of my head."

Erwin had taken photographs of the war in Crete, snuck them out past the censor and stowed them away, which incited the Wehrmacht to arrest him and throw him in jail, for treason. As soon as Erwin got out of prison, and gave his testimony at Nuremberg, he started a new life. That was the only life he ever told stories about.

Though he didn't tell stories about the war, he told stories where he dealt with the aftermath of it. For instance, years after the war, he went back to a tiny village in Crete. A tiny village that was the site of some thorough atrocities.

He went to a bar in that village and found the residents hospitable to him. He was honest with them, told them about his being there during the war, told them about that day, told them about the photographs he'd taken, hidden, and used for the testimony he'd hoped would bring justice. The villagers were kind to him, until one man finally stood up, said they'd fulfilled their duty of hospitality, and left. In no time, the rest of the villagers stood and followed, until it was just Erwin and the bartender, who didn't respond when—after the moment had passed—Erwin asked for his bill. Erwin said the bartender just rubbed at a glass with his back to him. Then, Erwin left.

Speculation backed by research says that this village was probably one of two in Crete that were hit hard in the war: Kondomari or Kandanos. Kondomari had a huge percentage of its population—mostly able and aging men—gunned down after the village was blamed for the deaths of several German paratroopers. The next day, Kandanos was razed, and most of its inhabitants were killed, for allegedly putting up a resistance to the Germans.

There's a photo online of a German soldier looking up at a sign they had placed outside the annihilated village. It reads: *Here stood Kandanos, destroyed in retribution for the murder of 25 German soldiers, never to be rebuilt again.*

But it was.

The more you walk through the memory palace, the more you think you have a handle on things, the more you believe you're not forgetting anything, even though you know you are. You curated the palace to fit an impression of everything—of you—perhaps because you knew that you didn't actually want to remember everything. You built it because you wanted a sense of control over these moments that you lacked at the time they occurred.

But in the end you know that life is nothing like remembering it. In this way, the palace skews things, makes you seem even more to blame for the life that you've led. The control you have in simulating pieces of your life, again and again, tricks you into forgetting how little you could do at the time. You look back at running away from Mother, from Genny, and though you know it was a matter of survival, you can see the moments where you could have stopped yourself.

You take your tour of the palace and resent your old selves for not having more control at the time. You resent them for existing within their own times, while you do your best to obscure your present with your past. So much so that when you get out of the palace, when you open your eyes at the bottom of the rope, you feel sick. Because as soon as your eyes are open, there you are. Here. So blazingly so.

I call the realtor and she comes over, sees the house, sees how partly fixed it is, sees how much stuff I'm going to take out of the house for the yard sale on Saturday. The armoire is still here, but I tell her it will be gone soon. Tonight. She says it can stay, but I say it can't, no.

"It's a family heirloom," I say, and she nods. She, too, knows how to weaponize sentimentality.

She agrees that enough has been done. I hand her a copy of the key, Mother's copy, because I know that I can't be here much longer.

"It's still a fixer-upper," she says, as we stand by the staircase, "but it will certainly move."

All the guts of the house, anything not nailed down, sit ready in the living room. A mess ready to be spit up. A hairball. The cat, I think, is hiding somewhere inside the jungle of old wood, sofas, and knick-knacks.

The realtor takes a gander at all the things, then smiles at me as I walk her to the door. "You've got a lot of lifting to do," she says, as she walks out and waves.

"Always."

When the monument vanishes, what still stands? Is it the things the world has decided should be upheld, should be visible? The high heroes and the villains, the moments of affection and the moments of shameful betrayal—the extremes?

If the world had its way, that's all we'd remember—the awful and the brilliant. But if the *real* world had its way—the world of hearts rather than intellectualized nerve clusters—we would remember what we want. We would carry with us through life only that which we wanted to identify ourselves by, not what we feel is obligatory.

If we could do that, we could, perhaps, carry with us a bit less fear and shame. We could glide forward on less fragile wings.

We would not forget all the tragedies, nor would we remember merely all the happy bits. We would cling more to the moments in between, the neutral moments of nearness—Mother sitting at the other end of a table with her camera opened up, cleaning it, while I scrawled an assignment for school on loose-leaf. Dropping Genny off at her office on the way to the university in the morning twice a week.

When the monument vanishes, we ourselves are tasked with keeping up the struggle. We're left with the impression of the monument's absence, with remembering what we want and need to remember. In pulling away from something, in obscuring its easy presence, you get a sense of what the thing really is to you. You get a more full view of it.

Mother is no longer my mother when I'm near her. It's only when I look away, when I close my eyes and step into the memory palace, that I really get a sense of her.

The sinking of a monument is not a surrender, is not a memory giving up, but rather a challenge, a passing of the torch. We must keep the memories we want alive, without relying so much on cold stone, metal, and placards, all of which—good and needed as they may be, at times—transmute the breadth of sensation into the finality of information. Most monuments, eventually, make their memories stuffy. They make you think that there is only one version of something that you should remember. They make you think the past is clean and over.

To me, Mother stands in for a host of incompatible memories. They don't add up to anything rational, don't add up to a finished product. They pile up into a convolution of honest loose ends and contradictions. There are many different versions of her that have lived and died, many different versions of her seen from different versions of me. Remembering her, to me, is watching two armies clashing in fury and love.

The same goes for Genny. Remembering her, the full spectrum is there: loathing and loving and everything in between—comfort and fear, confusion and conclusion.

The blankness of a monument hurts. In a monument's failure to fully portray loss there is a sort of tragedy. It's hard to feel anything but grief, because grief is the only appropriate reaction to loss. But what about humour, or relief, or anything out of the ordinary? There is a sort of policing, a lack of trust to most monuments. There are decided ways of relating to them.

You can't fuck in a graveyard. You can't smile on a tour through a death camp. You can't yawn at a confession. But why not? Most monuments don't let you revitalize a memory into your own code. They are too sacred; there's no place for your humanity to meet them.

I wasn't in Hamburg for the Monument against Fascism's final lowering. I only saw it in the middle, not at its peak, or its absence. But there were so many things written on its skin that were more than simply names. There was graffiti, incoherence, irreverence. I read in the papers that some officials were disturbed by this, the way people didn't follow the rules. But the supposed ruination of the monument energized me. I fed off it, how people had chosen to interface with the monument—with the memory, with the ideas—however they pleased. That was the beauty of that monument, how it was different from most other monuments. It stood against fascism, and what stands against fascism better than vandals? Better than not following the script?

I found scrawled in white paint on the thin lead skin of the up-shooting pillar the words:

PUNK'S

not DEAD

I stood there, in front of a mortal monument, a monument that would stand for less than a decade, myself living proof of a sort of anarchy of existence, and felt validated. I felt that every single human bit of me was important, and that any remembering I did was a personal responsibility rather than a social one.

I felt scrawled on, enigmatic and obtuse.

It's nearly eleven o'clock the night before the sale and Hudson is coming soon. The house is completely bare besides the armoire and everything in the living room. I've put a flat sheet down at the base of the armoire and I've been sitting here for a while now, thinking that I should have made coffee. I go down to the living room and find the box with the kettle, but then I remember there's no coffee in the house.

This house has never been so undone. There are so many things intrinsic to the house's soul that have been excised.

I stand in the living room looking out the curtainless window to the dark, curtainless lawn, freshly clipped. I stare at the back of the realtor's sign, freshly pushed into that lawn. I remember the photo of me, digging.

I go to the front door and kneel where the photo is in its frame. Where it is not. I close my eyes and it's there, in the memory palace, and I pick it up and carry it to the other room. I open one eye in a squint so that I can double expose the palace onto the house. I navigate around the things in the living room to an empty space on the floor and start a pile.

Hudson knocks when I'm in the middle of pulling Polaroids of me and Erwin and everything from the empty drawers in the kitchen. I yell at him to come in, but he doesn't, so I go to the door and let him in. He looks tired, unshaven, but gives me a nice, quiet smile. His arms are full of his tools, and I take some and help him upstairs.

"Coffee?" I say, bending out and into myself.

"My saviour," he says, setting his tools down on the sheet and putting a hand on the doorwood.

When I reach the banister, I close my eyes, and as I go down, everyone waiting around on the stairs comes along after me. I feel like some kind of duchess regally exiting a palace to go to a ball as the enemy knocks on the front gate. They take the photos of younger me and younger each other from the wall as they follow, and I show them where I'm making two piles in the only bare spot on the living room floor: take and leave.

I hear Hudson's hacksaw slowly beginning to growl through the hardware of the armoire as I open the back door. I get in my car and drive.

It's Friday night, but it's not busy out. This is Winnipeg, and it's not late enough. The younger versions of myselves are jammed in the back of the car. There's someone in my trunk, laughing. I drive through a Tim Hortons and get two extra-large coffees and turn back. None of them want anything.

I've decided that I'm leaving—I keep forgetting that I'm leaving, keep trying to forget it—in just a few days.

I park out front, behind Hudson, and almost knock before I come in. I open the door, the tray of coffees in one hand, and I can hear Hudson's saw, I can hear his humming. The coffee is heating my hand. My friends stay out in the yard, so I leave the porch light on and hit the stairs. My eyes are open because what's the difference now? The house is barren in both places.

Hudson is standing with the doors of the armoire open. I can only see his legs, and it looks like he's being eaten by it. He hasn't gotten far while I was out. I tap his shoulder and hand him a coffee. I am happy to see he is whole, removing the shelves from inside.

"Are you sure?" he says, looking at the armoire with the doors removed. The wood saw Hudson used to dismantle the loft bed is sitting on the sheet, its teeth so clean.

"What do you mean?"

"Are you sure you want me to do this? Take it apart? It's beautiful."

I look at it. "It's got to get out of here, and unless you get some more arms, it's the only way."

He closes the door and drinks some coffee. He could not look more tired.

"I could get some more," he says.

I do not say anything for a moment. I think about the cat looping through the rooms. "No, I don't think so. This has to be the way."

I put my hand on his shoulder and squeeze it. I could explain it, I could tell him what is gained, but there are too many words in the world I could use to say it. He drinks some more coffee and adds a very small twist to his head.

"Thank you," is all I say before I go downstairs.

I stand at the pile of things and look out to the yard, where all the rest of me are running around, getting in arguments, laughing at one another. I go to the door and let them in, take them to the living room.

"We've got to figure all of this out," I say.

They move like ants through the house, pulling at things remembered, dragging sensations and little favourite glimpses into our lives, putting them in the pile to keep. The rest—jagged, dim, heavy, and unincorporatable things—are torn out and left in the other, larger pile. Everyone has their favourite pieces. They clutch them and we listen as Hudson moves the saw through the wood again.

It takes him a long time to make it through, and while he does that I clear off the dining room table, clear it of the boxes, the lamps and whatnot, for the sale. Then I lie down on it like it's an operating table.

Corpse pose, Alice whispers in my ear, and I let my muscles fall dead.

My eyes rest, half-closed, half-open, as everyone takes up their favourite bits from the keep pile and places them on my body, massaging them into the gaps in my loosened flesh. I feel so refreshingly burnt down, like I've been dropped into a crucible and broiled away. There is a sea of hands on me, pushing, reshaping.

When I hear Hudson's feet on the stairs I come back to life, turn my head to him. He has large pieces of the reclaimed wood of the armoire in his arms, and he puts them down at the bottom of the stairs. He looks so tired. I stay where I am, on the table, and he comes over, clears the sofa, and curls up. I look at him, as he falls asleep, uncovered, and then notice the crowds from the palace circling us in the room. Populating and stuffing it.

As I nod awake I think I hear the darkroom door open. Hudson is walking out of the living room, toward the hall. The cat is in his arms, looking at me over his shoulder.

"Morning," he says, pausing to smile at me before disappearing down the hall.

I look outside and, yes, it is.

The story of Tantalus and his son Pelops is only alluded to in Ovid's *Metamorphoses*.

Tantalus—a mortal son of Jupiter—cut up and cooked the body of his son Pelops and served him in a stew as a sacrifice to the gods. Horrified, the gods did not eat Pelops—all except Ceres, who was blind to the truth of the meal in her despair over the loss of her daughter, Persephone, to the underworld. Ceres ate Pelops's shoulder before realizing what she'd done.

Jupiter instructed Clotho, the thread spinner of the Fates, to bring Pelops to life again. Meanwhile, Vulcan forged a new shoulder out of ivory.

Tantalus was punished with a fate of eternal dissatisfaction. He was placed deep in the underworld, where he still stands imprisoned in a pool of fresh water with a branch of fruit hanging above him. His hell is perpetual thirst and hunger, with the pool ever-receding from his cupped hands and the luscious fruits always just out of reach.

There may be nothing more terrifying than being shackled to a doomed action, than waking up in the morning and knowing that there is never going to be any sort of end to your desire. The scariest thing in life is living with a desire or a hope that will never be realized.

Like Pelops, who, despite the magic of the ivory, will never be complete again—sometimes stories don't come clean. Sometimes "why" is a piece of fruit, smoothly pulling away.

In the morning I go upstairs and clean the place where the armoire used to be. I stand there, staring at the space, remembering Mother standing there with her long, lost hair swirling down behind her, staring nude into the armoire's gut. I hit the shutter and take the last frame of *Shadows of the Prison House*.

11. The Armoire

Then I take the sheets from Mother's old bed—the only piece of furniture that is probably going to stay—out to the yard, where Hudson and I spread everything out. I carry the mirror out looking at me again, but this time I am carrying myself out of the house. I feel, in my skin, the places where my past is pressed in. I see, for the first time, in that mirror, the unmediated farness of sky.

A few older women show up as Hudson and I are setting up and I tell them they don't have to wait; they can take what they want. They stand in the yard, watching as Hudson and I carry the house outside of itself. They look at it all and don't buy anything. After we set everything up, Hudson goes to pick up Helena.

I walk between the sheets, looking at everything set up. I have a sign taped to a chair that says, *Everything must go, name your price*, because I do not want to put a value on any of these things. I want to take someone else's evaluation of their worth.

A clock strikes ten: the time the sale is meant to start.

The weather is clear and the traffic slow. A few people come by, walking dogs or strolling. Some stop and look; some glance as they pass and keep moving. I try not to put any pressure on anyone because I don't want them to know how heavy any of these objects are, how much they are a part of my life.

Hudson and Helena make it back. The bed of the little truck is empty. He must have dropped off the pieces of the armoire.

We all three loom around the yard. There is not much here, but enough. Helena makes conversation with people, and when someone makes her an offer on something, she takes it and tells me what she got, putting it in the cash box. I crouch on the dew-touched yard and write the price next to the item on my list.

Hudson sells the table and the chairs to a nice young woman. I watch from across the yard, near where Mother's phone is sitting, unplugged, on the sheet. He takes their money and points to his little truck; the young woman nods and smiles. They put the table and the chairs in the back and drive off.

He is back in twenty minutes, with sandwiches. People slowly draw their way to the yard. Some carry away pieces of Mother; others just come and touch them, then leave. Both actions cleanse the place. The more strangers handle Mother's things, the less they feel like hers.

Just past noon, the boy from the Neighbourhood Café comes by and looks at everything. As soon as I catch him noticing me, he doesn't look at me again. He crouches, grazing his young finger around the old, boring things: boxes of forks taped together, plates, a few lamps from the living room. Finally, he comes upon the little owl carving and picks it up. He stands, stares down at it.

"If you want that, you can have it," I say to him.

He doesn't look up at me, but looks over in my direction.

"My mom loves owls," he says.

For a moment, I can see his whole life stretched out in front of me on old bedsheets.

"Well, she can have it then."

As the afternoon progresses, things slip away more and more. The box of cutlery disappears, as well as one of the lamps, and both the couch and the loveseat.

When the time on the sale is running out, everything fits onto one sheet. All the big things are gone, and now there are just small, outdated things: the phone, a cracked jade lamp.

With an hour left, Helena and Hudson say they have to go. When they first arrived, Helena took a pile of picture frames, both empty and full. That was all she wanted. Hudson took nothing. As we stand on the sidewalk, I ask him what he would like to take, and he says he's not sure. Then he holds up his hand, says he'll be right back, and goes into the house.

The light in Winnipeg oranges through clouds. The wind seems to come out of the house when Hudson goes inside, and it runs through the leaves of the trees lining the street. It's like a loose spirit, searching for something in the green.

Helena says nothing, until she asks: "So you're not leaving too soon, are you?"

I imagine Hudson walking through an empty skull. I hear the saw and the humming. I wonder, *Do I ever really need to lie again?*

"I am, very soon. In the next few days, I think."

Helena, the beautiful young woman who does not know me at all, pouts. "It would have been nice if you could stay longer," she says.

I hear the door of the house open behind me. I see Helena's eyes light up, meeting Hudson.

"Hedwig," he says, and I turn to see him on the porch, glasses on, with the cat in his arms. "May I?"

I cannot speak for the lump in my throat, so I nod my head, hard. He carries the cat to us and I put my hand out to their little grey face and they lick it. Helena oozes over them.

"But what will you name them?" I say, finally.

Hudson looks down at the cat in his arms. His hair, tied back, spirals beyond the elastic holding it down. "I'll wait for them to tell me."

I walk them all to the little truck and thank them both for their help. I do not tell them that I will see them again soon, because I know that I won't.

"Have a good one, Hedwig!" Helena says from the open window.

"It's actually Alani," I say. "Hedwig was my mother's name."

"Whoever," she says, smiling as they pull away.

Hudson puts his hand out his window and waves—forward, as if he is waving at the future.

I turn back to Mother's house in their wake.

I wait with the last of the things. I try not to imagine the emptiness of Mother's house, as much as I also try to imagine it. I consider keeping these last things. I think about backing my car onto the lawn and filling it up. I imagine myself going to see Mother with all those things, and then walking out of the home with her, too, as if she were an heirloom.

Around the time the sale is supposed to end, an old man comes by: Blaine.

He smiles at me, but I'm not quite sure he recognizes me this time.

"Is this the last of it?" he says, standing up against the crick of his spine. I nod and he looks down at everything on the sheet. He looks up at the sign on the chair.

"The chair, too?"

"Everything."

He comes over to the chair and wiggles it, side to side. It's hard to tell how sturdy something is on soft soil. He turns back to survey the last sheet of things again.

"I'll give you fifty for it all," he says. "But you'll have to help me get it home."

"Of course."

I take the money, get some empty bags, and fill them with everything: the phone, the cracked lamp, old playing cards I found in a drawer, odds and ends. Blaine says I could just tie up the sheet and carry most of it that way, so I do. The fragile things, he carries. I take the bundled sheet and the chair. I crumple up the yard sale sign and let it fall to the lawn.

So we go. He asks me why I'm selling all these treasures, and I say because Mother moved to Ste. Agathe. When I say that he looks over at me. He squints at me and knows.

"My luck," he says, shaking slightly the bags in his hands.

We get down to the place where the street turns west into an avenue, along the Red. I think of the dead. How many times Blaine has probably heard these stories.

Eventually, he points to a house. It's old and the lawn is covered in bird baths filled with dirty water and clusters of old figures: gnomes, nymphs, plinths, flamingos. I recognize his truck in the driveway. There's almost no room for anything else on the lawn, even grass, though it's started to grow up in scant, long tufts. I follow Blaine as he navigates the worn path between them. He is so careful about not hitting any of them, and looks back as we go, perhaps to be sure that I'm being just as careful.

When he opens the door I'm hit with a wide, weighty smell: mildew, mould, dust, age. The sun is beginning to red on its way toward the horizon. Blaine turns on the light and everywhere are things. He turns to me and smiles, raising his arm with the bag to show his collection. He stops in the hall and I put the chair down behind me, with the bundle on it. He pulls out the cracked lamp from one of the bags and walks over to a place in the open, stacked living room that is a huge corner filled with lamps. He puts it there carefully and comes back. From the other bag he grabs the phone. Mother's phone. He cradles it, looks beyond me to the chair and the bundle of old junk.

"Can you bring that chair?" he says, smiling and moving along the little path through the house. I nod, pull the bundle from it, and follow him with it.

I hold my breath, not wanting to breathe in the mould, or the dust, or whatever spirits haunt these cherished-then-unwanted things. I oxbow through the rooms behind Blaine until we reach a door, free of clutter. He opens the door, turns on the light, and shuffles in. A bathroom. The toilet is free and seems to be functioning, but the sink is filled with what appear to be pewter ashtrays. The walls are covered in silk scarves tacked in with staples. In the bathtub, in a pile almost to the ceiling, are phones. Old phones through which so many people probably spilled their souls. He turns and gestures to me to bring the chair in, and I put it down next to the pile. Blaine climbs the chair with Mother's phone under one arm and adds it to the top. It fits there; it doesn't tumble down.

He lowers himself to the floor, puts his hands on the chair, then seems to decide to leave it there. He looks up at the pile, hands on his hips.

"Beautiful," he says.

13

NO EXIT

Sometimes after you've come back into the world from touring the memory palace, you can't stand the idea of the palace's existence, and you close your eyes and stand outside the front door again, only this time with a jerry can in your hand. Sometimes you just stand outside and watch it burn down. Sometimes you pull a tornado from the empty sky, bury it in a blizzard of ice, or quake the foundations. You never go in the palace when you do any of this, never let it crumble around you. You just watch and listen as all the lives and moments you've trapped there rise into an abstract concerto. You grimace in a fury as you watch your life go up, or break down, or get pulled away in the wind. You want to feel free of it, of the way that it defines you, haunts you. A lonesome house on a lonesome street on a lonesome planet, destroyed by the nature you brought to it yourself. You break it with your control, because the control you have of your memories in it feels so insincere. There's no getting out—the labyrinth falls into the maze falls into a pool, with neither air nor bottom. And so, once the palace is destroyed and the memories have let out their final cries, you come back out to the world, and you know that when you close your eyes, there it will be again, as usual. Which feels right, that your mastery over it is just another facade, that you're just your own history's angel being dragged back across this wasteland of yourself. You're relieved, even, that the destruction doesn't stick. Because wasteland or not, this is yours and this is you. When you open the door, to the first memory on—or not on—the floor of the landing, you sigh yourself into being. You're *someone.*

The sun is setting, and I'm tired of the drive, tired of pulling open the door of the home, tired of being struck by the lifeless, lavender smell of the building, of the smile that I give the nurse at the desk who says that Mother's asleep. I don't mind; I just go in and see her. She's breathing, peaceful, but foreign, too.

I have her camera, of course, but I take its burden from my neck and set it down on the bed, near her sleeping hand but out of her sleeping reach. I scoot a chair close to her and look at those hands, again. In their sleep, they don't move, though I can see the veins on the pink, scarred backs, like the dried-up delta of an old river, a river that has finally streamlined itself over the eons into her swollen, pulsing veins.

These hands lead up to a wrist, which leads to the mother who's gone, my mother.

This body is a memory of her, a memory that she's forgotten, that the disease has taken to pouring fuel atop and burning down. I abolish the rivers coming from my eyes, and feel a bit free, sitting beside her like this—asleep, free in the way that only your own death can grant you. Free in the way that taking off her camera and placing it between us does. Through Mother's dying, I feel partly untethered from a past full of guilt, of my leaving, of my own silence and my complicity in hers. Through the annihilation of her ability to recognize me I'm somehow cleansed of it all, in a sort of existential baptism. When her remembering hands are asleep, there's nothing left to regret. Nobody left to pull forgiveness from.

I pick up the camera, twist the knobs to grab the light proper, and frame her up.

I sit there, staring at her through the viewfinder, finger twitching at the shutter that is so desperate for her—then stop. I put the camera down on the bed again and just look at her. For a long time, taking her in, her breath rising and falling like waves, like the calm waves of the lake that one summer when we stayed in a cabin Asha's family owned, stilted on a slope with a far view of the water, the waves almost a mile away. They were unable to crest against us. I just look at her and I remember that summer, driving back to Winnipeg from the cabin, south toward the city in the evening through fields of sunflowers, millions of sunflowers curling their petals in over their eyes against the glowing, set horizon to our right—and I don't know if I've ever remembered this before, don't really recognize this part of my head.

I pick the camera up again and take her picture. Just like that. I take her picture over and over again, filling the roll, which was half-full of the frames of *Shadows of the Prison House*. I suppose she is part of that now.

12–24. Mother

She doesn't move.

I stand up, wipe my face, and go over to the window. The vertical slats of the blinds draw their prison on the grid of the floor, which slips over Mother. I rewind the film in the camera while looking out through these slices of window to the courtyard where I stood, trying to resuscitate myself in Mother's head.

It's not often a pretty sight, this world. I think about all the one-way roads, the cars, the buses, and the brutality that winds out and eventually meets a heartbeat that meets a street that arrives at the river. The Red. I think of the trees leaning into the river from the bank, their deep, old roots hanging on for dear life while it sucks at them, think of the little rivers that the Red consumes on the way to its end, consolidating. The big rivers, too: the Assiniboine.

Everything seems to arrive there, in that river, at its single end. The living. The dead. I think of it all as a sort of whole as I stand by the window, opening the bottom of the camera and removing the film. The little tapering tail wags from the cartridge like a tongue.

I turn back to Mother and put the camera down on the bed with her. I hold the film cartridge up into a bar of the afternoon sun that crosses her, and I pull the tail of the film out, exposing all the undeveloped shots: shots of her, shots of empty places in the house, shots that after all that effort, that intention, would now develop into a complete line of utter negative blankness—negatives which, when developed, would darken, and when printed, would become full white. But for now the film is a median blankness. There is nothing to see, and there never will be. And when the film reaches its end, I rewind it back up into the cartridge by hand.

I pick my camera up from the bed, and replace it on my neck.

It's heavy, but it should be. It remembers her and me both.

I sit down beside Mother again and breathe for a while.

"I'm leaving," I tell her without telling her, without saying anything, because she's not here to listen.

I grab her hand. She doesn't wake up. I pinch the rivers and can feel the surge pushing at me, pumping her up and forward, treading water. I let it go. My hands are slick and I'm smearing them all over her. My hands feels like the hands of a crowd. I pick up her hand again and kiss her fifty times at once. Mother. I kiss you on the head, lightly. I step back and watch you breathe.

I think first to myself, and then say aloud, looking down at your hand: "Whatever you wanted to tell me is whatever I wanted to hear."

The last photo I helped Erwin re-create involved the burning of a real house. He was going to light the house on fire and take a photo of me standing in front of it.

"I got a lot of flak for this photo," he said, as he stood behind the tripod, trying to find the composition he wanted. "Because I didn't capture the soldier correctly. Both the soldier and the court were separately upset that they couldn't tell who he was."

For this shot, he decided to use Mother's camera, because it was the exact kind of camera he'd used in the war. After Erwin got me where he wanted me, he stood up from behind the tripod.

"That man was my friend, and I watched him kill people, and I did nothing but shoot him with the camera."

Erwin walked past me to the house and I could hear him rustling things around, getting it ready to catch fire.

After a bit, Erwin came back around to the camera. He stood there, looking at me, and past me. I could hear the crackling. I slowly felt the heat hit my bare skin, a tickle until a wave.

"Almost," Erwin said. "Don't move, Sofia."

Sofia didn't move. The fire licked at the back of her arms and her neck.

In one split second, it was done. The photo was taken. He didn't take any others, not even in case the first was wrong.

He ushered me to come forward and I joined him by the tripod. We watched the shack turn into an inferno. Within twenty minutes it was gone.

"I exposed for the light of the fire this time, so you'll become a silhouette, Sophia."

That's what Erwin said to her then.

A camera works very much like an eye does. The aperture blades act like the pupil—the wider they are, the more light gets through, and the darker the things you can see; the tighter they are, the less light gets in, so you can keep your life from overexposing in the brightness. Both the eye and the camera are regulators attempting to make your life into a flatline exposure. But despite the efforts of the eye and the camera, sometimes there's too much or too little light. Engineering and anatomy fall short. When it's too bright, both the eye and the camera see everything. The focus is sharp; everything is noticed, everything is brought in. But when the light is too low, when you are trying to witness or document the darkness, the pupil must be wide, and the subject isolated in a sea of blur. In the darkness, there is only a sliver of focus in the field. Nothing else matters, nothing else can, if you want to see anything at all. Vision, human or photographic, is nothing but a transcription of light. Things do not disappear when light is absent, they're just not cooperating—not conversing in the universal language of light. In the dark, things do not communicate; things do not expose themselves. Things hush. In the light, in too much light, everything is screaming sharp. The brighter it gets, the harder it is for your eyes to discern one object's light from another.

So we slip between too dark and too bright, pretending we are getting it all.

I set the camera in the passenger seat, drive away from the home and toward Mother's empty house. I hit a street that strings along with a view of the river, and I follow it. I look at the bony shadows of the treeline that the setting sun is throwing into the river. I notice the greenery of summer coming in strong.

Finally, I make it to a thin park and get out of the car, walk toward the water and watch the Red run. In the distance, I can see the railway bridge, where the body was found. Where Mother took the photo of me as the train passed overhead, years and years ago. I look at the bridge, the speed of the river, and I realize: every river is long, and every river has an opposite bank to the one you find yourself on.

So I turn around, get back in my car, and drive to Mother's house. I pack the car with what's left of my things in my old room. I don't take a last look around the house; I just lock the front door, get in the car, text Genny, and drive.

My hands grip that cartridge of burnt, blank film all the way through the fallen, developing dark. The hours pass by unaccompanied, and the distance shrinks and widens. The farther I get, the less blurry Mother becomes, and the more and more I am no longer there with her, the more and more she comes back to life. The night has long overthrown the sky by the time I make it to Minneapolis, and in the rear-view mirror—and in the light bouncing on me from the headlights of cars behind me, from street lights—I can see in my skin the remains of the memory palace.

I look away from the mirror. I choose not to look at it.

The car gets to my house and parks. Across the street, the living room light is on. Genny is there, asleep, with the blinds full open. I leave everything in the car and go over. I imagine Mother in my house, pacing, standing in the dark and looking out at me, waiting, loving me far too hard and being loved by me even harder. I step over her slipper on the sidewalk, shaking.

When I get to the door, I don't knock. I take out my keys and unlock the door, like I always did Mother's, but I leave the door closed. I can see her shape rustle up in the light through the bubbled glass. She moves toward me, a shadow. Genny opens the door. I fall into her arms.

ACKNOWLEDGMENTS

It's difficult to look back and untangle to what and to whom you are indebted, but I will attempt it anyway.

This book has been with me for a long time, and I would like to first thank the friends and colleagues who have read this book (or excerpts from it) along the way. The biggest thank you to my partner, Melanie, who has been a kind and generous (and tough) reader for several different versions of this book. I would not be the writer I am without you next to me.

Thank you to my parents for endlessly supporting me along this strange journey.

Thank you to my thesis advisor at SBU, Susan Scarf Merrell, who encouraged me as I pieced together this book in its messiest, first-draft form. Thank you to my thesis readers, Sara Majka and Meg Wolitzer, for the kind and critical words that helped light the way forward.

I don't know that this book would ever have gone to press without Tony Wei Ling, who read the manuscript at a pivotal moment with such transformative care. This book would not be this book without intervention from your sharp, editorial mind.

Thank you to Arsenal Pulp Press—Brian Lam, Shirarose Wilensky, Jazmin Welch, Cynara Geissler, and the rest of the team—for helping this book become a reality in its leanest, meanest form. Thank you to my US publicist Alyson Sinclair at Nectar Literary for helping it find readers on this side of the line.

Joshua Whitehead, Chelsey Johnson, John K. Samson, Sara Majka: I cannot fully express my gratitude to you for spending time with my book, and for giving it such kind blurbs.

The version of Ovid's *Metamorphoses* referred to, and quoted from, in this novel is the Oxford University Press edition translated by A.D. Melville (first published in 1986).

Also, I would like to acknowledge that the character Erwin Egger took direct inspiration from the real historical figure Franz-Peter Weixler, who served as a war propaganda correspondent for the Wehrmacht. He was accused of high treason against Nazi Germany for leaking uncensored material that documented atrocities German paratroopers committed in the village of Kondomari in Crete. Weixler was arrested by the Gestapo, court-martialled, and imprisoned from 1944. After the war, he testified against Hermann Göring at the Nuremberg trials and, later, paid a visit to Kondomari that inspired the one described in this book. Although inspired by Weixler, Erwin Egger's similarities do not extend beyond these biographical details.

Finally, thank you to Winnipeg for fucking me up like no other city ever could. I will never get you out of my head. And thank you to all the trans, non-binary, and gender-nonconforming people whose work, or care, has helped educate me both on myself and in my writing. My highest hope is that this book might, in some small way, pay that gift forward.

Photo Credit: Melanie Pierce

JOHN ELIZABETH STINTZI is a non-binary writer who grew up on a cattle farm in northwestern Ontario. They are the 2019 recipient of the RBC Bronwen Wallace Award, and their work has appeared in the *Malahat Review*, *Kenyon Review Online*, and *Ploughshares*. They are the author of two previous chapbooks of poetry, as well as the poetry collection *Junebat* (House of Anansi). *Vanishing Monuments* is their first novel.

johnelizabethstintzi.com